From the expanse of her Pierson played her muscles, her bones, her skin like a violinist playing the notes of a classical song. He was magically familiar with the areas that held her aches, her pains and frustrations. Theresa willingly gave into the soothing rotations of his hands on her shoulders and down her spine to the small of her back.

Pierson concentrated hard on keeping his focus on her and not himself. Her skin felt so soft under his touch. With each circle of his caress, the towel over her hips moved lower and lower, until it was just above the hump of her behind. He wanted to throw the towel to the ground but that was not what he was here for tonight. Instead, he decided to move to her legs, hoping that would distract his current mindset.

He started at her feet, pulling each leg toward him and giving the back of each a thorough rubdown as he worked his way up. By the time he finished each, he had managed to work himself into a nice rage. Reaching the top of her legs offered more torment than the bottom of her back did.

"Turn over," he said.

moment his hands spread across the
shoulder blades. Thereto, was in heaven.

STOLEN JEWELS

MICHELE SUDLER

Genesis Press, Inc.

INDIGO LOVE STORIES

An imprint of Genesis Press, Inc.
Publishing Company

Genesis Press, Inc.
P.O. Box 101
Columbus, MS 39703

ISBN: 13 DIGIT : 978-1-58571-409-4
ISBN: 10 DIGIT : 1-58571-409-7
Manufactured in the United States of America

First Edition

Visit us at www.genesis-press.com
or call at 1-888-Indigo-1-4-0

DEDICATION

This book is dedicated to my children, my jewels:
Gregory, Tanisha, Takira, and Kanika.

ACKNOWLEDGMENTS

To my parents, Larry and Vondra Brokenbrough, for your words of encouragement and constant support. I love you.

To my friends, Cecilia and Cindy, for being there for me, beside me, and backing me up, no matter what the reason.

To my family, the Butchers, Sudlers, Brokenbroughs, and Heaths, for laughs, and good times.

To Sidney Rickman, thank you for all your hard work.

To the Genesis Press family and anyone who has ever read any of my books. Thank you.

And to anyone I might have missed, I'm thinking of you.

CHAPTER 1

Theresa Philips apprehensively walked into the classroom located in Building D of Xavier University's Art Village in New Orleans. She was nervous and very unsure of her decision to take the class, but she knew that she needed it if for no other reason than to be able to explain the past to her son. Theresa summoned her fortitude so that she wouldn't bolt from the room. Quickly taking the first seat in the back of the room, she ignored the questioning glances from the other students.

They probably wondered what she was doing there. And as confident as she was normally as a CEO for the multimillion-dollar corporation that she ran with her brothers, this group of young black students made her feel very uncomfortable. In all honesty, she wanted a reason to run out of the room as fast as she could and forget about the extra money she'd had to pay to take the summer African American Relations class and not a full curriculum. But she had never run from anything in her life, and she wasn't going to let the stares of a bunch of kids force her out.

So what if at thirty-four she was the oldest in the class? Or the only mother in the room? Neither was the reason for their stares, however. Theresa knew the reason they were staring was because of the color of her skin. By all appearances, she was a white woman. So why was she sitting in the back of their African American Relations class trying to act as though she were invisible? Talk about reverse racism. She didn't blame them; she thanked them because if they hadn't reacted this way she wouldn't have stayed.

Her skin was white. Until three months earlier, she had thought she was white. But she wasn't, at least according to the law, an old law she didn't really understand at all. Hence, her presence in the classroom. Three months ago, Theresa, along with her brothers Thorne and Michael, had found out not only that Thorne's long-thought dead mother was alive. They also learned that she was black, and their grandfather wasn't the man who was married to the white grandmother, Abigail Connor Philips, who raised them. Their real grandfather was also black and had grown up with Ms. Abbie and later worked as her gardener.

Her grandmother, who had died less than a year ago, and the gardener had kept their romance a secret forever. She and her brothers hadn't found it out until the truth was discovered about Thorne. A woman named Natalie had hired Thorne's company to do construction on one of her houses. Natalie was also trying to help her older friend Amanda, who had been in a recent car accident, find her long-lost son. During her investigation, Natalie stumbled onto information that linked their father Matthew Philips to Amanda and discovered that they'd had a son together who was born on Thorne's birthday.

With Natalie's help, they began to put together what turned out to be an elaborate plan concocted by their grandmother in order to protect Thorne and their family. Then the siblings went to their cousin who was the lawyer confidant of their grandmother for answers. The answers were revealed in a VHS tape from their grandmother herself. She explained how she and Michael, the housekeeper's son, had been the best of friends as children as he was nearly her only playmate. As they grew up, they had fallen in love, but realized they had to keep it a secret because their races were different.

During the time that Ms. Abbie's father was trying to marry her off, she realized she was pregnant by Michael, and together, they cooked up the dangerous scheme that had affected all of their lives. Ms. Abbie picked one of her suitors and practically threw herself at him, willingly having sex with him several times so that he would believe her baby was his. Of course he had to marry her, not that he would have objected. Ms. Abbie was the only heir of a very wealthy family. Fortunately, Michael was the illegitimate black half-brother to Ms. Abbie's husband. After the wedding, Ms. Abbie never let her husband touch her again, and Michael was kept on as the gardener so that he could be around his son in some capacity. Ms. Abbie named her son Matthew after her husband.

Their story was a very interesting one filled with a love so deep that both were willing to take serious risks to be together despite all the perils of that time. Theresa couldn't wait for that type of love to come her way. And she was happy that Thorne had already found it with Natalie.

Amanda Henry, Thorne's mother and Theresa and Michael's "adopted" mother by choice, walked into the classroom just then. Her confidence was something to envy. Her head was held high, and there was an easy way about her walk, a happiness. She smiled, acknowledging her students as she walked down the center aisle of the large room.

"Sorry I'm late, everyone." She glanced at her watch. "Oh, actually, I'm right on time, so anyone that comes in behind me will be late. I don't like it when you're late to my class." She looked around the room. There were approximately twenty-five students. That was normal. The kids loved to take her course. At Xavier University, she was one of the more popular professors. This was her last class, the late class, which ran from 7 p.m. to 10 p.m. twice a week, Tuesdays and Fridays.

Amanda looked around the room until her eyes came to Theresa, who was right where she knew she would be and right were she didn't want her. "First of all, since I don't bite and the chairs aren't all filled up, why don't a few of you move down here to the front row?" She used her hands to express her wishes. "Come on, not everyone at once," she replied, sensing that some urging was necessary.

Finally, one young man stood and moved forward.

"Thank you, sir. And your name?"

"Patrick, Patrick Downes."

"Mr. Downes, thank you. See, I didn't bite him."

Theresa sat in her seat. She didn't want to be in the front row. It was one thing to be in the class, but Amanda was trying to put her in the center of even more attention.

"Theresa?" Amanda said nicely, but Theresa knew it wasn't a question.

Even as her stomach sank, Theresa stood and moved to the front of the room. She refused to show that she was on edge so she smiled brightly as if it were her idea.

"Thank you, dear. Everyone, this is Theresa Philips."

The room was silent. Theresa knew it wasn't because of her name. Most of these kids probably didn't know of her. She was never in the local newspapers as much as Thorne and Michael. They probably wanted to know how Amanda knew her name. As she sat down in her black Vera Wang pantsuit, Theresa made a mental note to dress more casually for Friday's class.

Theresa and Michael had whole-heartedly joined Thorne in accepting his mother into their small family and had made Amanda their chosen mother. Their biological mother, along with their father, had passed away when they were very young. According to their grandmother's videotape, Amanda was Matthew's first wife. Matthew and his wealthy friends used to visit the little juke joints that spotted the New Orleans nightlife. Amanda worked at one in an effort to support her family. The two met, fell in love, and began to secretly see each other. When Amanda became pregnant, Matthew insisted that they marry despite the obstacles it would cause.

But before their son was three, Amanda left and filed for divorce. She loved Matthew too much to let him make the sacrifices he had just to be with her. Practically living solely from the support of his mother, Matthew had lost most of his friends and business colleagues who were either racist themselves or whose racist fathers demanded they distance themselves from him. Before they were married, Ms. Abbie told her son the truth of his birth, and he had developed a stronger relationship with his real father. Matthew figured that if his real parents' relationship could survive all those years, truly his marriage to Amanda could survive, but Amanda couldn't stand the pressure. She wanted a better life for him.

After Amanda filed for divorce, Matthew eventually remarried. Ms. Abbie raised Thorne, whose slightly tan skin color forced the high-profile family to start the rumor that his mother was an Italian woman who died at his birth. That was the story that they had always believed. On the day of Matthew's accident, the three children had been staying with his mother. Matthew was telling his second wife, Theresa and Michael's mother, the truth about his birth, Amanda, and Thorne. He was also telling her that he was taking Thorne back to live with them. An argument started and a brief fight before the car went off the side of the road. Their mother died instantly, and Matthew died a few days later.

Theresa and Amanda had spoken about Theresa taking one of her classes not too long after the whole truth came out. Theresa wanted help in explaining everything to her son, as well as finding out who she really was. And although their grandmother had made sure they were properly educated, Amanda had told her that there was a lot of important African history left out of the history books in America's schools.

Right after Theresa discovered she was black, a lot of questions formed in her mind. Did her black side, she wondered, have anything to do with the rebellious, outspoken, and intensely radical nature she had exhibited throughout her teens and early twenties? Was it the reason she never took any nonsense from anybody, except Ryan, who had been her downfall? It didn't make much sense to her, but when all of the stereotypes that she had heard all of her life came to mind, she knew she needed to educate herself. Of course, she didn't at first expect it would be in a classroom setting.

Once the local newspapers and TV channels got wind of the story, there was a huge frenzy. It mostly centered around Thorne because he was the face of the company, and his story was the most interesting of all. Before long, Thorne had to do interviews to make sure that the story was accurate. However, there were still a few crazy renditions of the truth out there. A few stories even managed to go national, and then for the company's sake, he had to have employee, management, and vendor meetings, and talk to the presidents of other companies more often than he would have liked. To escape the media circus, he and his girlfriend had taken a two-week vacation.

Four months ago any story about their company identified it simply as the Philips Corporation, but now they were the black-owned Philips Corporation, and the siblings were always such and such Philips, who recently discovered they were African-American. Theresa didn't have a problem with finding out that she was black. And the love and romance behind her heritage made her prouder of her grandparents than she could have ever imagined. But if she was going to take hold of her ethnicity, she had to get to know as much about her history as she could. This was the first class, and because this was important to her, she managed to make it on time despite the business of the office.

Amanda continued getting acquainted with her students. One by one she went around the room and tried to familiarize herself with their names and faces. Then she began a quick synopsis of the course. She explained what she expected from each student and what they should expect from her in return.

Theresa hadn't even contemplated the idea that she would have homework and have to take tests. She'd thought this would be more of a seminar. How wrong she had been.

"Each of you is here for a different reason," Amanda began. "The reason is personal and as diverse as all of you. As I look around the room, I see diversity." She watched as the students looked around and all eyes fell on

Theresa. "Yes, diversity," Amanda continued. "Young man, stand up." She signaled one of the students. He stood. "How tall are you?"

"Six feet, seven inches," he replied proudly.

"Basketball?"

"Yes."

"And you, sir." Another student stood. "How tall are you?"

"Five feet, five inches," he humbly whispered.

"No, no," Amanda replied. "You didn't answer me correctly, Thomas. Why do you lower your voice as if being five feet, five inches is something to be ashamed of? This course is about pride. Pride in your history, pride in your present, and pride in your future, pride in yourself. God created all of us differently for a purpose. Your height is your height for a purpose. Whoever said that tallness was more of a positive than shortness? Both have their advantages and disadvantages. The same with race. White, black. The hypothesis that white is better than black has been successfully proven, not by fact, but by people, both white and black. It must stop. The only way that can be done is for each of us to work to expel the myths and stereotypes that have befallen us. And to that end, let's all stand up in a circle around the room."

Theresa wasn't the only one who wondered what this exercise was supposed to show them, but she obeyed willingly.

"Okay," Amanda said, "I want everyone to look around the room at your classmates. Now, everyone in this room is a black person." Again, the eyes fell on Theresa's golden blonde shoulder length hair and her green eyes.

Theresa hated her reaction to their disapproval, but her stubbornness wouldn't allow her to show it affected her. Despite her self-consciousness, Theresa returned each of their gazes.

"Do you see the diversity that blackness is? As you look around the room, you see light skin, dark skin, even white skin. You see brown, green, hazel, and pitch black eyes; brown, black, blond, and hints of red hair in dreads, braids, feathers, and perms. This is blackness. This course is about getting to know yourselves, and there is no better place than the past. However, I wouldn't be the professor if I didn't assign some kind of homework, so part one, due next week, is a one-page report on yourself. I want you to tell me how you define yourself as it pertains to being black. Also, be prepared to give a two-minute introduction of yourself to your classmates explaining why you have chosen this course. Now let's take our seats and learn something."

As soon as Theresa opened the book to the first page, she was engrossed in the class. It was simply a map of Africa with pictures of African kings and queens surrounding it. Amanda spoke passionately of the continent, commanding the interest of the students.

Almost at the same time, all the students, including Theresa, opened their notebooks and began taking notes. By the end of the class, Theresa knew more about Africa and the beginnings of the slave trade than she could imagine. But not only did she know about it, she felt almost as if she had been standing in the middle of the African plains as natives ran past her to avoid being captured. She saw the African warriors capturing African children and women and dragging them to be loaded into the small confines of the slave ships. At one point during the class, Theresa was so captivated that she felt a tear run down her face. There had been so much cruelty, so much mistrust.

Amanda gave so much more to her class than the course description indicated. When class was over, they had a total of three assignments due for the next class, and Theresa almost couldn't wait to get home and complete them.

"So, how did you like the class?" Amanda asked as they walked out to their cars.

"Mom, I am so glad I took your advice and signed up for this class. Natalie said that you were an awesome teacher, but I would have never guessed. You were excellent. And I am so interested that I can't wait for Friday's class. At first, I was a little upset about having to give up a Friday night, because you know that's my nightgown and robe night with a little coffee on the side and a proposal to change something in one of the hotels." They laughed. "But now, I actually have something to look forward to on Fridays for the next twelve weeks. Granted, it wasn't exactly what I had in mind, but it's a start."

"I'm glad you enjoyed it."

"I did, and I'm going to suggest it to Michael and Thorne as well."

"Please, those knuckleheads will only talk me into teaching them the class privately."

"You need to learn how to tell them no, especially Thorne. The two of you haven't done anything but spoil each other rotten, and I suppose Michael and I haven't helped any."

"Nonsense, I am so blessed to have all of you in my life. God has not only given me back the son that I lost, but also two more children and a grandson. There is no such thing as spoiling too much. And a grandson. Now, if we're lucky, Thorne and Natalie are working on getting me a few more grandkids."

"Well, they'll be home Sunday night. Hopefully, they can at least give us a wedding date so we can start making arrangements."

"I can honestly say that since he's been on vacation, I've been getting much more rest. He worries about me so much that I start worrying about him. Something's not right about that picture."

"That's a son's love. He'll stop once he and Natalie are married and some children start popping out," Theresa said with a laugh, walking Amanda to her car first. Once she was inside, Amanda gave her a huge hug and watched as she walked to her own car.

Before going to her apartment, Theresa stopped by her secretary's house to pick up her son. Stephanie's daughter occasionally babysat for her. Mikey, named after his uncle Michael, who was named after their biological grandfather, had insisted that he didn't need a sitter. He thought he was old enough to take care of himself, but at nine, Theresa wasn't about to let him stay alone.

"Mom, I was having fun there," Mikey said as soon as they got into the car. "I was helping Stephanie's son with his math homework. He's learning how to add and subtract. Then we played video games and baked cookies."

"I'm glad you had a good time. Friday, you'll stay with Uncle Michael until I get out of class."

"Okay. Uncle Michael said I could work with him tomorrow. He said he was going to have a desk put in his office for me and everything."

"Oh really? Don't you already have a desk in Uncle Thorne's office?"

"Yeah. I think he's jealous that I pay Uncle Thorne so much attention when he's around. I really like them both the same."

"I know you do, but your uncles like to compete against each other all the time. Believe me, your Uncle Michael knows that you love him, too. They're really just big babies at heart."

"How is my grandmother doing?"

Theresa looked at her son.

"She's doing just fine. She asked about you, too. I'm sure that you'll be seeing her soon. But you have to understand that since she started teaching again, she's been very busy. She has to grade papers and such. Not a lot of time for visiting."

"But I'm her grandson. She has to miss me."

"And she does, baby. She misses you, but she has to work, and we have to understand that."

"Okay."

Eventually, he quieted down, and she knew he was starting to get sleepy. She just hoped that she made it home before he was fully knocked out. He was too big for her to be carrying.

CHAPTER 2

Two days later, Theresa sat at her desk. The manila folders had piled up on her mahogany executive desk so high that she wondered if she would ever make it to the bottom. She kept her determination high as she meticulously signed her name on invoice after requisition after memo after pay increase confirmation forms. She figured that it would take her a week to get caught up on the backlog. That's what she got for volunteering to oversee operation of the family business while her older brother Thorne took a two-week vacation. Luckily, the first week had steadily moved along. And although he deserved it, she would think twice before she volunteered again to handle his workload on top of her own.

It would have been different if their business were a small mom and pop store or even a mediocre franchise, but what they were in control of was a corporation, a large corporation with at least five major businesses under its umbrella. And those businesses were all successful, employing thousands of people in several different parts of the world.

Her younger brother Michael was busy himself taking care of the oil fields and cruise lines, which were the largest of the corporation's businesses. She was overseeing her usual charges, the hotels and interior decorating agencies, which were her favorite. But in addition, she was also now in charge of the majority of the paperwork, which Thorne usually handled, and his baby, Phillips Contractors, Inc. It was so large and overwhelmed with business that Thorne was going to have to open another office in the state and one in Mississippi just to meet the demands for his service. She smiled as she thought of how Thorne had taken that particular business under his wing and fine-tuned it so that it ran perfectly.

After Hurricane Katrina practically turned New Orleans and the surrounding area into shambles, Thorne had managed to secure a majority of the reconstruction contracts by lowering his rates and hiring a number of the victims. He had also gone through great difficulties to get acceptable housing for them. One of the requisitions she had just signed was for the electric bill on the apartment complex he had built next to the daycare center he'd donated to the City of New Orleans the year before. Sometimes, she wondered if his generosity was a little excessive, but for the most part, she and Michael both agreed with his actions. They did plenty of charity work.

Just as she put her hand on the next folder, she heard the wheels of the mail cart coming down the hallway toward her office door. She tightened her resolve and pushed deeper into the files. She would look at her mail later. It was probably just more inter-office deliveries to add to her misery.

"Hey, Mom," Michael Thorne Philips yelled to his mother as he came whirling around the corner. His squeaky pre-teen voice caught her off guard, causing her to jump and drop her folder.

"Mikey, what are you doing in here?" she asked curiously.

"I'm helping Samuel with his deliveries," he replied innocently.

"Samuel? I thought you were supposed to be working with Uncle Michael again today."

"I was, but Uncle Michael got called away on important business. He won't be back until later. He told me to help Samuel and stay out of your way because you had a lot of work to do."

"And are you slowing Samuel down?" she asked, nodding at the tall and lanky young man who came into her office just behind her son.

"He's no problem, Mrs. Philips," Samuel remarked. "If anything, he makes the day go by faster."

"Okay, but if he gives you any trouble, you send him up here," she said, giving her son a warning look.

"I will. Mikey, you can stay in here for a second while I run this heavy box down the hall. I'll be right back to get you."

"All right," Mikey answered, walking around Theresa's office, looking at pictures of himself. "Mom, you sure do have a lot of pictures of me."

"Of course I do. You're my baby," she replied before returning to her pile of work.

Mikey remained quiet for a moment, letting his mother work until he couldn't take it any longer. His curiosity was getting the better of him, and he had to know. "Mom, can I ask you a question?"

"Sure, Mikey," she answered without looking up from the stack of folders in front of her. "I'm listening."

"Well, I was just wondering what our classification is now?"

"Uh, our classification?" she asked, her head moving from left to right in an effort to find a letter of recommendation that she had let slip out of its folder. "What are you talking about, baby?"

"You know, our classification. What do we mark on stuff? Like a census or application? Are we black now?"

"Huh, oh . . ." Theresa dropped the folders that she was about to shuffle into yet another pile on her desk. She sat back after looking up into her son's confused face and released a long sigh. She realized that this was a subject that needed to be broached, a subject that she hadn't really thought about herself. What would she mark? How did she classify herself?

Glancing at herself in the small mirror on the corner of her desk, she realized that physically she didn't see herself any differently. Her eyes were still that sparkling shade of emerald, her hair was the same honey gold, and her skin was still ivory white with just a few freckles sprinkled here and there. It was inwardly that she felt different, and that was the part of her that she needed to know better.

Over the past few months, she and her siblings had learned a lot about their past. With Natalie's help, they had discovered a lot of secrets kept from them by their parents and grandparents. As children, they had been told that Thorne's mother was different from theirs and Italian. Hence, his darker coloring, dark hair and eyes. It was a tangled web that had been necessarily woven for their grandmother's time. So, although Thorne was technically "blacker" than she and Michael, by all accounts, she and Michael were technically black, too, right?

After a moment of uncomfortable silence, she looked up at her son. Mikey reminded her so much of her younger brother with his light blond hair and bright green eyes. She was so thankful that he bore no resemblance to the miserable bastard who was his biological father.

Pushing back in her chair, she stretched an arm toward him and beckoned him to join her. She watched him hesitate and smiled to herself. At nine, he was so intelligent, a math wizard, and picked up on things that other kids his age just didn't care about. How many nine-year-olds cared what to check on a census? But then, not all nine-year-olds had recently had their lives turned around by such a sudden change in their families. He happened to have a black grandfather and a new black grandmother whom he loved to no end, but for all his life he had known himself as a little white boy.

Theresa had never kept anything from him if possible. So, he knew that she had left his father when he was two because he tried to beat her. Mikey had been there. He also knew that he was from a wealthy family, which gave him certain privileges, but many responsibilities. He knew that he had a close-knit family filled with love and support for each other.

Theresa saw no reason not to talk to her son honestly about events that affected his life. "Come here, baby. Your school friends aren't around. And I won't tell anyone that you sat on my lap."

"Do you promise, Mother? Because if Uncle Thorne saw me sitting in your lap, he wouldn't like it." Both his uncles enthralled Mikey, but it was Thorne who he was always trying to make proud of him.

"Cross my heart and hope to die," she replied, crossing her heart with her finger.

Satisfied, he smiled and hopped onto her legs.

"Mikey, I'm sure you're a little confused about what's been going on around here lately, huh?"

He nodded. "Just a little. Samuel said that I've been passing all these years, but that it's okay because I'm a good person. I asked him what he meant by that, and he told me that I was black, but letting everybody think I was white."

"Oh, did he really? Well, you are a good person, but whether a person is black or white, they can still be a good person." Theresa made a mental note to have a talk with the young mailroom attendant about his conversations with her son. "Okay, let's get this all out in the open, because I'm a little confused about it myself. Maybe you can help me figure it out."

"Okay," he eagerly agreed, glad his mother needed his help with a problem.

"So, if you were filling out a census and they asked you your race, what would you answer?"

"Mom, I wouldn't be filling out a census, but when I go back to school, some of the kids might have heard about my new grandmother. Remember when the newspaper ran that big article about Uncle Thorne finding his mom and about her being black?"

Theresa smiled to herself. He was almost too smart for her. "You're right. Okay, what if when you go back to school somebody asks you about your race. What will you say?"

"I don't know. I'm white," he said, lifting his hand up high in the air for them both to look at. "But," he continued, "just because you can't see that I am black doesn't mean I'm not, right? Just like we can't see the air, but we know it's there."

"That's right, but where did you get that from?" she asked, amazed by his statement.

"That's what Samuel said. He said that I've got the best of both worlds in me. Do you think he's right?"

"I think Samuel is a pretty smart kid," Theresa replied, throwing the idea of a promotion for Samuel around in her head. "But what would your answer be?"

Mikey raised his index finger to his chin, deep in thought, then gave an honest answer. "I'm going to tell them that I am both black and white, because I am. And if they don't like it, then that's just too bad."

"You know what? You're right. That's what I'm going to do, too. Besides, we have to respect all of our ancestors. They're what made us who we are."

"So, when you do the census, will you mark us as white or black?"

"Well, the census is a bit different. Legally, if you go by the laws, then we are now black. The law says that if one drop of black blood can be traced through your lineage, then you are considered black. And your grandfather and his mother's family would be our black blood, so we're black. But now, since there are so many interracial relationships of all kinds, the census requires you to check any of the race categories that apply."

"So you'll check both black and white?"

"That's right, because now I know I'm both. What do you think about that?" she asked just as Samuel walked back into the office. She wasn't surprised when Mikey quickly jumped off her lap and moved a step away from her.

"It's cool, Mom. I gotta go," he said, embarrassed at having been caught lounging like a baby against his mom.

"You ready to get back to work, little man?" Samuel asked, ignoring what he saw for Mikey's sake.

Theresa smiled at him and nodded her head. "Thank you."

"Yeah," Mikey replied, "I'm ready. Mom, see you later," he called out behind him as he walked out the room.

Theresa shook her head. He was already pulling away from her, trying to be a little man. She wasn't sure if she would be able to handle the years to come.

"Theresa?"

"Yes," she answered, hitting the button on the silver intercom system built into the corner of her desk. "What is it, Stephanie?"

"Michael just called and said that he will meet you at one o'clock at Mr. Connor's office to go over the last of the paperwork for your grandmother's estate."

"Oh, hell," she whispered to herself. She had forgotten all about the meeting. Looking at her watch, she began shuffling the folders again, moving the completed ones into the out bin. "Thanks. I'll be leaving in an hour. Could you please find Mikey and Samuel and let them know? Tell Mikey to stay with Samuel until I return, and let me know when you've told them."

"I'm stopping them right now. They're about to get on the elevator."

"Thanks, Stephanie," she sighed. Blowing out a long stream of air, Theresa wondered what had possessed her to do Thorne's work. "Ugh . . . I hate paperwork."

The doors of the garage elevator opened as Theresa pushed her wallet back into her Coach bag, which she was picking up off the floor. She was in such a rush that, as usual, nothing was going her way. After leaning over her desk for the majority of the morning, her back and neck were stiff and sore. She reached up with one hand and lightly massaged her neck.

"Afternoon, Mrs. Philips," Christopher, the garage attendant, yelled cheerfully.

"Hello, Christopher. How are you today?" she answered.

"Just fine, ma'am."

"What did I tell you about that ma'am business? You're three years older than me."

"Sorry about that." He smiled. "Leaving for the day?"

"No, just a meeting. I should be back in a couple of hours," she said, unlocking the door of her navy blue Chrysler 300 and sliding in smoothly against the cool gray leather interior.

Pulling out into the flow of traffic, Theresa reached over to turn on her radio. After a moment of finding nothing to her satisfaction, she decided to put her Mary J. Blige CD in to relax and enjoy her ride, automatically skipping to track number three, "You Know How I Feel," her favorite song. She didn't think of anyone in particular as she sang the words loud and with feeling. There was no one to think about. She just loved the beat and the rhythm of the music.

Oh, Lord. I hope this meeting doesn't take too long. I've got so much work to do. A little further down the road, she had to bring down her speed when she saw construction signs indicating that one lane of the highway was closed ahead. *Just my luck*, she mused as the speed limit steadily decreased until she came to an almost complete stop.

After ten minutes of creeping, Theresa had the car back up to fifty miles an hour, but then, to her dismay, she had to pull over to the side of the road. Getting out of the car in a huff, she walked around her car wondering what was making the strange sound and causing the car to bump.

In disgust, she realized that the front passenger tire was flat. *What to do?* There was no way she was going to try to change it. Not that she didn't get the concept of changing a tire, but she had never done it and never wanted to. Not that she was too good to do it, but if she didn't really have to do it, why do it?

She dug into her pocketbook for her cellphone. Pushing the speed dial button, she waited for her secretary to answer.

"Hello, boss lady. Everything okay?"

"No, Stephanie. I got a flat tire on the way to Howard's office. I'm on Brentford Station Road, about half a mile south of Drexel Avenue. Do you know the number of a repair man?"

"No, not off hand, but give me a second to grab the company's insurance policy. I'm sure they have a twenty-four-hour service number. Just hold on."

"Please hurry. I hate this," she replied, waiting for a car to pass so that she could get back in her car.

A moment later, Stephanie returned to the phone. "Okay, Theresa, I called the service number, and they're sending someone now. The name of the company is Brooks Repair and Towing Service."

"Thanks, Stephanie. I don't know what I'd do without you."

"No problem. Do you want me to stay on the line until someone comes?"

"No, I'm all right. It's daytime, and there are plenty of people around," she replied, looking around her at the cars going by filled with people looking over at her. "I'd better call and let Howard and Michael know that I'll be running late."

"Okay, I'll see you when you get back, and I'll stay here with Mikey until you get back."

"Thanks again, Stephanie." She hung up and called Howard's office.

By the time she hung up the phone from Michael and Howard, a big tow truck was pulling up behind her. Grateful for the fast service, Theresa climbed out of her vehicle as soon as he came to a complete stop. "Hello," she began. "I believe that it's just a flat tire. Will it . . ." She stumbled as soon as he stepped out of the truck, at a loss for words.

"Afternoon, ma'am," the handsome black man said, walking toward the side of the truck to retrieve his tools from behind the metal panel. "Name's Pierson Brooks. What seems to be the problem?" he asked, having not heard her first statement.

"Um . . ." Theresa quickly swallowed. "Hi, I'm Theresa. I think it's a flat tire."

"No problem. I can fix that in a jiffy," Pierson replied, walking towards her carrying a big tire iron. As he walked, he took the opportunity to give Theresa a thorough once-over. Class, money, snob, he assumed. From her glossy sandy blonde locks with their assorted highlights to her French-manicured nails to her tailored business suit and pricey two-inch heels, he could tell that she was either a businesswoman or a rich somebody's housewife who was in the middle of a busy social-affairs day. Around this time of the day, he always got a call to help some damsel in distress. Best to get this done and over with as soon as possible, he figured.

"I'm sorry to inconvenience your busy day," Theresa apologized as she followed him around the side of the car to the flat tire. He was a big man, taller and stockier than even her brother Thorne, who had been her picture of an ideal male specimen, *until now*. Not that she lusted after her brother, but she knew handsome when she saw it, and both of her brothers were the most handsome men she had ever seen, *until now*.

"No inconvenience. This is what I do for a living," he said, keeping his replies short and to the point. She looked like the type of lady that could get him into a hell of a lot of trouble. And that was something that he didn't need right now. His business was just starting to make a decent profit. The last thing he needed to do was piss off some rich white man by flirting with his wife.

"But still, I'm sure that you have more important things that you could be doing," she returned, wondering why he was trying so hard to be unsociable. Maybe he just wasn't a friendly conversation type of guy. But by the looks of him, he had to have a lot of friends. The laugh lines around his thick lips showed that he smiled often. So, why wasn't he smiling now? "Are you from New Orleans, Mr. Brooks?"

"No, ma'am," he answered, as he used the iron to loosen the first lug nut on the wheel.

"And you're not going to tell me where you're from?" she asked.

"I'm originally from Delaware," he said, continuing his work.

"Delaware? Don't think I've ever been there. What's it like?" she pried, trying to make small talk.

"Small, ma'am," he answered.

"Theresa," she corrected.

"Well, Theresa," he stood to his full height, looking down at her and giving her his undivided attention. "I'd really like to get this tire fixed so that I can go back to work. So, if you don't mind, please, just stand back over there and let me finish."

"Are you having a bad day or something?"

"No, and I don't want to have one. Please, the last thing I need is for your jealous husband to think I'm trying to hit on you while fixing your car here. Please, let me finish and get you on your way."

"My husband?"

"Yes, ma'am. Your husband. I know how jealous and racist some of these Southern men can be. And I don't want any trouble." He bent again and started working on the second lug nut.

"For your information, sir, I don't have a husband. I'm a single mother of one," she answered smartly, standing behind him with her arms crossed.

"Well, that's nice to know," he laughed, physically relaxing and leaning back on one knee. He looked up from his kneeling position, taking in her physical appearance one more time. She still looked like some rich lady that didn't do a damn thing for a living but shop, but she was attractive.

"So, Pierson Brooks, from Brooks Repair and Towing Services, you related to the owner or something?"

"Actually, I am the owner," he said, getting back to work. It was time to stop this conversation. He had plenty of things to do.

"Owner?" she asked. "Do you get a lot of business?" She wasn't trying to be nosey. In fact, her head was always working on business. Maybe she and Mr. Brooks could work out some sort of deal that would give her employees a discount on his services. Her company employed over two thousand people in New Orleans alone. That could help his business substantially while giving her employees another perk. She liked making sure her employees were happy.

"A fair amount," he answered honestly.

"How many shops do you have?"

"Just two. One just north of the city and one here."

"I think that I could help your business, Mr. Brooks," she said, waiting for his reply.

"Thanks, lady. Just recommend me to a friend if you like the service. That would be appreciated." He finished loosening the last lug nut and placed the jack under the side of her car to lift it up.

Theresa didn't say anything while she watched the muscles in his back and arms strain against his shirt as he pumped the jack until the car was high off the ground. When he finished, she remembered what she'd been thinking about.

"I have a suggestion for you," she said.

"Are you asking me for a job? Because by the looks of this car, I can't afford to pay you more than you're used to making."

"No, I'm not asking for a job. Maybe we could get together somewhere and discuss what I have in mind." Theresa wanted to stop herself. It sounded even to her as if she might be stalking him. But when he stood up and turned to her holding the flat tire in his arms as if it were as light as a deflated balloon, she decided not to retract her statement.

"Do you have a spare? This one has a nail in it," he began. "If you have a spare, I can put it on so you can be on your way. I can take this to the shop and repair it, then either you can pick it up or I can deliver it to you."

"Sure, I think there's one in the trunk. I've never been in it. But you didn't answer my question."

"Look, um, Theresa, was it? I have to be honest with you. And, mind you, I'm not racist or prejudiced myself, but I make it a habit of not dating outside my race anymore."

"I wasn't trying to ask you out on a date," she half-lied. Then she thought about his comment. "And why not?"

"Bad experience once. It takes me only one time to learn my lesson."

"Is that so?"

"Yes," he replied, taking the spare tire out of the trunk and carrying it to the front of the car. "I don't knock anyone else for doing it. I just don't anymore."

"Couldn't take her home to your mom?"

"Actually, I could and did." Pierson wasn't sure why he was telling her all of this. It wasn't any of her business. He had just met this woman, what, ten minutes ago. "Most of my family really liked her."

"Then what happened?

"Well, once we had a big argument, and when she couldn't have her way, a lot of vulgar comments were made. That pretty much put an end to anything we could have ever had."

"She used the 'N' word?" Theresa asked knowingly.

"That was one of many. But it wasn't what upset me the most." Pierson paused and glanced at her. He was talking too much. "To make a long story short, I was out of there that night. There were just some things said that I cannot forgive."

"I understand," she said.

"Do you? I don't see how you could?" he laughed, shaking his head.

"That's because you don't wish to see." Theresa liked this light banter she was having. "What if I told you that I was black? Would you believe that?"

Pierson turned around and stood slowly looking her up and down. He answered honestly. "I've heard of stranger things. Just because you don't look it doesn't mean it's not true. I wouldn't think it if I passed you on the street, but you don't seem like the type of person to lie."

"I see you're a pretty good judge of character, Mr. Brooks. No, I don't lie. And I am black. One-fourth. My grandfather was half black." Theresa wondered why she felt a need to supply him with this information.

"Then that would make you one-eighth, wouldn't it?" he corrected, looking at her more closely.

"So, I stand corrected. But does that make a big difference? I mean, by all appearances, I still am white, aren't I?"

"Like I said, it's not that I'm prejudiced or anything, I'm just very cautious nowadays."

"I understand." She smiled to herself, moving aside as he walked past her. Theresa hadn't played this game in a long time. Since she had finally gotten Mikey's father out of her system and her life, this was the first time she'd even wanted to play.

"Okay, that's it. I hope you don't have too far to go. I wouldn't ride on this spare for more than thirty miles."

"Thank you very much, Pierson Brooks. How much do I owe you?"

"Actually, your bill was already paid over the phone. But fixing the tire is a separate bill. It will be ready by tomorrow morning. We can call when it's ready. Then you just let us know if you're going to pick it up or have us bring it to you. Either way, it can be mounted back on your car. However, at the shop balancing your tires is also part of the service of mounting the tire."

"Thanks. Yes, just call. I greatly appreciate this," she reiterated. Glancing at her watch, she realized that she had practically missed the whole meeting with Howard and Michael. She got into her car and saw that the light on her cell phone was blinking. After she picked it up, she saw that she had missed four calls because she'd left the phone inside the car while she was outside flirting.

Picking up the phone, she watched Mr. Pierson Brooks walk back to the tow truck in her side mirror.

That man looks good enough to be dangerous, she thought. Pushing the speed dial number to Michael's cell phone, she watched as the truck pulled away from the side of the road and moved past her.

Theresa smiled to herself, knowing that she would see him again soon. She probably wouldn't be the one taking her car to get repaired, but she would see him again real soon.

CHAPTER 3

Ryan Courtney slammed the manila folder he was holding down onto the desk in front of him. As he fought the truth in the report he had just read, his anger mounted. He stood and began pacing across the worn carpet of his private investigator's office, wondering what he was going to do about this new situation.

His latest client, an older black woman, very distinguished looking, very strong, independent, and dangerously serious and angry, had left the folder with him the day before, agreeing to give him time to review the information before taking the case. Now that he'd read the files, he had no choice but to take it.

His first instinct was to pick up the phone and call the last person on Earth who would want to hear from him, Theresa Philips, his ex-wife. But what if this woman had purposely picked him as an investigator because she knew of his relationship to the Philipses? According to this folder, she knew that the Philipses were somehow tied into the disappearance of some very valuable pieces of jewelry, which she claimed rightfully belonged to her son.

Ryan sat back down in his chair and thought for a minute. He had known the Philips family for a long time, and the one thing that they were was honest. He knew that if Theresa and her family did have any of this jewelry it hadn't been gained by ill means. The Philipses didn't take anything from anyone. If anything, they gave more often than not.

Mrs. Surgen, his client, wanted him to find out for sure that the Philipses were in possession of the jewelry. That was a tall order to fill, considering that he and Theresa had been through a messy divorce and were about to be in the middle of a nasty custody battle. So, how was he going to find out answers from a person who couldn't stand him and wouldn't find herself within a mile of him?

Opening the folder again, he shook his head at the information that the older woman had preserved over the years. On one large, quadruple-folded paper was a large family tree that had been magnificently drawn. Its branches were long and elaborate, sprinkled with leaves in various places and names in others. Someone had obviously taken great care to keep track and document names reaching back almost five hundred years, since before slavery.

At the top of the tree were the names Nadi and Ursulene, topped by golden crowns. So where the names on the next few lines, but eventually as the names changed from African to American, the crowns disappeared. There had to be some sort of symbolism there, he figured.

At the bottom of the tree, on the last branch filled out, was the name of his son, Michael Thorne Philips. That name. Each time he thought of how Theresa had denied his wishes for his son to be a junior, his anger at her mounted all over again. Not only did she not name the boy after him, she named him after her two brothers, both of whom he'd had more run-ins with than he could count. And although their marriage had been brief, it was a marriage, even though she never took his last name and didn't give their son his last name either.

He knew that Theresa was greatly influenced by her grandmother, but he was her husband. Though granted, he hadn't been the best husband by a long shot. Until she burst open the door of Room 72 at the Holiday Inn, he had actually thought that he was getting away with his philandering. That was when he found out that she was a lot stronger than he had taken her for. Not just physically, even though by the time she had left the room, she had gifted him with a broken arm and shoulder and the lady a black eye and swollen lip.

By the time he had left the hospital and gotten home, Theresa had already cleared out their house and bank account and gotten all the utilities turned off. The funny thing about the whole situation was that Theresa was already a millionaire. She didn't need the little bit of money that was in their joint account or the furniture, but she took him for everything. Her excuse later was that he didn't deserve anything.

Ryan sat back in the chair behind his desk and laughed to himself as he thought about the past. He had been stupid enough to believe that he had her wrapped around his finger. He'd always had grand plans for her money once the old lady died. Thanks to him, their marriage had died long before her grandmother did.

"Mollie!" he yelled, calling to his secretary. She was probably painting her nails. That was how she spent much of her time in the office.

Poking her head into his office, Mollie, living up to her M.O., held one of her hands up high with her fingers spread apart, blowing on them as she shook her hand through the air. "You call me, sugar?" she answered.

"Yeah, and didn't I tell you not to call me 'sugar' while we're in the office?"

With a sarcastic expression, she looked around both offices. "Um . . . we're here by ourselves."

"It doesn't matter. Don't call me sugar here," Ryan said, looking at her, trying to figure out why he kept her around.

"Huh, you didn't say that this morning when you were screwing me on the sofa," she said with a smirk, placing her unpolished hand on her hip.

Oh, right, that's why. "Um . . . look." Ryan shook his head from side to side, shaking the image of that morning's interlude out of his head. "I need you to see if you can get me any information on something called the Umergodia Jewels."

"Umergodia Jewels? What's that?"

"That's what I want you to find out," he exhaled in disgust. This wasn't going to work out. He needed a secretary, and she needed . . . she needed a lot of help.

In a huff, Mollie turned around and walked out the room, causing her short flowing skirt to swirl high, giving Ryan a quick glance at a mocha butt cheek partially covered by a pair of lacey pink panties.

Just a little while longer. Turning away from his desk, he looked out the small office window, wishing he could figure out the best way to approach Theresa. For the past six years, he had wanted to see their son, but Theresa always said no. As far as he was concerned, Theresa was still under the influence of her grandmother. She thought he wanted his son just for the boy's money. That wasn't necessarily true. His son was nine years old and already a multi-millionaire while he struggled to make ends meet with this semi-successful detective agency. The money would help, but he did want to get to know his son.

Either way, he felt a need to find out exactly what this client was talking about and how it involved his son. Knowing he would have to go through Theresa, he prepared himself for another battle. This was not going to be easy. Theresa could be a barracuda when she wanted to be.

Exhaling deeply, he picked up his old desk phone and punched in the numbers to Philips Corporation. He knew the number by heart even though he had never used it before.

"Philips Corporation. How may I direct your call?" the receptionist answered in a cheerful voice. Automatically, he envisioned a body to go with her voice. He'd been doing that for years, and on occasion, even came pretty close to the real thing.

"Um, yes," he began, snatching his mind out of the clouds. "Theresa Philips, please."

"Hold on minute. I'll transfer you to her secretary."

In the next instant, the sound of elevator music floated through the phone line. Ugh, he hated elevator music. But Ryan forced himself to remain patient until the next voice came through.

"Good afternoon, Mrs. Philips's office. How may I help you?" This voice sounded raspier than the first. Raspy, but sexy, he thought, again picturing a beauty, an older beauty.

"Yes, I need to speak to Theresa Philips," he answered and waited.

"I'm sorry, Mrs. Philips is not in the office at the moment. I do expect her back, however, before the end of the day. Can I take a message?"

"Yes, could you tell her . . . you know what, that's okay. I'll just try to catch her before she leaves for the day. Thank you very much." He finished the statement cheerfully, knowing that she would remember his voice when he called back and be more likely to put him through to her. If he left his name, there would be no way for him to talk to her.

Surely, by now, she had already let her secretary know to be on the lookout for his calls. At any rate, he had to honestly admit that it was a relief not to have to talk to her at the moment.

"Mollie!" He grabbed his jacket off the back of the chair. "Mollie, I'll be out for a while." He walked past her, stopping for a brief second. "Find something?"

She didn't move her head from in front of the screen, just moved her eyes up and looked at him, irritated by his presence. Ignoring him altogether, she turned her attention back to the game of FreeCell that occupied one corner of her computer screen. "Yeah, I'm on it," she commented sarcastically.

Mollie hated her job, but she hated actual work even more. Where else was she going to get paid for doing nothing? Occasionally, she did have to lie on her back, but that wasn't all bad. She'd had worse, and it never lasted for longer than twenty minutes.

✧

Ryan's footsteps slowed as he neared his car and saw the large figure sitting on the hood. This is not going to go well, he thought, sizing up the man in front of him. Ryan wasn't a small man by a long shot. He didn't work out often, but his body hadn't gone to the wayside yet. His waistline lacked the tightness that once held it taut, and his pack consisted of ten instead of six, but he wasn't completely out of shape.

The thug on the hood possessed all of the qualities that he didn't. With arms that filled his sweatshirt as if it was a fitted tee and a neck the size of a tree trunk, Harp Jones could be a man's worst nightmare. Luckily, he and Ryan went back a way, and Ryan knew Harp's talent stopped at his physique. You just had to know how to talk to him.

"Harp, what you doing around this part of town?" Ryan asked, his arm extended to let his welcome seem genuine. Surprise brightened his face like a Christmas tree.

"Johnny D sent me down here for his money, Ryan. He said . . ."

"Johnny D? What you talking about?" Ryan rushed to interrupt him. "I just got off the phone with him. I'm on my way over there right now. You want a ride?" Five thousand, that was all he owed Johnny D. You wouldn't think he'd send out the heavy hitters for that little bit of money, but Ryan knew that Johnny D had killed people for much less.

"No." Harp stood his ground. "Um . . ." He didn't know whether to believe what Ryan was saying or not. "I can save you the trip," he stated, finally remembering that Johnny D had told him not to believe anything Ryan said.

"Uh, no. That's all right." Ryan laughed nervously. "I'm going that way."

"Good, I'll follow you," Harp proclaimed proudly.

Ryan shook his head. Somebody must have been giving Harp lessons. He wasn't letting up fast enough. So many times, Ryan had used the same excuse to get away from him that it was pathetic. He hunched his shoulders, wondering if it would work one more time.

"Hold on, Harp. I gotta piss. Stay here while I run up and use the bathroom real fast." He whirled around, hoping his walk was believable. For the first five steps, he held his breath, listening to see if he was being followed. Then he heard Harp's voice.

"Just make it snappy, Ryan. I ain't got all day."

Ryan let his breath out, knowing he had gotten away, momentarily. He would still have to call Johnny D and beg for an extension. Angrily, he marched back up to the second floor of the office building, then to the roof and slowly climbed down the raggedy fire escape ladder. *This is more dangerous than facing Harp.*

With no car, Ryan headed toward the bus stop at the corner of the next block. Why was he in this predicament? His son and his ex-wife were loaded, millionaires thirty, forty, fifty times over, and here he was riding on the city bus because some loan shark had sent his thug after him over a measly five thousand dollars. This was going to change. There was no reason why he should be living like this.

With determination in his mind, Ryan stayed low in his seat in the back of the bus with his destination set. He wasn't going to get anything from Mollie. In all honesty, he didn't think she knew how to do anything on the computer but click the icon for games. The printer never sounded, and when he'd told her to google something last week, she asked if she would need money.

ॐ

"You had a phone call while you were gone," Stephanie started, getting out of her seat and falling into step behind Theresa's long strides. "It was a man, nice voice, interesting."

"What was the name?" Theresa casually asked, taking off her pink cashmere business jacket and throwing it across one of the chairs near her office door. She placed her purse on the counter behind her desk before looking up at Stephanie for an answer.

"He wouldn't say. Just said that he would call back." She sat down in the chair across from Theresa nonchalantly. They had more than a boss and secretary relationship. They were friends. It had taken a while to get to that point, but they both enjoyed the fact that they were now there.

"Is there something else?" Theresa asked impatiently as she looked at her secretary and picked up the folder on the top of the pile. She had a lot of work to get back to doing.

"Somebody else called, too." Stephanie sat back, smiling when Theresa's eyes darkened with curiosity. She continued, "It was a Mr. Brooks, from the towing company."

"Okay, and?" Theresa said, irritated with the tone of Stephanie's voice.

"Your tire is ready," she replied.

"Really? He said it wouldn't be ready until tomorrow." She hunched her shoulders, not giving it a second thought. "Have one of the guys from the garage go pick it up."

"If you want me to. I thought that maybe you'd want to go yourself." Stephanie had watched her closely during the whole conversation.

Theresa looked up at her from the open folder in front of her. "What makes you think that?"

"Because he said that you'd probably want to come pick it up yourself. According to him, you were trying to pick him up today."

"I what?" Theresa almost yelled. "I know you're joking."

"No," Stephanie replied, carefully keeping her smile to a minimum. "He definitely said that you were coming on to him."

"How long did you talk to him?"

"Not long at all. Once I introduced myself as your secretary, he kinda said what he had to say. I tried to question him, but he didn't change his story. And I told him that he had to be joking, too. Apparently something happened to make him think you're after him. And you know what, I think he's interested in you, too."

"Why do you say that?" Theresa tried to hide her interest in the man, but she already knew that Stephanie's nose was wide open with curiosity and the prospect of possible matchmaking. "I mean, did he say something to make you think that?"

"Not in so many words, but he didn't sound disappointed by it. Now, you tell me. Does he look as good as he sounds?"

"Girl, yes," Theresa rushed out before getting a grip on herself. "Get away, Stephanie. I have way too much work to do," Theresa said, laughing.

"Okay, so do I, but just give me a hint."

"He's a very nice looking man. There, are you happy now?"

"Yes," she smiled, getting up to return to her desk. "I told you that you were going to meet someone nice this year."

"Stephanie, just because you go to that psychic of yours every week doesn't make you a psychic yourself."

"Well, since you won't go with me, I've appointed myself your personal psychic."

"In that case, I'm glad I don't pay you for those abilities. However, I do pay you for other abilities, none of which you are performing at the moment."

"Hint taken." Stephanie smiled as she walked out of the office.

Theresa waited until Stephanie was out of the room before she put the folder down and relaxed back into her chair, allowing the image of the handsome mechanic to creep back into her imagination. All six-feet-something of him. At that moment, she knew that she was going to get her tire herself. And her excitement rose, knowing that she was going to work for only a couple more hours.

Putting her head back down, she made herself work harder than before just to make the time go by that much faster. When she looked up again, two hours had passed and her brother was poking his golden blond head in her office door.

"I see you, girl. Getting all this work done, aren't you?" Michael laughed, walking into the room and taking a seat across from her.

Whenever she saw either of her brothers, she couldn't help thinking how handsome they were. She would never tell them in a million years, but she loved that they were related to her. It was strange how they favored each other so much, but were also as opposite as night and day. Thorne was ruggedly handsome with lumberjack shoulders and steel-gray eyes and dark hair; Michael was lean and rangy, and also ruggedly handsome but in an Armani suit sort of way.

Michael was impeccably dressed, as always, except when he was with his girlfriend, or not girlfriend, Tamia. She was the only person Theresa had ever seen him off-balance with, if that was the right term. All she knew was that when those two were around each other sparks flew. And she honestly admitted that she was a little envious that both of her brothers had seemingly found that one person that was for them.

Even though she received a lot compliments, she never felt herself to be as attractive as her brothers. That might have been because for all the years she was involved with her son's father, he tried his best to keep his compliments low and her self-esteem lower. And despite her millions of dollars, she'd never felt her own self-worth until she was rid of him.

"I'm trying my hardest to get out of here," she commented absently.

He looked at her strangely, noticing her excitement, "Why? You got a hot date or something?"

"Of course not," she laughed nervously. "Don't be silly. I just refuse to be stuck here until ten o'clock again tonight."

"Well, what's the good mood for?" He watched her closely.

"I just got someplace to go after work. Could you watch Mikey for me for a minute? It shouldn't take me long."

"Sure," he said, looking at her funny. "But I got a date with Tamia at nine. Will you be back in time?"

"Oh, way before that," she said, steadily skimming papers, signing what needed to be signed, and working her IN pile down. She felt him still watching her. "What are you looking at me like this before. What's going on? Where do you have to go?" he asked curiously.

"I've just never seen you like this before. What's going on? Where do you have to go?" he asked curiously.

"Like what? I said no place important. Now," she said, standing and smoothing down the sides of her shirt, "excuse me while I run into the bathroom to freshen up."

Michael watched her walk past him with her head held high. He wondered what had gotten into her. "Like that. All 'let me freshen up.' Where you going or who are you going to? I'm going to find out," he yelled to her as he watched her reapply her makeup in the bathroom mirror. "And when Throne calls tonight, I'm going to tell him that you're up to something."

"Michael, Thorne's not my dad. He's my brother, and so are you. Therefore, I don't have to answer to either of you or tell you my business if I choose not to. I am a grown woman. And when I say that it's none of your business, I mean just that."

"Oh, it's like that now. We used to be the three musketeers," he reminded her.

"Yeah, when we were five and six, Michael. I'm thirty-four. It's time for you to stop being all in my business."

"Fine. Don't tell me," he laughed at her. "It'll all come out in the end." Deep down, he didn't want to let the matter rest, but she was right. She was grown, and it was time for him and Thorne to both stop being so protective of her. The past was the past, and she hadn't had a man in her life so far as he knew since they had finally gotten Ryan out of the picture. She had to be lonely, and it couldn't have been easy for her to watch the womanizers that he and Thorne had dedicated themselves to becoming over the years. Luckily, Thorne was now settled and engaged, and he considered himself in a semi-serious relationship, although he would never tell Tamia that.

"If you must know, I'm going to the library. I have a homework assignment due tomorrow night." That wasn't too much of a lie.

"You're this excited about the library?"

"Yeah, so mind your business. What are you and Tamia up to tonight?" Theresa asked, deciding to change the subject and catch him off guard. "Going out or staying in?"

"Romantic evening in," he replied. "One of those 'she needs to talk to me about something' nights."

"Oww . . . that sounds serious."

"Yeah, it does. I've been wondering what's going on all day," he said, walking toward her desk to get a peek at her calendar. Maybe there was a clue somewhere on it about this meeting.

"Well, is everything all right?" Theresa asked, walking out of the bathroom and smiling once she realized what he was up to.

"Huh, yeah, yeah. Everything's great." Looking up, he noticed her watching him. His face turned a soft shade of red from the slight embarrassment of having been caught snooping. But Michael simply hunched his shoulders and moved away from the desk. He didn't know anybody who got that excited about checking out a library book.

"You ought to be ashamed of yourself, but I know you're not," she stated.

"No, not really. I want to know what you're up to, and so will Thorne."

"Yeah, but Thorne's not here, and neither will I be in a few minutes." Theresa stuck out her tongue and walked toward the office door. "Let's go, little brother. Go find my son. I'll be back in a couple of hours, no more."

"All right. Just be careful."

"Always, but it's not that serious." She smiled as she walked out the door behind him. As she pulled the door to, Theresa heard her office phone ring. She was about to open the door and quickly answer it, but after a brief hesitation, she decided that to let the machine answer it. She'd save whatever problem it was until tomorrow.

$\mathcal{SP}$

"Philips Corporation. This is Theresa Philips speaking. Unfortunately, I am unable to take your phone call. Please leave a number and message at the beep, and I will return your call as soon as possible."

Ryan slowly moved the phone from his ear, expelling a long breath. Shaking his head, he mentally admitted to himself that a part of him still held very strong feelings for the woman whose voice made a hard shiver run up his spine. Mixed emotions played throughout his body.

Relief filled him as he thanked the Lord that he didn't have to speak to Theresa because he knew an argument would have been the end result, especially after he asked her about her heritage and the jewels.

He listened to whole the voicemail message before hanging up, even though he knew that he was not going to leave a message. He just wanted to hear her voice. He was almost tempted to call back, but thought better of it. Ryan decided to just be glad he didn't have to talk to her at that moment. He wasn't sure if he was truly ready.

CHAPTER 4

As she sat in her car in the large parking lot of Brooks Repair and Towing Service, Theresa wished that she didn't have the sudden flash of hesitation. Her self-esteem wasn't the problem. She was sure that she was interested in this man, at least interested enough in a little harmless flirting. He was interested in her, too. She could feel it. No, her self-esteem wasn't the problem. Her problem was plain old fear, she assumed. Fear of making a fool of herself doing something that she hadn't done in years.

For ten minutes, she sat behind her steering wheel talking to herself, pushing down her anxiety, and making her task of just walking into the building seem like nothing. That was how her grandmother had taught her to handle her problems. Make them smaller.

The knock on her driver side window startled her bad enough to make her jump. She looked up to see Pierson standing next to her with his hands on his hips.

"Is everything all right?" he asked, a look of bewilderment on his face.

"Uh . . . yeah," she quickly replied, nodding her head as she opened the car door and stepped out. Her face glowed with the bright red telltale of embarrassment. "Everything's fine."

"I thought you were going to sit out here all day." He laughed. "What are you doing?"

"You wouldn't believe me if I told you," she replied.

"Sure I would. Tell me," he demanded, jokingly. At her hesitation, he continued, daringly, "Unless you're afraid to."

Theresa stood to her full height beside him. She knew a challenge when she heard one. "First of all, I'm not afraid of anything."

He snickered.

She thought it was sexy, but she continued, "Secondly, challenges don't work with me. I was sitting in the car talking to myself. Is that a problem?"

"No problem," he answered, trying to hold his laughter, "you look good at it. Do you do that often?"

"Mr. Brooks, you don't know me." Theresa began to walk away from him, heading toward the shop door. "I'm just here to pick up my tire," she finished, not nearly as agitated as she pretended.

A gasp escaped her as his hand reached out to lightly grab hold of her arm. Again he had surprised her, caught her off guard. She hadn't had a man dare be so bold with her since Ryan. But instead of feeling the tension that bound her when Ryan did it, she was stunned by the flutter of butterflies that filled her stomach and made the bottom of her spine tingle.

Pierson turned her around and looked down into her face. He knew exactly who she was. It didn't take a scientist to figure that out after he called the corporation to let her know that the tire was ready. Who hadn't heard of the

Philips Corporation, especially with all the volunteer and charity work they had been doing since the hurricanes? Her brother Thorne was talked about practically every night on the news.

"I know exactly who you are, Ms. Theresa Philips," he replied, looking at her closely with amusement. He was waiting for the surprise and shock to come over her face, but to her credit, Theresa's posture and facial expression remained exactly the same. She didn't move away from him as he expected.

"Just call me Theresa," she said, determination making her stand her ground. Determination and curiosity. Theresa glanced down at the hand that still warmed a spot on her forearm, then looked him square in the face and put the ball in his court. "Are we going to stand here all day, with your hand on my arm? Or am I going to pick up my tire?"

As if just remembering that he had hold of her, Pierson put his arm down to his side and casually looked around his parking lot. He didn't need anyone to see him with his hands on the white woman dressed superbly in the shapely pink outfit that she was wearing earlier when he had seen her. Taking an easy step away from her, he let his eyes peruse the parts of her body that he wouldn't allow himself to look at earlier.

Her strong, shapely hips and thighs held him captivated for a moment, but it was her calves that made his heart skip a beat. She had to work out or do a lot of walking for them to be so thick and muscular, sticking out from her legs like the bulging muscles in his own arms.

"Are you looking at my legs for a particular reason?" Theresa asked. He was looking so closely that she felt any minute he would bend down and start inspecting her like one of his vehicles. Besides, his close appraisal was making the tingling between her thighs almost unbearable.

"I like your legs," he answered matter-factly. "I could look at them all day. But thanks for stopping me. I do have work to do. You ready?" Without another word, Pierson turned and began walking toward his building. As he had expected, Danielle was standing in the window watching everything that was going on.

On a long expel of breath, he opened the door to the reception office. Luckily, it was close to quitting time, and there weren't any customers in the waiting room. She was going to be the last customer of the day. Actually, he had planned it that way. He held the door open and stood to the side, allowing her first entrance, just as a gentleman should. He was a gentleman.

Theresa entered the room, glancing around with interest. "This is a nice setup," she said. "Comfortable and spacious. Nice décor, totally separate from the work area."

"Always business?"

"Forgive me," she apologized. "I'm an interior decorator. I guess it's hard for me to go into a room and not picture what it could look like." Taking another look, she finally saw the young lady standing next to the front windows. "Oh, I'm sorry. Hello." Something, maybe the slightest hint of anger in the girl's eyes, gave Theresa the impression that she wasn't too welcome.

"Hi," the girl replied almost as if it was forced out by manners long homed in.

Pierson quickly stepped forward to make the introductions. "Theresa, this is my younger sister, Danielle. Danielle, this a new friend of mine, Theresa."

"What kind of friend?" Danielle asked without hesitation as she moved forward, looking Theresa over thoroughly.

"A good friend, so don't start," he replied, a look of warning crossing his face. The last thing he needed was for Danielle to act like a spoiled brat. She was starting to get real good at it and it was getting really annoying. Instead of staying around for her to start the fireworks, he quickly guided Theresa down the hall to the door that led to the garage.

"Everything okay?" she asked, once they were in the garage.

"Yeah, she's just spoiled, and has some issues that she's dealing with. She doesn't like living here."

"Why is she here and not with your parents?" Theresa decided to be as nosy as she wanted to be.

"My mother passed away a few years ago, and Danielle got to be too much for my father. After he caught one of the neighborhood boys running out of the house when he came in from one of his meetings, he gave me a call. She's been down here ever since, and like I said, she hates it. I think she's starting to hate me a little, too."

"No, she doesn't. She's just a teenage girl. Teenage girls resent being held down, but she'll be grateful for it later. Believe me."

Pierson looked her up and down. "Somehow, I get the impression that you're talking from experience."

"Well, don't let these $500 shoes and this Donna Karan business suit fool you. I used to raise a little hell back in my day." She crossed her arms, daring him to doubt her.

"What did you do, hang out at the local bar one time too many?"

"I don't think you're ready to know the truth about that time in my life. You'd probably have a coronary if you knew." She laughed and crossed his path to step into the back garage, causing her right shoulder to brush against his chest. *Hard,* she thought.

"Yeah, right. I'm sure it won't be that hard to figure out. Anyway, here's your tire. I repaired the puncture and cleaned it for you."

"Well, I truly appreciate it," she replied, standing next to him and looking at the tire as if it were going to walk to the car by itself.

"I'm going to carry this out to the car for you, but if you really want to show your appreciation," he started as he bent to pick up the tire, showing off his firm butt cheeks and strong leg muscles, which Theresa took extra care to give the once-over, "why don't you consider the possibility of going someplace with me." Walking past her, he made sure he looked her directly in the eye to let her know how serious he was.

Theresa was happy, excited, thrilled, all of that. With just his voice, just making that suggestion, he had made her feel good inside, too good. It surprised her a little.

She hadn't felt that way in a long time. She smiled to herself as she retraced her steps out of the garage, down the
hall, through the reception area and past his sister, who
still looked to be mad at the world, and to the front door.

Theresa said goodbye to the girl as she left, but didn't
hear a reply. She wished that she could have cheered her
up in some way, but who was she to be saying anything
to her? As far as that girl was concerned, she was just supposed to be another customer. But as far as that girl's
brother was concerned, Theresa was going to be much
more. The smile returned as the evening sunlight hit her
face.

She loved this time of year, mugginess, gnats, mos-
quitoes and all that New Orleans entailed in the summer
months. Even the heat, as hot and humid as it was,
seemed to be pure pleasure to her. But all that could be
because she had a reason to want to enjoy the rest of her
summer—the tall, muscular man standing near the trunk
of her car holding a tire in one hand.

"Are you asking me out on an official date, Mr.
Brooks?" Theresa tried playing coy, though it had never
suited her. "If you are, I'd like that." She moved near him
to open the trunk.

Once he pushed the tire down into the trunk, Pierson
turned to face her. "I wasn't actually asking you on a date,
it was more like a favor. But if you want to call it a date,
it's okay with me."

Theresa's mouth fell open slightly. Her shock, she
realized, showed her as more vain than she would have
wished. She had never been treated so nonchalantly, and

she found that she liked it. This man kept her more on her toes than any of the CEOs, CFOs, or VIPs she'd dealt with over the years.

"I'll give your secretary a call with the details," he continued.

"No," she retorted, digging into her bag for her personal business card. "Call me directly, please."

"Will do." Pierson walked her to the driver side of the car and watched her slide in. He stood in the parking lot until she pulled off, and then walked back into the shop. Of course, his sister was standing at the window.

Theresa stretched. She smiled. She prayed. She thought of him. Regretting that she couldn't snuggle back down in her bed and finish her dream about Pierson, Theresa got up and went into her son's room. Mikey was sleeping so peacefully she hesitated to wake him, but she knew that if she didn't they would never get to the office. The fact that her apartment was on the second to the top floor of the Philips Corporation Building made it that much easier for her to be lazy and late. Thorne, being the oldest, had the penthouse, which he sometimes shared with his recently discovered mother. He had wanted her to give up her own house and move in with him, but she'd refused, saying that they both needed their space. Michael's apartment was on the floor beneath hers.

"Wake up, sleepyhead," she said to her son softly, running her fingers through his hair.

"I'm awake, Mommy," he replied, refusing to move from beneath the sheets.

"You've got five minutes to get up. And you have to hurry if you're going to work with Samuel again today. I know he's already on his way to work."

"Okay."

Theresa smiled. She'd thought the mention of Samuel's name would wake him, but her plan seemed to have backfired.

"Five minutes."

He didn't respond, and Theresa realized he was asleep. She would give him another half-hour while she worked out.

Theresa moaned as she pushed in the workout tape that was supposed to be helping her lose weight by using it for eight minutes three times a week. She hadn't lost any weight yet, and she'd been using it for a year now. But in the tape's defense, she hadn't gained any either. She was still the same 155 pounds she was last year.

Eight minutes later, she was breathless.

In the shower, she let her mind wander to Pierson Brooks and wondered where he wanted to take her. She had no idea what he had in mind, and apprehension tightened her stomach when she thought about it. But after being alone for so long, Theresa felt it was time for her to get out a little. During their marriage, Ryan had treated her so badly that when she was finally free from him, the last thing she'd wanted was another man. Of course, she'd never thought the feeling would last six years. Her separation from Ryan lasted a year before she was able to divorce him, but with the help of her grand-mother's friends, her divorce went in her favor even though he fought to get as much money as he could. It had been the custody battle that took forever.

At any rate, that was the past. And Theresa was looking forward to her future, the possibility of getting to know Pierson and having some male companionship. But could she manage her job, her son, and a friendship?

She hunched her shoulders as she wrapped the extra large towel around herself. *Women do it every day*, she mused. Theresa dried off and put on her robe before going back to her son's room. They really had to get a move on. She had stayed in the shower longer than she should have, daydreaming about a man that she had met only twice.

"Mikey? Come on, baby. We gotta get ready for work."

"Okay," he replied, obeying his mother. He walked into his bathroom, which was decorated to look like a coral reef. The wall was illustrated with replicas of different types of fish. All of his bathroom accessories expressed the same theme. It had been his birthday present last year, and he loved it after having watched the movie *Nemo*.

Theresa went to the kitchen and made him a bowl of cereal, a toaster strudel and a glass of orange juice. When he followed her, he was wide awake with a clean face and mouth.

"Mom, I like working with Sam. I can learn a lot from him."

"I already know that, dear." Theresa glanced at her son. She knew what he was up to. "And just so you know, I don't have a problem with you working with Sam just so long as you don't slow him down. He has a job to do, and you can't interfere with it."

"I just think that I could do a better job if I was there all the time. I could really learn a lot about the business."

"You think that's necessary? I don't think you have to worry about that right now."

"Well, what if something happens, and I'm needed. I think I should stay close to you."

"Don't worry about me. Uncle Thorne and Michael will help."

"That's not good enough," he said, suddenly standing up from the table and running to his room.

For the first time, Theresa stopped buttering her toast. She decided that it was time for them to have a serious talk. She'd had no idea that he took this subject so seriously. This was supposed to have been just their routine banter.

Following him back to his bedroom, she found Mikey lying across his bed crying. "Hey . . . come on now. Sit up here and talk to me, please," she urged him up as she sat down on his bed. "Tell me what the problem is, Mikey. You know that you can talk to me about anything."

Between sobs, Mikey did as he was told. "I don't want you to be alone."

Theresa was speechless. What was he talking about? Where had he gotten these ideas?

"Mikey, I appreciate you worrying about me, but I am fine. I am only lonely when I miss you. But I have you at the academy because it's a very good school."

"But there are good schools here. I could transfer. If you don't get a husband, you're going to be lonely and sad."

"Is this about you changing schools or about me getting married?"

"Both," he replied, wiping his eyes. "I need to change schools, and you need a husband." He said it so easily that it sounded like a to-do list, not a statement.

"Mikey, if you really want to look into a private school in the area, I don't have a problem with that. You know your education is first and foremost to me. We can look into it. But if we don't find something quickly, before school starts in September, you might have to go back to the academy for another year."

"Okay, but I'll help so we can find one fast. I'll help you find a husband, too."

"No, you will not!" Theresa yelled.

"But . . ."

"Mikey, darling, that isn't something that you can help Mommy with. That's something I'm going to have to do on my own."

"Well, when are you going to? You are always working, and now you're going to school. I think you need my help."

"What did I just tell you? There are some things that I have to do myself. Now let's get dressed, we're late."

"Okay, but next year, I'll be ten," he said as he stood up and walked to his closet. "Before you know it, I'll be gone, and nobody will be here with you."

Theresa didn't reply. She walked to her room and silently contemplated his statement. Time was going fast. It seemed like just a few years ago she was bringing him home from the hospital. Was she truly running out of time?

The idea of moving her son to a closer school wasn't necessarily a bad one. She had originally picked the school in Texas to keep Ryan from being able to see him on a whim. Ryan had never been particularly caring to Mikey. He saw his son as a meal ticket, and Theresa was not going to allow her son to be used. But it was time to stop running. Mikey was older, and she now had full custody since Ryan had failed to show up for numerous custody hearings. The day after the verdict was put in place and her full custody was granted, her lawyers informed the judge that Ryan had been located and provided an address for his notification of custody hearing letter to be sent.

CHAPTER 5

Theresa was deep in paperwork by the time her brother Michael decided to pop into her office.

"Hey," he said, flopping himself in the closest chair.

"Hey yourself," she said, giving note to his five o'clock shadow. Michael always shaved before coming to work unless something was troubling him.

"Did you get that homework done you were so anxious to get to the library for?"

"Yes, I did, thank you. And thank God it's Friday. I can't wait for Sunday to get here so I can hand Thorne's work back over to him."

"Well, I'm glad you did it. Remember when I had to cover for him because he didn't know 'who he was'?"

"Yeah, well, now I know. I hope he and Natalie don't get married anytime soon, or we'll be stuck with the work again."

"Don't hold your breath. I think that we'll find out Sunday that they are officially engaged and have a date set."

Theresa signed a few more forms before realizing that Michael was quiet and in deep thought.

"So, how did your evening with Tamia go?" she asked, guessing that was the cause of his meditation.

"Um, I guess it went okay," he answered, then grew quiet again.

"Michael?" Theresa had given him a few minutes to sulk, but this was getting ridiculous. She didn't know what his problem was, but she didn't have all day for him to tell her what it was. She had work to do.

"I'm going to be a father," he blurted out. His voice sounded torn between excitement and anguish.

Theresa smiled until she looked at his face closely. "Well, is a 'congratulations' or an 'oh, damn' in order?"

"It's both. I'm not ready to be a father."

"Most men aren't. But you love kids. You'll make a wonderful father."

He ran his hands over his face, sitting forward with his elbows on his knees.

"You didn't act this way around Tamia, did you?"

"No, I wrapped her in my arms and told her that I loved her, and—"

"Do you? I mean, I know you did all of that because it's what you were supposed to do. Having been New Orleans' bachelor of the year a number of times, you must know your way around the mind of a woman, but do you really love Tamia?"

"I ask myself that all the time. We've only been seeing each other four or five months. There is definitely something about her that keeps me snagged more than I've ever been before with anyone. It's like when we are together there is an electricity that's between us, you know?"

65

Theresa remained quiet because she didn't know. She only wished that she did.

"And she doesn't want to marry me. Says that I only asked her because of the baby."

"That's true."

"Yeah, it is, but my child won't be born out of wedlock. I can't have that."

"Michael, you do know that this is the twenty-first century, right? You will have partial custody, and the baby can still have your last name. You don't have to be married to Tamia before she has the baby. Stop being so old-fashioned. With our family history, you and Tamia not getting married is not the worst thing in the world."

"They had their reasons for doing what they did, and I have mine for insisting that Tamia marries me."

"This is not going to be pretty. You know that Tamia is going to fight you to the death before she gives in to you. I think that's why you are so enthralled with her. She doesn't bow down and kiss your feet like all those society pinheads you and Thorne used to date. Isn't it funny that it was sisters from the same family, both very opinionated and independent women, who captured the hearts of the Philips boys."

"I see that you're not exactly the best person to be speaking to about my situation. You seem to be getting a lot of enjoyment out of it."

"I don't enjoy seeing you in pain, no. But I do think this is going to play out so interestingly that I won't be going anywhere anytime soon. I've seen you and Tamia together. This is going to be more interesting than anything I've ever seen before."

"She's just going to have to marry me."

"Do you really think that's the best solution right now? You said it yourself. You've only been dating for a few months, and for one of those months, you were both dating other people."

"Well, Thorne and Natalie haven't been dating long, either."

"Thorne and Natalie are very different people than you and Tamia. If I were you, I'd tread very lightly. If not, you might end up losing her."

"Not with my baby. The way I see it, she's tied to me forever, and vice versa."

"Like I said, this is going to be interesting," she stated. Then she changed the subject before Michael's anger grew. "Oh, don't forget that Mikey has a basketball game tomorrow at the Boys and Girls Club."

"What time?"

"Ten. Don't be late."

"I won't. Has he been practicing? You know he's not the most coordinated. I told him to practice dribbling. He dribbles like Thorne used to."

"Leave my son alone. You still got him tonight for me, right?"

"Yeah, I got him. Is this for school or the library again?"

"Hah, hah. I have school tonight. Michael, you really need to sign up for the class. When Natalie said that Mom was a good teacher, she wasn't lying. I'm telling you, this is one of the best decisions I've ever made. It would help you learn a lot about our history."

"I know enough about my history."

"I'm talking about the history of our black ancestors."

"I know that they were slaves. What more is there?"

"You big dummy. There is so much more to know. And I'm not talking about our specific ancestors. Hell, I know that blacks were slaves, but I'm talking about learning specific events and names. I'm talking about learning of their persecution and resilience, and knowing the names of people who made a difference in the world, who persevered although the odds were against them."

Michael watched as her face lit up and her eyes grew expressive. "Wow, it must be a good class. I haven't seen you this passionate about anything in a long time. Maybe Mom will educate Thorne and me a little at home. I mean, we are black. I think we should learn a little more about ourselves."

"Isn't it funny how as soon as the media found out that our grandfather was black, we became black, at thirty-four and thirty-two?"

"Yeah, Tamia and I were talking about that ourselves. I guess it's all about labeling in America. Either you're white or black, not both. Even Thorne, who is half and half, is black. But hey, look at President Obama. They don't call him the first biracial president; he's the first black president. It's like the white side just goes away when it comes to classifications."

"Look, I've got to get back into this pile because I'm going to have this done by the end of the day. When Thorne comes in Monday, I want him to have a fresh slate. I want you to think hard about pressuring Tamia because I don't want it to backfire on you."

"I will. Hey, do you need any help finishing this up? I've got some free time, I could help. Mikey is down in mailroom following Samuel foot to foot. We could order lunch and work on it together." Michael stood up and picked up Theresa's phone.

"Yes," Stephanie answered.

"Hey, Steph, it's Michael."

"Hi, Michael," Stephanie answered. She had always had a small crush on him, but because he was her good friend's brother and one of the bosses, she knew it could never be. "What's up?"

"Could you order Theresa and me some sandwiches? We're going to work in here through lunch."

"Sure. I'll order them right away."

"Thanks," he replied, and then turned to Theresa. "Okay, let's get this done."

Theresa could barely wait to get to class. With Michael's help she had managed to finish the whole pile of paperwork. Thorne's desk was cleared, and so was hers. Michael had an appointment Monday morning that he couldn't reschedule, but aside from that Thorne's homecoming should be uneventful.

She was second in the classroom and proudly took her seat in the front row. Smartly, she'd taken the time to go up to the penthouse to change before going to class. Tonight, she wore a pair of Gucci jeans and sweater. Luckily, she'd found the outfit in the back of her closet. She hadn't worn them in years, but her confidence soared when she could still fit in them.

"Hi," she said as she sat down in her seat.

"Hi," the girl replied. "Nice jeans."

"Thanks," Theresa said.

"I'm Dottie."

"Theresa."

"So, are you rich or something?" Dottie asked.

Theresa turned toward the young girl, who was almost half her age. "Why would you say that?"

"Well, Tuesday, you had on an expensive suit. Today, you got on Gucci jeans. I love fashion so I know they cost a pretty penny. Either you're rich or you have a sugar daddy."

"Sugar daddy?"

"Yeah. Blonde hair, green eyes, white skin. I know you have black men falling all over you. Hell, men, period, for that matter."

Theresa felt this girl was invading her privacy. She had never had a conversation like this, especially with a stranger. Theresa realized that because of her busy schedule hadn't had a lot of time to maintain relationships with other women. Stephanie was her only 'girlfriend' besides Natalie and her sisters, who were more like family. And they were still in the process of getting to know one another. She struggled to find the right words.

Dottie mistook her silence for confirmation and figured she had hit the nail on the head. "It's okay. A lot of the girls here have sugar daddies, but obviously yours is more generous."

"Dottie, I don't have a sugar daddy," Theresa stated simply. "I'm sorry to disappoint you."

Before Dottie could make another statement, other students began walking into the room. Theresa was thankful because she had no idea where the conversation might have gone.

"Class, welcome back. I assume that everyone enjoyed their assignments and had no problems. Am I correct? Did anyone have trouble?" Amanda gave the students a chance to respond. No one answered. "Good. You can pass your worksheets and your essays forward. We'll go around the room for the introduction presentations and then move right into tonight's lecture."

After everything was passed forward, Amanda did a quick roll call, and as she did, Amanda asked each student to stand and give their presentation. Theresa was relieved that she wasn't first so that she could get an idea of what was expected of her. But as her turn approached, her nervousness grew. Amanda, she noticed, tended to ask questions based on her student's responses, which caused others to ask questions as well.

Theresa stood when it was her turn. She didn't understand why she was having such a problem with this. During the day, she was tough, straightforward, and rubbed shoulders with men with more power than these college students. But in the boardroom, she didn't let people into her personal space. This was personal, this class, the whole reason why she was there, and it was a subject that was close to her heart.

"My name is Theresa Philips. I am the single mother of a nine-year-old son named Michael, and I am black. I know that when you look at me, you don't see it. Honestly, I never saw it myself. I never knew it before a few months ago. So, I honestly don't know how to define myself as anything but a woman struggling to raise my son correctly, because I want him to be strong and confident with himself. I want him to know his heritage, black and white. I don't want him to have to choose between his races when both make him the person that he is. I don't see color in a person. And even though I grew up thinking I was a white woman, I was taught that all races are equal, and that people are judged by their actions, not the color of their skin." She tried to keep it as simple as possible without giving away too much of herself or her life, but before Amanda could ask anything, two hands went up in the air.

Amanda pointed to one student.

"So, what's changed in your life since finding out that you were black?"

Theresa had to think for a minute before answering. "Nothing has changed in my life, but everything has changed within me. I've always had friends and associates of different races. I still have those. The most important change in me is that I want to become more educated about my black side. I want to know more than the little I learned in school."

"So, the only reason you want to learn about black is because you found out that you are black?"

"Is there something wrong with that?" Theresa asked, becoming defensive. "I mean, have any of you signed up for White American History lessons?"

"No, because that's all we ever learned in school."

"Well, that's not my fault. I'm not going to say that if an African American History class had been offered in high school that I would have taken it, but I am also not going to say that I wouldn't have. As far as I'm concerned, this is my time to learn about my history, my black history, and that's what I'm doing. It's not to prove a point because you may think that I'm not black enough. This class is all about me. What I've found is that if I walked in here in a dashiki with my hair in braids, it would offend most of you more because all you see when you look at me is a white woman. So, I'm kinda stuck between a rock and a hard place, aren't I?"

"I think she's right." Patrick stood up next to her. "We," he waved to the students, "judged, um, Theresa as soon as she walked in the door Tuesday night. We all saw her as a white woman and wondered why she was in here. Not one of us fathomed that she was black. I think it was a little judgmental on our side, and I think there is still resentment that Theresa here could have passed when we could not have."

This spurred a heated debate that every classmate had an opinion on. Amanda had to stop the conversation in order to cover the required class material, dealing with slavery sales and the difference between house slaves and field slaves. Teams were formed in the room, all of the light-skinned blacks on one side, the dark-skinned blacks on the other. Lists were made of how each side thought they would have been treated in slavery times and the outcomes were discussed. For homework, there was another worksheet and another essay. This time, they had to write on how they thought their lives would have been in the year 1780 as a slave.

Theresa loved this class. She loved the debates, the honesty, and the information.

In the dark, Ryan sat contemplating his life. A lot of things had been happening lately to make him wonder if all the decisions he had made were valid ones. Namely, he should never have let Theresa divorce him so easily. If he was still married to her, he wouldn't have Harp lurking around every corner waiting to pound him to death, and his business could be more successful.

Confusion fell over him as he tried to think of a way to crawl out of his troubles.

Not even Mollie and the performance she was putting on could help take his mind off his problems, although she was helping him release some of his tension. He probably would have told her to dismount if he could figure out a solution.

"You like that, baby?" she whispered in his ear.

Ryan liked the mocha beauty because she was attentive to his needs, but that was where the line was drawn. "Yes, right there, love," he replied.

Ring. Ring.

"Hello," Ryan answered the phone after placing a hand on Mollie's hip to slow her movement.

"Ryan, I got the word on your son."

"Give it to me."

"He's got a basketball game tomorrow at the high school gym."

"Basketball?"

"PAL League."

"How'd you find out that information?"

"Don't worry about it. Just be there at ten o'clock if you want to see your son."

"Thanks, Jim."

"Just have that bill to me by tomorrow."

Ryan hung up the phone. It was a damn shame when a private investigator had to hire another private investigator to track down his own son. But his problem was solved. Now, he could relax and enjoy.

Mollie felt herself flung on her back as Ryan grew inside of her. The smile on her face was one of relief. She now knew that this wasn't going to be a waste of her time. With his first plunge, Ryan focused his attention on bringing her as much pain as possible. That was how Mollie liked it, rough. And he didn't disappoint her as her screams filled the night air, building louder and louder until her final climax.

"Agh, thank you, baby," she said after he rolled off her. Her fingers played teasingly in his hair. Mollie loved to twirl her finger in the brown mass. His body was covered with tattoos, not as many as Tommy Lee from Motley Crew, but enough for it to be sexy and not nasty. She traced a few before he got up and left the bed. That was what he always did once she paid too much attention to his markings. She knew he had a large-ass tattoo on his back of his first wife. And there were at least two different 'Theresa' tattoos on him. By now, she had seen his whole body. Mollie knew that she could never compete with his imagination, so she never tried. She wasn't in love with him anyway.

Ryan did just as she expected. He stood and headed toward the shower. Under the hot water, he tried to think out the next day. What would he say when he saw her? How would she respond? How surprised would she be that he'd found her? He couldn't wait. He should take Mollie with him just to show her that he was doing well and in a loving relationship, whether it was true or not. Then again, that would ruin any chance of them possibly reconciling, if he had to play that angle. No, he would go alone with the assumption that he wanted to spend time with his son. It was time for the boy to get to know who his father was.

But how would he find a way to work in a discussion on the Umergodia Jewels? It wasn't as if he could just blurt it out. No, this was going to take some delicate handling on his side, and the first thing he was going to have to do was show how much he was dedicated to getting to know his son better, at least until she trusted him. This could take a lot longer than he thought.

CHAPTER 6

"Hello?" Theresa whispered into the phone. She was still a little drowsy from sleep. It had to be early. She glanced at the clock, 6:45 a.m.

"Hello, Theresa. It's Pierson, Pierson Brooks."

She sat up in the bed immediately. "Hi, Pierson. How are you doing?"

"I'm fine, and yourself?"

"Good. Good. What do I owe the pleasure of this phone call?"

"I was just thinking that maybe if you aren't busy today, we can get into something."

"So, this is the not-date that you were talking about? How did you get my number?"

"I called your office yesterday, and your secretary, Stephanie, said that you had just left to go to school so she gave me your cell number."

"Did she?"

"Yeah, she's very nice. I guess I would not have gotten your cellphone number if she hadn't answered. I tried your office first, thought you might have been working overtime. So, what you got planned for the day?"

"Actually, I am taking my son to his basketball game today."

"Oh yeah. Where?"

"I signed him up for the PAL League after my brothers insisted that he needed to get around other kids and broaden his horizons. He's not overly enthused about it himself."

"Is he a shy kid?"

"No, not really. Unfortunately, I believe that I've had him around adults for most of his life."

"What about school?"

Theresa laughed. "Most of the kids at his school acted like adults. They suffered from the same situation. It was a military school, so it was strict and very discipline-based."

"You said 'was'? Does that mean that he no longer goes to that school?"

"Well, we had a little talk the other morning and he would like us to find a school closer to home. His old school is in Texas."

"I can understand him wanting to be close to his mother."

"My son is worried that I'm lonely." Theresa was not about to mention that Mikey insisted that she needed a husband. That was a surefire way to have Pierson running for the hills.

"He wants to protect you. Commendable. Every boy should feel that way about his mother. So, where is his game? I mean, if you don't mind me coming."

"No, of course not."

"Does he know how to play?"

"Not very well from the looks of it, but this is their first game. I definitely see an improvement from the first night's practice, though."

"Can I meet you there around 10:30 a.m.?"

"You don't have to go to the shop today? I figured that today would be one of your busiest days."

"Saturdays usually are, but I gave those to my manager when Danielle moved down so I could spend time with her. She used to play basketball. Maybe she'll want to come. She's been in a funk with me lately because I won't let her run wild like her friends do."

Theresa didn't respond right away. She remembered those days very well. "I have a little experience with rebellion. She'll come around. All you can do is stay strong, pray, and keep talking to her. Eventually, she will see that you are only looking out for her best interests. I know that I was responsible for half the gray hairs my grandmother had in her head when I was a teenager, but she never gave up on me, and I thank her so much for that."

"I hope you're right. I think she has a lot of bottled-up anger. She's still mad at my mother for dying and my father for sending her down here. In Philly, she basically had free rein over the household. My parents had her too late in life, so she was spoiled from the get-go. They couldn't run after her like they did me or my older brother."

"Well then, it's a good thing that you took her in. She'll be graduating soon. Hopefully, she'll realize soon enough that her actions have repercussions. Why did you come to New Orleans?"

"Honestly, I didn't mean to. My father was a mechanic in Philly, so my brother and I grew up working in his garage. I was a policeman in Philly, so was my brother. One day, he was killed in the line of duty . . ."

Theresa remained silent as he gathered himself.

"I'm sorry. Um, he was killed in the line of duty. After that, I kinda lost a feel for the job. I continued to work, but we never found the person who did it. It was supposed to be a regular traffic stop, but they shot him and left him in the middle of the street. I quit two months later and moved.

"I was headed toward North Carolina because I thought I wanted a quiet country life, but I couldn't deal with that small town living. A friend of mine asked me to visit here, to go to her sister's house with her. I came along and saw a for sale sign on this garage. I talked to the owner, made him an offer from my savings, went home, packed up and moved on down. Been here ever since. Can I ask you a question? What are you going to school for?"

"Why do you ask that?"

"Because I'm sure you already have a degree, and even if you don't, you're already successful and established. So why would a woman as busy as you go back to school if she doesn't need to?"

"I am not going back to school. I do have my degrees, a master's in business and a bachelor's in interior design. I'm only taking a couple of classes. African American Relations classes."

"You don't say."

"Yep. I'm taking the summer session for the first class, then I'll go one semester for the second class."

"So, you're taking these classes to—"

"To educate myself on the history of my people, of course. Why else would I be taking the class?"

"What do you want to learn?"

"Everything. This class is so interesting and intense. I would suggest it to every black person. I'm not the only black person who doesn't know all of the history of blacks. It's not something that we are born with. Regardless that I just learned that I was black, there are plenty of other black people who know less than I do about our history."

"Okay. I didn't mean to put you on the defensive."

"I'm sorry. It seems like I've had to defend myself more than I ever had to in my life. In the first two sessions, I was so on edge I couldn't bear it."

"But you stayed in it."

"Yeah, because I wasn't about to let a bunch of kids make me feel as if I didn't have a right to learn about my history, my ancestors, or my people. They really helped me more than they know."

"That's because you're a fighter, and fighters never quit."

"You're right." Theresa turned as her alarm clock rang in the background. "I've talked to you for almost an hour. Look, I gotta get my son up, dressed, and fed before we head out to the school. So, I'll see you at the high school later."

"Okay, good-bye."

"Good-bye."

ঞ্চ

"Mom, I'm a little nervous about playing in front of all those people."

"I'm sure that it's not going to be that many people, baby. Probably just the parents that were at the practice Wednesday night." Theresa tried to comfort him as they pulled into the school's parking lot.

"But the other team's parents will be there, too."

"Mikey, you're only here to have fun with the other kids. That's what all the parents want. Nobody expects you to be Michael Jordan."

"Michael Jordan? I want to be LeBron James."

"Well, if you go out there and practice, maybe one day you'll be like LeBron James. And don't forget to have fun."

"Okay. Are Uncle Michael and my grandmother coming?"

"Yes, they both said they would be here. Come on before we're late. You know you're making me later and later every day," Theresa said as she helped him out of the car and nudged him with her hip.

"You're the parent, and you do the driving," he responded, pushing back against her hip.

They were laughing as they walked hand and hand toward the gym door. Suddenly, she stopped in her tracks and tightened her grip on her son's hand.

"Mom, what is it?"

"Nothing, dear," she replied, unwilling to alarm her son. "Just come on, don't worry about it. I want you to have a good time today, okay?"

"Okay."

Cautiously, she moved to the door, putting herself between her son and the man waiting for them to approach. Her intention was to walk right past Ryan, but he stepped in her path.

"Hello, Theresa," he said, daring her to cause a scene. "Hello, son," he said, looking down into a face that was very similar to his own. "I haven't seen you in a long time. You sure have gotten big. How old are you now?"

Mikey was about to answer, but Theresa's hold on his hand tightened, and she stepped between him and the man.

"What the hell are you doing here?" Theresa asked through clenched teeth.

A bright smile crossed Ryan's face as he let a couple of people walk by before he answered. "I came to watch my son's game. And I figured you would be less likely to cause a scene with all these other people around. You don't want to embarrass our son, do you?"

"Stay away from us."

"Now, I can't do that." He reached around and brushed the locks on the top of Mikey's head. "I want to spend more time with my son. Look at him. He doesn't even know who I am. Do you?" he asked Mikey. He knelt down to Mikey's level.

Mikey shook his head; his confusion could not be hidden.

"Well, I'm your father. But don't worry about it. We're going to start getting to know each other very well. Would you like that?"

Mikey didn't know how to answer. His mother was obviously not happy about the meeting. And Mikey wanted to be happy about meeting his father again, but he didn't really remember him. If his mother wasn't happy, then he didn't think that he should be either.

When Ryan stood back up, Theresa gave him a dangerous look. He knew from that moment that he was going to be in for a serious battle. He had seen that look before, and it had always had a bad event following it.

"Come on, let's get Mikey inside. We don't want him to miss the game."

She allowed Ryan to walk in with them until she was able to direct Mikey to his team's bench. She was going to let Ryan have it just as soon as she got a chance. She didn't know what he was up to, but this was sure to get ugly.

"Mikey, you have a good time and remember to have fun."

"I will," he answered, running off to join his team.

Theresa turned to walk toward the bleachers; Ryan followed until she stopped and turned to face him. Right in front of the other parents, she pointed her finger in his face and said, "You are not sitting near me so I suggest you find your own spot."

"We need to talk."

"No, we don't." She turned and walked away.

"I want to spend some time with my son."

"Like hell," Theresa said, turning and walking back in his direction. "If you ever come near my son again, you'll regret it."

"Is that a threat? My lawyers will be happy to hear that."

"If I thought you could afford a lawyer worth a grain of salt, I might be worried. Ryan, go to hell." She turned and took a seat on the bleachers next to Amanda, who had been waiting for her.

Ryan stood in that same spot until he noticed everyone staring at him. Then he found a seat not too far from her. He realized that he had to prove that his main reason for being there was his son, so he focused his attention on Mikey. He cheered when the game started and when Mikey went out onto the court.

"You okay, Theresa?" Amanda asked after a few minutes.

"I'm all right." She knew that Amanda was waiting for an explanation of the scene that had unfolded. "That's Mikey's father, my ex-husband, Ryan."

"I thought he wasn't around."

"He's always been around New Orleans, just not around us. I worked very hard to keep him out of Mikey's life these last six years since the divorce. He never cared anything for Mikey. All he ever saw was a fat purse. And he's not going to use my son or try to get a hand on his money." Theresa was so upset that her leg was shaking uncontrollably. Her hands gripped the edge of the bleachers tightly. She feared that any minute she was going to attack him.

Amanda put a wrinkled hand over hers. "Theresa, you need to calm down. As long as he's here, we can keep an eye on him. He's not going to do anything. He'd be a fool. And look, here come Michael and Tamia now. Stop worrying. You don't want your son to pick up on it. Smile and watch his game."

Theresa forced a smile on her face and tried her best to ignore Ryan. Michael came up into the bleachers with Tamia, making sure she carefully maneuvered the steps. Theresa and Amanda both smiled at him. He surely wasn't acting the way he had when they'd had the conversation yesterday in her office. His uncertainty seemed to have disappeared. They both bent over to place kisses on Amanda's cheeks.

"Hello, Mom," he said. "How are you feeling today? Did you ride with Theresa? I could have picked you up."

"I know, baby, but I have some running around to do after the game. And I didn't want to bother you young people."

"Oh, nonsense, Ms. Amanda," Tamia answered. "You know we'd do anything for you."

"Thank you, dear," Amanda said, hugging Tamia, who sat next to her. "You just have me a healthy grandbaby, and I'll be happy."

Tamia blushed. Theresa was surprised. She had never seen Tamia blush before, didn't think it possible. Pregnancy changed some people right away.

"How's little man doing?" Michael asked.

"He's doing good. Having a lot of fun."

Just then Mikey threw the ball up high and it somehow found the rim of the basket and rolled in. Michael stood up at the same time as Ryan, and Michael finally noticed the man in the white T-shirt, unbuttoned blue and white checkered oversized button-up and blue jeans. He visibly stiffened. His applause stopped.

"What the hell?" He looked down at Theresa, anger making his brows furrow. "What's he doing here?"

"Michael, please sit down," Theresa urged. "Not in front of Mikey. I don't know what he's doing here, but I'm not going to ruin Mikey's day or let him do it. We'll handle it later." She pulled on his pant leg to take his focus off Ryan and the smirk on his face.

Ryan watched as Theresa subdued her brother and asked him not to make a scene for Mikey's sake. He turned his attention back to his son. The game was actually more fun to watch than he'd thought it would be. Ryan was not going to let Michael ruin his enjoyment or his plans. He would worry about him later. Knowing that at least part of Theresa's family would be present, Ryan realized he was taking a chance at a confrontation. He and her brothers had a long history of battles. Luckily, only one of her brothers was present. He stood a much better chance against Michael than he did Thorne, although a battle with Michael could be nasty, too. Either way, they had a common weakness, Mikey. No harm would come to him in front of Mikey. Ryan decided to figure a way to use that bit of knowledge to his advantage.

By halftime, Mikey had six points and the score was fourteen to ten in favor of the other team, but the kids were having a good time running up and down the court. Once Mikey started to relax, Theresa could tell that he was enjoying himself, and she was glad she had listened to her brothers and signed him up.

When she saw Pierson walk into the gymnasium, her heart stopped, or at least she thought it had, and then a heavy thud against her chest reminded her that it hadn't. He was casually dressed in a pair of jeans and polo shirt. The only problem was that the shirt showed off a powerful chest and his jeans hugged his thigh muscles at every step. Pierson could have easily passed for a fullback with the Saints. His cleanly shaven face and curly black hair drew attention from a few female admirers, but he paid them no attention as he scanned the bleachers for her.

Right before he found her, Theresa forced herself to stand and motion him over. Tia, Michael, and Amanda all turned in his direction once she gestured. Ryan watched as well.

"Oh, my," Tamia said as Pierson walked forward.

"Oh my, what?" Michael scowled, turning from his position one seat lower, between her legs.

"Nothing, baby," Tamia said, putting her arms around Michael's neck and bending to kiss him on the side of the head. "I was just surprised. I didn't know that Theresa was seeing anyone." She giggled.

He didn't. "Yeah, okay."

"My what a nice-looking young man," Amanda commented.

"Yes, he is, isn't he?" Theresa asked just before he approached them.

Pierson zeroed in on Theresa and walked confidently to her. He ignored the comments he heard as he walked by a group of women clustered together near the front of the gym. Maybe some other time he would have been flattered by their comments.

One guy was staring at him so long and hard that Pierson had to take note of him. He had never seen him before, but by the look he gave him, Pierson thought that they could have crossed paths before.

Theresa stood as he approached.

"Hello," she said.

"Hey, hey. You look more beautiful every time I see you."

"Thank you," she replied, blushing a little. She tried to hide it because she knew Michael's eyes were glued to the back of her head trying to take in everything to tell Thorne.

Pierson surprised her by throwing his arms around her and placing a light kiss on her cheek. "How are you doing?" he asked as they sat down together. He hadn't even noticed the people sitting beside her until introductions were made.

"Um, Pierson, this is my mom, Amanda Henry," Theresa said. She didn't know him well enough to put all her business out and she wasn't about to disrespect Amanda by calling her anything less than what she'd been calling her these last months. She'd explain everything to him later.

To his credit, Pierson didn't act like he needed an explanation. He didn't bat an eye, stutter, or look confusedly from one face to the other. Theresa had said that was her mom, so as far as he was concerned, Amanda was.

"Ma'am, it's very nice to meet you. Pierson Brooks," he said, extending his hand towards her.

"Please, call me Amanda."

"Thank you, I wish I could. But if you don't mind, I'll call you Ms. Amanda."

"I see there are still nice men out there, raised properly by their mommas. That will be fine."

"And," Theresa interrupted, "this is my brother Michael and his lady Tamia."

"Michael, nice to meet you. Tamia." He shook their hands as well. Then, out of the blue, he said, "Noah's Ark, right?"

"Yes," Tamia answered. "You been there?"

"Sure, me and the guys meet up there sometime to watch the games."

Noah's Ark was the name of the restaurant and sports bar co-owned by Tamia and her twin sister Tamya. Tamia was an accomplished chef; her sister was a popular bartender. She usually performed during happy hour, showing off the skills she had learned while working in New York.

"So," Pierson diverted his attention back to Theresa, "which one is yours?" He pointed to the group of boys huddled near the bench.

"Number 11 on the red team, McDonald's."

"How many points does he have so far?"

"Six."

"That's great. I thought you said he couldn't play that well." As he situated himself on the bleacher, their thighs rubbed together. They looked at each other.

"I guess he plays better than I thought."

"Looks that way. By the way, you look more relaxed today than you did at the shop."

"Speaking of the shop, where is Danielle? She didn't want to come?"

"Actually, you'll be happy to know that she is volunteering at the girls' club down the street from my house. That's why I'm late. I had to stop by there and make sure she went."

Theresa turned to him in a panic. "She didn't see you, did she?"

"No," he smiled, "I'm not a complete idiot. I snuck in and snuck out. I just wanted to make sure she was there."

"And if she hadn't been? You have to start trusting her sooner or later, you know."

"I know, and I will. So, what are you two doing when you leave here?"

"I don't know. I figured that he might want to go out for lunch."

"How about pizza? Chuck E. Cheese? Kids love that place, and he won't feel too awkward about meeting me."

Theresa smiled at him. "What makes you think I want you to meet my son?"

"Ms. Philips, if you didn't want me to meet your son, you wouldn't have allowed me to come here today."

"This is a public place. I couldn't stop you from coming here if I wanted to." She glanced in Ryan's direction, wishing that she did have that ability. "But I think that he would enjoy getting to know you."

"And you? Would you enjoy getting to know me, too?"

Their voices were low, but it was obvious that they were flirting with each other. Whispered words were exchanged close to their ears. Strain as he might, Michael couldn't hear a word of what was being said. It didn't really matter; he was going to have an earful for Thorne when he got back.

Theresa's giggle almost made Michael turn in disgust. He had never seen Theresa acting so much like a high-school teenager. Not even when she was a teenager. He happened to look in Ryan's directions and saw that Ryan was no longer paying attention to the basketball game either. Instead, he was watching the interaction between Theresa and Pierson. Michael smiled to himself and watched his nephew make another basket.

As Pierson leaned close to whisper into Theresa's ear, Ryan felt his jaw muscle tighten. And she was giggling. *What the hell was that?* He had never seen her do that before. From their actions, he could only assume that this was her man or boyfriend. He wasn't ready to entertain the thought that there was anything more serious than that going on between the two. But he was going to find out if it was the last thing he did that day.

As the game wound to an end, Theresa knew that she had to tell Pierson what she had been putting off since his arrival. Although they weren't in a relationship, she felt that she owed it to him to be honest.

"I have to tell you something," she began during the last minute of the game.

"What's going on, Theresa?" Pierson looked at her questionably.

"The man sitting over there in the blue and white checkered shirt. That's my son's father, my ex-husband."

Pierson didn't hesitate turning in the direction she referenced. Ryan's venomous gaze hit them.

"Oh," Pierson smiled, "that explains a lot. I was wondering why he looked as if he wanted to kill me when I first walked in here. Why is he sitting over there? I assume the divorce wasn't amicable."

"Hardly." She stood and applauded the teams as they lined up to shake hands. "This is the first time he's seen Mikey since he was about four. I successfully kept him away from my son until now. I don't know how he found out where we were going to be today."

"If you don't mind me asking, why is he not allowed to see his son?"

"It's a long and complicated story, but the bottom line is that when he sees Mikey, he really sees dollar signs." Theresa ended the conversation when she saw Ryan stepping down the bleachers to greet Mikey. She couldn't get down the steps fast enough. Michael was right on her heels.

Pierson stood back, a little stunned at how fast the situation had changed. Keeping his eye on Theresa, he offered his hand to Amanda to assist her down. Then she and Tamia joined him and followed Michael and Theresa.

Ryan got to Mikey first. He grabbed his son's hand and simply led him to the bleachers to sit down. He might have been able to get out of the gym with him, but Michael would have caught up with them fast enough. What purpose would that serve? Instead, they sat down so Ryan could talk to him.

"Wow, son. I didn't know you could play basketball so well." Ryan didn't have to pretend to be proud. He truly was impressed. Although he didn't know Mikey well at all, a small part of him wished that their circumstances were different. But right now, it had to be about the money because his life depended on it.

"Me, either. I was afraid at first, but then I started having fun. I can't wait until next Saturday. Will you be here?"

"I sure will," Ryan answered, just as Theresa came to her son's side. Ryan stood up, carefully watching his son's uncle, who no longer looked calm, cool, and collected. He was ready; Ryan had to make sure he was, too.

"What's up, Michael?" Ryan said.

"You tell me, Ryan. Do we need to talk or what?"

Ryan smiled slightly. "No, we don't need to talk. I just came here to watch my son play, have a little talk with him and tell him how proud I am of him."

Theresa pulled Mikey with her. "Say goodbye."

"Bye," Mikey said as he was pulled away. He didn't ask any questions, but Theresa knew some were forming. Her son was very observant.

"Everything okay?" Pierson asked when she walked back to him.

"Fine," she said, watching Michael walk Ryan out the door.

"Are you sure?"

"Yeah, I'm okay," Theresa said, feeling his hand slide from her shoulder to the small of her back. Her spine tingled, but Theresa pushed the feeling aside to focus on her son. She bent down to kiss him on his cheek.

"Mom, not in public," he said, trying to remind her the guys were around.

"I just wanted to congratulate you on a good game." She sighed, wondering what he thought about his father's sudden appearance. Mikey seemed less concerned about it than she was.

"Can we do it later? Like when we get in the car, please."

"Oh, okay, baby, sure."

"Well, little man," Amanda said, putting her hand around his shoulder, "I just love to watch you play, and I can't wait until next weekend." She bent down and gave him a kiss on the cheek, which he gladly accepted.

"Hey—"

"I'm the grandmother," Amanda said. "Grandmothers are always allowed to get their kisses. Don't you know the rules?"

"Obviously not."

"Mikey," Tamia said, "I thought you said that you couldn't play? You looked like Templeton Conquest out there."

Mikey smiled, confirming his mother's suspicion that he finally had his first crush on his uncle's girlfriend.

"Mikey, I want you to meet a friend of mine. His name is Mr. Pierson. Pierson, this is my son, Mikey."

Pierson was surprised when as he put his hand out for a handshake and Mikey was doing the same thing. A smile came to his face. Of course, he would have a professional side to him. He was probably meeting people all the time. "It's very nice to meet you, Mikey."

"And you, Mr. Pierson," Mikey replied, causing Pierson's smile to widen.

"I must voice my agreement with the ladies' observation. You played a very good game. I was only able to make the second half, but I saw how you guys came back from behind and then you made the winning basket. Very impressive."

"Thank you." Mikey looked Pierson directly in his eyes, just as his uncles had taught him. Mikey thought Pierson was a basketball player; he was so big and tall.

"I was wondering if you and your mother would like to celebrate your victory today with me at Chuck E. Cheese."

"Chuck E. Cheese? Oh, Mom, please, please can we go?"

There he was, Pierson thought, there was the nine-year-old he was looking for. Mikey was right against his mother looking up in her face, almost hopping up and down to plead his case.

"I guess it's settled. To Chuck E. Cheese," she said. Sometimes, she was caught off guard by how quickly he changed his demeanor.

"Tamia, you going to walk out with us? I don't know where your man went."

"He's probably outside having a word with your son's father."

Theresa didn't say anything, but she knew it was true.

"So, what's the real reason for you being here, Ryan?" Michael asked, having followed Ryan outside into the school's parking lot. To Michael, this was serious business. Nothing was more important to him than his family. Ryan had hurt his sister one time too many the last time. As far as Michael was concerned, he had no reason nor right to be in their vicinity, regardless of whether Mikey was his son or not. He gave up any rights to his son when he took the money their grandmother offered him and left town instead of trying to build a relationship with his son from the beginning.

"I'm only trying to see my son."

"Man, why are you coming around here? What do you want?"

"Michael, no matter how much you try, you and your family can't stop me from seeing him. I don't care how much money you have."

Michael looked him straight in the eye. The tension between them showed in their stances. Both were on the offense and ready for defense.

"We both know you better than that. You don't give a damn about that boy. That's why it was so easy for you to take the money and run the last time. Is that what this is all about, money? You need money?"

Ryan smiled sarcastically. He wished that he could take the money and run just to get Harp off his back, but in the long run the jewels would bring him a bigger prize. Maybe even big enough for him to finally get out of New Orleans altogether. No, he would never get as much from the Philipses as he would from the jewels, especially if he decided to hold out for more money, which was his plan once he had them in his hands.

"You keep your money, Michael. I'm just fine. Why can't I just be a father interested in spending quality time with his son?"

"Because then you wouldn't be you, now would you, Ryan? Just remember that I will be keeping an eye on you, and I'm sure that Thorne's eye will be even closer. You need to stay away from our family."

Ryan unlocked the door to his car when he saw Theresa walking out of the building with Michael, Tamia, and the stranger. "I'm not trying to be near your family, Michael. I'm trying to be near mine. Tell me one thing, though. Who's the guy with Theresa?"

Michael smiled. "Wouldn't you like to know? Get in the car, Ryan," he said as he walked away.

CHAPTER 7

Chuck E. Cheese was crowded, just as Theresa knew it would be. She had taken Mikey there only once before when he was much younger and was thankful that he'd never asked to go there again. But thanks to Pierson, here the three of them were, looking for an empty booth. Her discomfort with the atmosphere didn't matter, however, when she looked into her son's face and saw his happiness.

They found a booth, but Mikey didn't want to sit down at all. He was ready to play. Being the smart kid that he was, Mikey knew that his mother was not going to be playing any of the games that were in the restaurant. Theresa Philips didn't play games.

"Mr. Pierson, are you ready?" he asked just as Pierson was about to sit down across from Theresa.

"Uh," Pierson looked at Theresa who was smiling and hunched his shoulder. "Sure, little man, let's get busy."

Pierson followed the brown-haired, green-eyed kid from game to game until they could find one that was to his liking. If he thought that their first meeting was going to be awkward, Pierson had been seriously mistaken. He and Mikey got along famously. They moved from one arcade game to the next, playing each competitively, and cheered each other on when they had to take turns. They were racing cars when Theresa found them and told them that their pizza had arrived.

"Pierson, I have to thank you for this. I can't remember seeing him have so much fun. Besides wrestling with Michael or Thorne, he doesn't really have a lot of male bonding. And they're often too busy at work or whatever to spend time with him, not that they don't do their share."

"What about his father?" Pierson questioned as Mikey took a bite of his pizza and walked over to the air hockey area where a serious game was taking place. "He was there today. Obviously he wants to spend some time with his son."

"No, let's not start that. I don't want Ryan anywhere near my son."

"Well, he is Mikey's father. Maybe he should spend more time with him."

Theresa gave him the didn't-you-just-hear-what-I-said look. "No, I'm just saying that despite whatever problems you had in the past, maybe he's had a change of heart, mind, or circumstances."

"Okay, listen. So as to avoid an argument on our first meeting, I suggest that we change the subject. You don't know the man you're trying to defend at all, and I know him too well. Let's talk about something else, please."

Pierson smiled. He liked the fire that lit up her eyes when her anger was sparked. That told him that she was a fighter despite his first impressions of her as a rich woman separated from the real world by her money. The fact that she was sitting in Chuck E. Cheese with him should have given him the idea that his impression was incorrect. For that matter, Pierson figured that if she was that snobbish, she would have never come to his shop or allowed him to attend her son's game. She probably wouldn't have had her son playing in the PAL League in the first place.

"Okay," he agreed. "Can we talk about when you are going to allow me to take you out?"

Theresa blushed. "Are you sure you want to do that? I mean, I'm still white on the outside aren't I?"

"I guess you're not going to let me live that down, are you?"

"You were pretty forward in telling me your thoughts. Why should I let you forget them? Now that you've met some of my family, you think it's all good between us?"

"No, but I think that it could be," Pierson answered truthfully, causing another blush to spread across Theresa's cheeks.

Just then, Mikey came back to the table. "Hi."

"Hi," Pierson said, moving over to make room for Mikey.

Mikey took the seat and pulled another piece of pizza on his plate. "This is fun. I wish we could come here every Saturday."

"Every Saturday?" Theresa said. "I think you'd get tired of it pretty fast if you came here that much."

"No, I wouldn't. I love it here. And Mr. Pierson could come and play games with me, and we'd have a lot of fun."

"Mikey, I'm sure Mr. Pierson has more to do on Saturday than be in Chuck E. Cheese every week."

"Actually, I don't," Pierson chimed in. "Mikey, I'd be glad to come to Chuck E. Cheese with you whenever your mother says it's okay. Or we could go to the gym and practice some. Hey, you know what? Since I know you like basketball so much, maybe we could go to see the Hornets play some day."

"Oh, could we? Basketball season starts in a couple of months, you know."

"I do know," Pierson replied.

"If you really want to do that," Theresa said, "you can use the company tickets. We have season tickets on the floor, second row."

"Are you kidding me?" Pierson asked, his face lighting up just as brightly as Mikey's. "We are there, little man." He put his hand up for a high-five, which he quickly received. "You don't go to games?"

"No. Usually, if Michael or Thorne are too busy to go, we rotate our seats through the staff. My seats are usually available. We each have two seats."

"So would you go with me and Mikey?"

"I don't know. Do you need me there?"

"No, but we want you there. However, I understand that you have school on some nights and wouldn't be able to go with us. But then again, Mikey, we don't want no girls with us, do we?"

"Eww, no."

"I'll be going when the Celtics come to town, though. That is, if you two big strong men don't mind. I have to see my 'Big Three' when they come to town."

Pierson laughed. "What do you know about a 'Big Three'?"

"Excuse you. Ray Allen, Paul Pierce, and Kevin Garnett are the best 'Big Three' in the league, and Rajon Rondo is a beast."

Pierson stared at her, speechless. "Your brothers been schooling you?"

"No, dear. I've been schooling myself for twenty years. I might be a bigger basketball fan than either of them. I just don't get to the games. I don't want to go by myself."

"Well, you can call me anytime to help you with anything you don't want to do by yourself." He smiled.

Theresa blushed and looked at her son. He was busy with his third slice of pizza.

"Mr. Pierson, as soon as I finish this, I'll be ready to play some more."

"Don't you think we've used up enough of Mr. Pierson's time, Mikey?"

"Aww, Mom, it's still early. We got all day. Mr. Pierson doesn't mind."

"How do you know that?"

"Mr. Pierson, do you mind?"

"Not at all, Mikey."

Mikey looked at his mom. "See, I told you. We were having a good time." He quickly ate his remaining pizza, and he and Pierson left Theresa to sit alone and watch them run around the room again.

Theresa didn't mind watching them at all. She was glad that her son was enjoying himself with Pierson.

Theresa hadn't realized until that day that she might have been doing more harm than good to her son by keeping Ryan out of her life. She was sure that she was doing the right thing, but on the other hand, what if Pierson was right? What if Ryan was genuinely coming around because he wanted to get to know his son? What if he had changed his ways? She had.

It seemed like an eternity ago that she had been hanging out in the streets with Ryan as an act of rebellion against her grandmother's control. She had hated that they had so much money, and that money kept her from doing what she wanted and going where she wanted when she thought money was supposed to do the exact opposite. She had met Ryan by accident one day when she was at the mall buying shoes. He'd introduced her to the different world that was New Orleans nightlife at an early age. There were parties, people, and events that she would never have known about if it hadn't been for him. When she openly asked her grandmother about attending some of the events, her grandmother firmly put her foot down in refusal. Ms. Abbie, her grandmother, knew what Theresa didn't know. Those parties were filled with drugs, alcohol, and prostitutes. New Orleans was filled with teenage runaways trying to survive on the streets, not to mention the tourists.

But Theresa rebelled, and it seemed that Ryan had some kind of spell over her for years. Finally, the last straw for their grandmother was her elopement with Ryan. Ms. Abbie practically disowned her; she left her to live her life and learn from her mistakes. Theresa survived only because of the money Thorne and Michael made sure she had, which Ryan often stole from her. When she found out that she was pregnant, she stopped smoking whatever Ryan had her smoking and she stopped drinking altogether. It wasn't that she was ever a drug addict or an alcoholic; she was neither. In fact, Ryan was the only drug that she was ever under the influence of until she had Mikey. Ryan had her strung out bad, but she started to come out of it when she realized that she had someone else to look after. She was still willing to work it out with Ryan until she found him at the motel with someone else. Then she was done. She just didn't think it would take so long to get him out of her life completely. Now, here he was again.

Was she doing wrong by her son? That was Theresa's biggest question and worry. According to Pierson, maybe she was, but was she really willing to take the chance on Ryan that he might deserve?

The guys came back to the table with hands and pockets full of prize tickets and threw them all on the table. Pierson was pulling his out just as excitedly as Mikey was. She couldn't do anything but smile.

"So how many do we have?"

"I don't know, but it's a lot," Mikey said. "Are we about to leave now?" His voice indicated his sadness.

"Baby, it's almost three o'clock."

"But we're having fun. Can Mr. Pierson come to the house with us? We can play Play Station?" Then before she could answer he added, "Please, please, and we can order pizza for dinner."

Theresa looked at her son in disbelief. "Mikey, we just had pizza."

"I know, but Mom, you can never have enough pizza."

"That's right, Mom," Pierson concurred. "You can never have enough pizza."

"I don't care, if Mr. Pierson doesn't have something else to do. It seems as if I'm going to be outvoted at any rate."

Pierson winked his eye at her. He didn't have any plans for the day; in fact, he had cancelled all of his plans in order to spend some time with Theresa and her son. However, he hadn't thought that he and Mikey would get along so well or that Mikey would want to occupy so much of his time. "I'll follow you. I want to give Danielle a call. I'm sure she's loving the fact that I'm not around trying to calculate her every move."

He picked up the receipt and fished in his wallet for money to pay. After leaving a tip on the table, they left the restaurant.

$\mathcal{HP}$

"He's out like a light," Theresa said after walking a tired Mikey to bed and tucking him in. "Thank you so much for today, Pierson. I don't think he's had this much fun in a long time."

"It was fun for me, too. I can't remember the last time I've enjoyed myself with a kid. He's very bright. And a whiz at those video games. I was playing to what I thought was the best of my ability, and he still whipped my tail."

Pierson was walking to the kitchen in his stocking feet carrying an empty bowl of popcorn. He had really enjoyed himself sitting on the plush pillows on the floor playing with Mikey. Glancing at his watch, he saw that it was seven o'clock. It was probably time for him to start getting home.

"Would you like something to drink? I mean, I know you've been stuffed with pizza all day and then popcorn and ice cream, but I was wondering if you wanted a glass of wine or some coffee?"

"Sure. I thought maybe I should be on my way home."

"No, not unless you need to go. It's still early. I was hoping to spend a little time getting to know you better. I guess the truth is that it's been a long time since I've had any type of male companionship."

"Has it really now?"

"Well, since before my divorce. Over three years ago." She followed him back into the living room with two glasses and a bottle of wine. "I want to thank you again for showing Mikey so much attention. I could tell that he was truly enjoying himself."

"Heck, I was enjoying myself. I haven't been around kids in a long time. Mostly teenagers. Up Philly, I worked with the PAL League a lot and I got to know a lot of the neighborhood kids. It's not that different up there than down here. Here they move just a half a beat slower, but you basically have good and bad people everywhere you go."

"You don't miss it up there?"

"Not really. Too many bad memories. I'm trying to talk my father into moving down here with us, maybe work in the garage a few days just to give him something to do, but you know how the older generation is. He doesn't want to sell the house, doesn't want to leave the old neighborhood. Says it was the house that he and my mother made a home and he couldn't just leave it. But he knows that it's going to be sold when he passes. I have a cousin who checks in on him for me and lets me know what's going on."

"It must be hard on him, though."

"He's just being stubborn. He'll come down for a visit every year, but that's about it, and only for a week. Then he's ready to go back." Pierson hunched his shoulders as he took a drink. He actually hated wine, but to spend more time with her, he would have drunk oil.

"Nasty, isn't it?" Theresa smiled as he made a sour face. "It's an acquired taste. I used to hate wine myself, but business meeting after business meeting, they serve it, so I had to get used to the taste just to keep up appearances. Here, I'll get us some juice."

He laughed. "That sounds much better. Thanks." Pierson followed her into the kitchen. He watched her pull down two more glasses. "Don't dirty more glasses on my account. Here, I'll wash these." Pierson had dumped out the wine in the sink and begun washing the glasses when Theresa came up next to him.

"I'll do it," she said, reaching over to grab a glass. Their hands touched and both froze. That was when

Theresa realized how close she was standing to him. Their thighs touched, and Pierson reached behind her so that she was in the circle of his arms against the sink, standing between his spread legs. He moved close behind her.

"We can do it together," he whispered next to her ear.

Theresa closed her eyes quickly, but leaned back against him. Her heartbeat increased as he put the glass in both of their soapy hands. It had been so long since Theresa had any physical contact with a man, and even with Ryan it had never been so sensual, so provocative. Just with Pierson standing close, breathing on her neck, running his hands over hers, Theresa felt her tummy fluttering.

"Am I making you uncomfortable?"

"No. I rather like it," she replied.

"Turn around."

Theresa shook her hands off the best she could, and then did as she was told. She turned and faced him, looked up at him, anxiously waiting for whatever was to come next. Her breath caught as she watched him lower her head. The kiss was slow and soft, like two nervous kids kissing for the first time. It seemed to start out innocently, but quickly heated up as both let their anxiety go and felt something close to serenity moving in. Theresa's hands went around his back as she moved further into his circle. She returned his kisses eagerly.

Pierson had to put the glass down before he dropped it. His wet hands went to her hips as she pulled him closer and deepened the kiss. Moving down to her chin, he said, "I think we had better stop before I don't stop."

"Yeah," she sighed, "maybe you're right."

But neither of them moved; Pierson continued his nuzzling of her neck, and Theresa's eyes remained closed in rapture.

"You'd better stop me because I can't stop myself."

"What if I don't want you to stop?"

"Theresa . . ." he began as he moved back to her lips, engulfing her in a long, passionate kiss.

Theresa was breathless once he finally stopped. He was breathing heavily. They both stood in their spots, wondering if it was wise to take it to the next level.

"Follow me," Pierson said, taking her hand and leading her into the living room. He sat on the couch and patted it, suggesting that she join him. "Look, Theresa, the last thing I want to do is make a bad decision or cause you to make one. We don't really know each other that well right now, and, although the sexual attraction is very strong, we can wait. I'm not going anywhere. You know where I am, and I will definitely be in touch with you. Like I said, I want to get to know both you and Mikey better. So, I'm going to. Maybe we can go out to dinner one day next week. You got school Tuesday and Friday, right? I know you probably have homework, so Monday's not a good night, but I'm free Wednesday, if you are."

"I should be good Wednesday, too. Why don't we plan to meet at Noah's Ark? My brother will be back in town tomorrow. I really want you to meet him. His fiancée is the twin's older sister. They could meet us there."

"You sure you want us to meet? Your brother Michael didn't seem too bad about meeting me, but seriously surprised."

"That's because I don't let them in on my business. They are so used to seeing me without anyone that it's going to take some adjusting for both of them. And they're a little overprotective. Thorne, being the oldest, is protective of us both as you can imagine. It would just be better if it appears that I'm not trying to hide you, that is, where Thorne's concerned. It's not that I'm afraid of him or anything, but I do give him a lot of respect because he is basically the patriarch of the family."

"So, is he going to be upset because I'm just a mechanic?"

Theresa looked at him. She couldn't believe he'd said something so silly. "Why would you say something like that? First of all, you are more than a mechanic, and if I can see that, why can't you? Secondly, Thorne doesn't judge people by what they do. He judges people on their character."

"Theresa, I'm just kidding. I don't think of myself in that way, really." He tried to pull her close, but Theresa resisted.

"No, seriously, Pierson. I really don't like that." She looked him straight in the eye. "I can't even consider being with anyone who isn't confident and sure of himself and his abilities. I promised myself a long time ago that I would never deal with anyone like that again. And it's a promise I have to keep for myself and for Mikey's sake."

"I understand." Pierson looked her. He hadn't thought that she would react this way to his comment. "If I wasn't confident in myself, I would have never moved down here and then brought my sister down. Believe me, there is nothing wrong with my self-esteem. I know we don't know each other very well yet, but you have to at least know that much about me."

"I just wanted to let you know how I felt. That's all. Any man who is going to be in my life has to be a strong man because I'm a strong woman."

Pierson continued looking at her. "Oh, I know how strong a woman you are. Strong minded, strong spoken. I personally don't find anything wrong with that, and I supposed you've had to be strong, as a single-mother and all, but please rest assured right now as I say this and then don't mention the topic again." He moved in very close to her face, making sure that he had her undivided attention. "I am a very strong, confident, dependable, and positive man. If you can believe that, then we'll be just fine."

"I believe you," Theresa whispered as her spine shivered with excitement.

"Well, we need to change the subject. Who decorated your house?" he asked with a laugh. "I need to lighten up the mood."

She had hoped that he was moving in for a kiss, but instead Pierson stood up and walked to the mantle on the other side of the room. He was acting as if he was shy, of all things. Theresa knew that wasn't true.

"I did all of the decorating. I have a degree in interior design. I also own a small business."

"You own a large corporation," Pierson said matter-of-factly, looking at her.

"Well," she laughed, "there's an interior design company in there somewhere, which is my favorite business. But besides all of that, I have a better topic. Why do you act like you're all hot and bothered for me one minute and then cold as ice the next? Or have you always missed the perfect opportunity to take advantage of a willing woman?"

Pierson knew it was time for him to leave before he would have to prove a point. He wanted Theresa more than anything in his life, but rushing into a situation wasn't always the best way to achieve what you wanted. Pulling his keys out of his pocket, Pierson walked toward her. He helped her off the couch where she was still sitting and motioned to the door. Holding her hand, he led her in that direction.

"Theresa," he began, placing both hands on her shoulders, "I don't think that the things I may or may not have done in the past pertain to our situation. For some reason, I think that with you I need to take a different route to get what I want." Pierson pulled her close, kissed her on her cheek and walked out the door.

CHAPTER 8

Monday morning came too soon for Theresa. She had spent all day Sunday camped out in her office at home working on her schoolwork after sending Mikey to hang out with his uncle. She had been up late finishing her paper. How would she have been treated in 1780 as a slave?

The answer to the question, although it was one that she wasn't too proud of, was easy. There was no way that she could even begin to imagine how harsh slavery was, but from what she had heard and learned, she knew that she would have "passed" easily and taken advantage of the fact that her skin was as pale as it was. She would have most likely married well, and her husband might have been a slave owner. She hoped that she would have married a decent man, but not even white women had a lot of choice in those matters back then. Theresa knew that she would have willingly done whatever was necessary to survive those terrible times for herself and any children she might have had. Pride had nothing to do with it. In that situation, she would have used her skin color to her benefit, and she was sure that other women had done the same. It didn't make them weak; it made them smart.

Glancing at her watch, she rushed Mikey to get dressed, as usual, for his work day with Samuel before she missed her breakfast meeting with Thorne. He and Natalie had arrived late last night and called her to let her know they were in. Thorne made sure to let her know that he had already spoken to Michael when he called Tamia's house and that their meeting was still on. Theresa was just glad he was back and that she had finished all of the paperwork that was on her desk Friday with Michael's help. Anything on his desk now would have been put there late Friday night by his secretary.

"Good morning," Theresa said, walking briskly into the room past Michael and right into Thorne's arms. "Welcome back, big brother." She threw her purse in her chair. "I am so glad to see you." She kissed him and gave him a tight sisterly hug.

"I hope it's not because of all the work I left you with," Thorne said, standing to his full six-feet, two-inch height. His grin spread across his face as he took his sister in his arms, showing perfectly aligned teeth that appeared to gleam even whiter next to his bronze skin. Her brother's handsome face had caused him a lot of pleasure and pain over the years, until Natalie that is.

"Of course not. I missed you."

"Really? I heard you were complaining." They both glanced at Michael, who had put his head down.

"Nonsense. Where did you get a ridiculous idea like that?"

Michael's head stayed down. Thorne smiled, but pushed her out of his arms and looked at her seriously for a minute. Theresa had always been a social butterfly, more beautiful than most of the other daughters, socialites, he and Michael had grown up around and dated heavily in earlier years, but Theresa's true beauty and what attracted so many unworthy suitors was her spunk. Thorne had hoped more times than he could count that someone would come and sweep her off her feet, especially after she hooked up with Ryan, but that guy had never come, until now, it appeared.

"I heard a couple of things happened while I was away."

"Did you really, now?" Theresa cut another eye at Michael. She should have known that he would try to see Thorne before the meeting so he could tell all her business. Probably suggested that they meet early on the phone last night.

"Yes." Thorne motioned to her chair. "We might as well have a family meeting before we get started with business. Seems as if I've missed a lot these past two weeks. Ryan back in the picture?"

"Hey, that wasn't my doing." Theresa wondered why she allowed Thorne to treat her as if she were his daughter instead of a sister. "I have no idea how he knew about the basketball game."

"So, what are you going to do about it?"

"There is really nothing that I can do about it. As long as he doesn't try to hurt Mikey, I'm not going to worry about him watching a few ball games."

"Okay, but don't be too trusting. You know he's got something up his sleeve."

"For that reason, I am also looking for a local school. Mikey wants to transfer closer to home. I was against it at first, but with Ryan being closer, I fear that he might be able to track Mikey in Texas when I'm not around. I'd rather have him here."

"That's a good idea. Michael, I understand that congratulations are in order for you and Tamia."

Michael smiled from ear to ear. He had taken the idea of being a father to heart and was growing more excited by the minute. "Yeah, the only problem is that she won't accept my marriage proposal."

"She won't?" Thorne was shocked, and rightfully so. Michael practically had women breaking down his door to get a marriage proposal. "Well, you might have to work a little harder than usual to get this one, Michael. But if it's not worth fighting for, it's not worth having."

"It's a fight I'm prepared to win. No child of mine is going to be born out of wedlock." Michael banged his fist on the table, determination filling his voice.

Theresa wanted to stay quiet, but the words seemed to slip out before she could control them. "Michael, do you really believe that Tamia wants that kind of proposal?"

Both men turned to her. Thorne leaned back in his chair.

"I mean, really. No woman wants to be asked to marry a man just to give his child a name. Are you in love with her or not? Because if you're not, you shouldn't be asking anything of her except a relationship with your child."

"She's right, Michael. If you want to marry Tamia, it should be for the right reason. Not just because of the baby."

"I do love her."

"Does she know that?" Theresa asked. "I know that you love her. I know that the two of you are like yin and yang. You complement and complete each other nicely, but have you honestly showed her that you are in love with her? Have you done anything differently with her than any of the other hundred women you've dated?"

"Well, in Michael's defense, she does call him Mike, and he does act more normal, I mean relaxed, around her than I've ever seen with any of the other women."

"That's right," Michael agreed. "I'm immensely jealous when I see anyone else around her because she's mine. I want her for myself, and I can't stand that she's not. She's the one woman that I can't get just by throwing out my name or my money, because she doesn't care about either. The only thing that I have in my favor is the baby."

"That's not true, Michael. You can give her your love, your heart. Show her how much you love her."

Michael simply nodded his head in agreement.

"Okay, now that we've discussed Michael's love life and everyone knows that Natalie accepted my proposal, why don't we move on to you, Theresa," Thorne said without batting an eye. Theresa's eyes went right to Michael, who was wearing a smirk. She snapped her eyes from him and faced Thorne.

"There is nothing to move on to," she stated.

"Oh, really? I've heard differently from two different people. And I'm sure that when I have lunch with my nephew, I'll hear a third story." Thorne gave her time to answer. He wouldn't take no for an answer, and Theresa knew they could be there for quite a while waiting for her response. Thorne seldom played games, especially when it came to her.

"Well, there is really nothing to tell. I have a friend who seems to be a good man, and hopefully, we will work on getting to know each other a little better."

"What's his name?"

"Why? You going to run a check on him?"

Thorne gave his sister a look that said do you think I'd do something like that and you know that's exactly what I'm going to do. She didn't know which was more prominent a statement.

"Pierson Brooks."

"Thank you." Thorne smiled.

"He's a mechanic. You know, I'm not a little girl anymore, Thorne. I can take care of myself, and I am a pretty good judge of character."

Both brothers looked at her skeptically.

"Ryan was a long time ago, and that was just out of rebellion. You can't hold that against me."

"Theresa, he was your only boyfriend. Who else would we use?" Michael asked, laughing. "But all joking aside, Thorne, I met this guy, and he seems to be very honorable. And he doesn't appear to be a slouch. He's a big dude, built, looks like ex-military or something."

"He was a policeman up Philadelphia. Moved down here a few years ago and is now raising his younger sister, who actually reminds me a lot of myself at her age."

"And Mikey?"

"Mikey adores him. Saturday, he didn't want Pierson to leave us. And—"

"And what time did he leave?" Thorne interrupted.

Theresa looked at him in disbelief. "That's none of your business, Thorne. If he stayed all night, that's none of your business, either. What do you think, I'm a virgin or something? I don't understand you two sometimes. And I might let you act like you're my father, but please don't make the mistake of thinking that you really are." Theresa's anger was obvious. She was seething. How could he ask her a question like that after all the things she had seen and heard about him and Michael? Compared to them, she was a saint, or a nun, rather. Theresa got up from her position at the table and prepared to leave the room.

"Sit down." Thorne smiled. "You're overreacting. I just asked because I love you. I'm not trying to be your father, but I am your older brother and it is my job to make sure you're okay. And maybe I do take my job a little seriously, but you know that's how I am. Okay . . . I apologize."

Theresa eased back down in her chair.

Thorne changed the subject. "So, how are the classes going? I spoke to Mom last night, and she said that she thought you were really enjoying it."

"Oh, I'm having a very good time. I told Michael that I think you two should take the class as well. Mom is such a good teacher, and we have discussions where no one holds back questions. I wish the class was more than twice a week. It's very educational, and it's not so much about history as it is conscience. We do learn a lot about the past, but the class makes you put yourself in the shoes of those who came before you. You figure out what they felt, why they made the decisions they did. You know, at first I was taking the class for Mikey, so I could talk to him about questions that he might have, but now I realize that I'm in it for me."

"That good, huh?"

"And so much more. Michael said that you would probably talk her into giving you a private class, but I really think that the classroom atmosphere would be better."

"Yeah," Thorne commented. "We'll see. Natalie has been telling me the same thing. Okay, well, if that's all, let's get down to business. What do we need to discuss before this afternoon's meeting with the company heads?"

"Hello, Theresa." Stephanie smiled as she walked into the office. "How was your weekend?"

"It was very nice, thank you. How was yours?" Theresa watched her pile a handful of envelopes on her desk.

"It was good. Hey, there's a letter on top from Family Court. I thought that you would want to see it first."

"Thanks, Stephanie. Why don't you just tell me what it's about?" Theresa knew that her secretary scanned all of her mail first. It was part of her job.

"You better read it. You're not going to like it. Ryan is trying to enforce his visitation rights."

"What?" Theresa snatched the paper off the top of the pile and ripped the envelope trying to pull the paper out. She read the paper twice before tossing it across her desk in disgust. *He sure does work fast,* she thought. *The bastard.* Ryan had filed papers requesting visitation with his son twice a week and every other weekend. Quickly, she picked up the phone and dialed her cousin Howard's law office. Howard, their grandmother's first cousin, and four of his six sons handled the Philips Corporation legalities. She spoke to Joshua, Howard's second oldest, and immediately began running down the situation.

"Theresa, calm down. Calm down. Why don't I come over to the office and speak to you directly? I'm sure there is something we can figure out. I'm on my way, just calm down and let me handle this, okay?"

"Okay." Immediately, she dialed Pierson at his shop. She knew that was where he would be, and she needed to get this off her chest, just needed someone to talk to.

"Brooks Repair and Towing," a voice said on the other end, less than enthused. "How may we help you?"

"Hello, Danielle, this is Theresa. How are you today?"

"Fine." Danielle was silent for a moment, trying to remember who Theresa was. When she remembered, her tone seemed to get nastier. "I suppose you want my brother."

"Yes, if he's available."

"Well, he's not here at the moment. He had to run over to Alluvial City to pick up a car."

"Oh, well, I wanted to talk to you about something. I find myself in need of an assistant, someone to help me out both on the job and at home. I was hoping that you were looking for a job."

"I already got a job."

"Yes, I realize that, but it being your last school year coming up you'll probably get out, what? Half a day? I was hoping that you might want to work for me. I would make the pay comparable for your time. But of course, if you prefer answering the phone and helping your brother out, I understand."

"How much?"

"Well, enough to save up for your first year of college, maybe your second. Of course, your brother would have to approve. I don't want him thinking that I'm stealing his employees from behind his back."

"Wouldn't I have to get a paycheck to be an employee?"

"Uh, yes."

"Then I don't think I'm an employee. I'm working here for my bread and butter. I'm sure he won't have a problem replacing me. I basically just stand around anyway."

"Good, well, how about you talk to your brother, and I'll give him a call later. I will also give you a call and let you know what time you can start if everything meets with his approval."

"Okay." Danielle was silent. So was Theresa. "Thank you," Danielle said reluctantly, as if it was a phrase she didn't like to use.

"You're welcome, Danielle," Theresa acknowledged before hanging up the phone. At least that little exchange had helped get Ryan off her mind temporarily. Glancing at her watch, she realized it would take Joshua at least another thirty minutes to get there. She focused on the other envelopes Stephanie had put on her desk.

Two hours later, Theresa was more distraught than ever. She and Joshua had butted heads for more than an hour; Thorne and Michael were both in her office as well. Still the final answer was the same.

"Theresa," Joshua said, "the only thing we can do is request that the visits be supervised. We can state grounds that Mikey does not know his father and they have never spent any time together. A case can also be made that Ryan has never had any interest in him up to this point; however, no court is going to prevent a father who absolutely is showing interest in his child from seeing him."

"What about the child support that he hasn't been paying? Can't we use that in some way?"

"We can try, but honestly, with the amount of money you're worth, and Mikey's worth himself, it is unlikely that the courts will even consider it a viable enough excuse to disallow Ryan's right to visitation. Technically, Mikey doesn't need the little bit of money Ryan's child support would provide. It's minute compared to Mikey's inheritance."

"So," Thorne interrupted, "there's nothing we can do to stop this?"

"I seriously doubt it, but I will meet with a judge first thing in the morning anyway."

"Well, thank you very much, Joshua," Theresa said. "I really appreciate you coming all the way over here."

"I'll do everything I can, Theresa. Don't worry too much about this. Most times fathers visit once or twice and then things go right back to normal. I will make sure that the visits are monitored. Ryan won't be able to take him out of your sight if I have anything to do with it."

"Thanks again."

"No problem, cousin. You know I love to come over to see you guys."

"Us," Michael said, "or Stephanie?"

Joshua smiled with surprised but longing eyes. He wasn't aware that his cousins knew of his crush on Theresa's secretary. Waving a warning finger in Michael's direction, he walked out the room and down the hall, stopping in front of Stephanie's desk.

"Is everybody around here trying to hook up or what?" Thorne asked. "What's going on?"

"Well, you know it will be wintertime soon. Everybody needs someone to cozy up to." Michael stood. "I'm going back to my office. I've got a few phone calls to make."

Thorne came up behind her. "Don't worry, Theresa. We'll handle this." He put his hand on her shoulder. "Ryan won't have a chance."

"Thanks, Thorne."

"Hey, as a matter of fact, why don't you let him stay with us tonight? You need a break, some time to think. Natalie and I will spoil him to death, and I'll bring him to work with me tomorrow. We're going to stay out at Gladewinds."

Theresa smiled and nodded. Gladewinds was Thorne's country home. Their grandmother had left each of her grandchildren a mansion in her will, along with seven other family estates around the country and in England, St. Thomas, and Paris for all their use. Theresa rarely got out to Rosegate, and she knew that Michael had closed Oaktrees down for renovations. She needed to make time to get away.

After Thorne left, she picked up the phone.

"Hello."

"Hi."

"Hi, how are you doing?" Pierson's deep voice soothed her immediately.

"Not so well. I was wondering if I could see you tonight."

"Um, sure. I thought we agreed to meet Wednesday. Is everything okay?"

"I've just had a very bad morning, and I need—"

"Some company?"

"Yeah, company would be nice."

"Sounds like you need more than that. How about I pick up some dinner and come by around seven?"

"No, no. I want to cook. It's been a long time since I've had company."

"Okay, I'll bring the wine and soda for little man."

"He won't be here. He's staying the night with his Uncle Thorne."

"Okay. And I want to say thank you for offering Danielle the job. She's not going to let you know, but she's very excited."

"Well, let me ask you this. Can I stop by and pick her up today? I feel like I need to work off some frustration, and I can't think of any better way than to shop 'til I drop. I have to get out of here."

"I'm sure I'll have to twist her arm, but I don't mind. And Theresa, do not buy her a whole lot of stuff."

"Who, me? I wouldn't think of it."

CHAPTER 9

Theresa struggled through the front door of her apartment loaded down with more bags than she knew she should have. She laughed at the memory of Danielle dragging four bags of her own into the front door of the repair shop. The look on Pierson's face had been priceless.

He had tried to stop her in the parking lot, but Theresa knew exactly what he was going to say, and instead of stopping, she rolled down her window, waved, said that she would see him that evening and that she was going to cook dinner. She and Danielle had had a wonderful afternoon, and she wasn't going to ruin it by taking a thing back.

When Pierson got to the apartment, Theresa had the table set up with her best china, stuffed shells were in the oven, and a tossed salad in the refrigerator. She was dressed in a black wrap-around dress with black fuzzy slippers on her feet. Both the atmosphere and her attitude pleasantly surprised him.

But Theresa was in for more of a surprise when Pierson walked into the house carrying a massage table and a bag filled with lotions, candles, and music CDs.

"What's all this?" she asked as he went into the living room and began setting the table up.

"Well, I figured that you would probably be tense and need a good massage to help you relax and get rid of all this negativity. But after the piles of clothes that I left Danielle hanging up at the house, you might have worked out your frustrations on your own. Probably don't need me at all."

"You'd be wrong to think that. I would love to be treated to a massage. I was going to make appointments for Danielle, Natalie, Amanda, Tamia, Tamya, and myself this weekend. I never imagined that I would have a personal masseuse. Are you sure you know what you're doing?"

"We'll make a bet. If you don't enjoy my massage, I'll pay you for your time."

She smiled. "And how will you pay me?"

"However you want me to."

"You're on. Let me go check on the food." She walked to the kitchen. "So, do I get rubbed down before or after dinner?"

"After. You can sip on a glass of wine, smell the candles, and soak in the aura as I do my thing."

"Your thing? Mmm, that sounds exciting."

"That food smells exciting. Do you need me to do anything?"

"Thank you," she said, smiling at him, "and no. Just finish putting up everything. You have it looking almost like a spa over there."

"I aim to please you, Theresa. Or like my dear mother always used to say, if you're not going to do it right, then just leave it alone."

They both laughed.

"She sounds like a smart woman."

"She was the best."

As she put the food out on the table, Pierson walked over to the sink and washed his hands. He was famished, and the stuffed shells looked so good with the thick sauce poured over them. Then Theresa pulled garlic bread out of the oven, and his mouth started to water.

The meal was magnificent. Pierson couldn't give her enough compliments. He ate to his heart's content, and Theresa drank just enough wine to be completely comfortable in his company. They talked about the day's events. And although Pierson didn't like the idea of Ryan around, he did say that a boy had to get to know his father and have the opportunity to make his own decisions about the man.

"I don't agree with that, Pierson," Theresa said after taking her last bite and clearing both plates from the table. "My job as Mikey's mother is to protect him. I will do that until my last breath. Mikey is only nine years old. He doesn't even know who Ryan is, besides the fact that he's his father. Ryan will lie and try to manipulate him into believing all kinds of lies."

"About you? Is that what you're worried about? Let me tell you something. I've only been around Mikey one day, but he's the smartest kid I know. Very observant. And Mikey is very loyal to you. He's not going to let a stranger come into his life and bad talk his mother. Theresa, you are not going to lose your son to Ryan."

"I know, but . . . I know."

"Please don't think that I agree with this whole situation by what I'm about to say, but maybe Ryan has changed. I mean, I can remember all of the kids I used to work with in Philly whose fathers left them and didn't give them a second thought. Boys literally walked past their fathers every day on the way home from school, and these men, some even boys themselves, were too busy trying to make that street money to give their own flesh and blood a second glance."

"I understand what you're saying, but that doesn't make it any easier to forget. I know Ryan. He doesn't give a damn about his son."

"I'm not saying to go in this with a blind eye. Hope for the best, but be prepared for the worst. I got your back regardless what happens. Now, are you ready for this massage?" He handed her a large towel that he had gotten from her closet earlier. "Here, go change into this, and I'll set the atmosphere. I don't want you to think about any of that stuff anymore tonight."

Theresa did as she was told, walking back into the living room five minutes later wrapped in only the white towel. He had sheets covering the massage table, candles lit around the large living room, and soft classical music playing in the background. When she walked close to him, Pierson guided her toward the table. She could tell that he wasn't nearly as nervous as she was.

Pierson looked into her eyes. He had promised himself that this evening was going to be all about her, so he pushed his desire down as he reached over to loosen the towel. He held the towel up in front of his eyes and told her to lie face down on the table. *Damn, he wanted to see her nude.*

From the moment his hands spread across the expanse of her shoulder blades, Theresa was in heaven. Pierson played her muscles, her bones, her skin like a violinist playing the notes of a classical song. He was magically familiar with the areas that held her aches, her pains and frustrations. Theresa willingly gave in to the soothing rotations of his hands on her shoulders and down her spine to the small of her back.

Pierson concentrated hard on keeping his focus on her and not himself. Her skin felt so soft under his touch. With each circle of his caress, the towel over her hips moved lower and lower until it was just above the hump of her behind. He wanted to throw the towel to the ground, but that was not what he was here for tonight. Instead, he decided to move to her legs, hoping that would distract his current mindset.

He started at her feet, pulling each leg toward him and giving the back of each a thorough rubdown as he worked his way up. By the time he finished each, he had managed to work himself into a nice rage. Reaching the top of her legs offered more torment than the bottom of her back did.

"Turn over," he said.

Theresa hesitated slightly, wondering how far this was going to go before one of them gave in. It was really Pierson who seemed to be fighting an internal battle. Theresa had willingly offered herself up to him. She was lying nude under one sheet on a massage table, for God's sake. How much more of a sign did she have to give him that she wanted him? She turned over when he lifted the towel, noticing that his eyes were averted. She closed her eyes and hoped that he wanted her right now as much as she wanted him.

Pierson stood above her head and worked on her shoulders. But each time they moved, the towel shifted lower until the tops of her breasts showed. He reached for her arms, and brushed against the side of one breast, noticing immediately that the nipple formed a hard circle that he could see even through the thickness of the towel. He went to her legs, and was about to lift one over his shoulder, but the towel slid down and made the nestling of curly hairs visible. Without thinking, Pierson dropped her leg, and her ankle banged against the table.

Theresa sat up as soon as she felt the pain shoot up her leg. Her ankle had come down hard against the metal edge. She screamed in pain and grabbed her ankle.

"Oh, I'm so sorry. I must have lost my grip. Are you okay?" Pierson moved closer to her until he noticed that the towel had fallen completely away when she sat up. He stood still for a second, but when she continued to grab her ankle, he realized it was more serious than he thought.

"I think hit directly on the ankle bone," Theresa said through painful gasps.

"Let's get some ice on it," Pierson suggested.

"Wait, move me to the sofa first," she said, "then get the ice."

Pierson did as she said, without giving a second thought to the towel. Holding her in his arms, he allowed himself the brief pleasure of enjoying her naked body.

"Maybe we should get you to the hospital," Pierson said a minute later, placing the freezer bag of ice wrapped in a kitchen towel on her ankle.

"I don't think it's that bad. It just hurts like hell. I guess it caught me off guard. I was so relaxed, then all of a sudden all I felt was the pain. I might have overreacted."

"No, it's my fault. I am so sorry."

"It's okay," she said, "I'm not dead or made of glass. I'll be fine."

"Well, um, here, cover yourself up with this." Pierson retrieved the towel from the floor and handed it to her.

"You know what, Pierson?" she laughed, "you are hilarious. You're the only man I know who would be trying to cover up a naked woman. You know you had me right in the palm of your hands, could have had your way with me. And what do you do, worry about my modesty."

"I told you my reasons behind all that. Now here, cover up and stop tempting me to break my own damn rule."

"You know, you're very hard on a girl's ego." She took the towel and placed it over herself as best she could. "Makes me think you don't want me at all, like there's something wrong with me."

Pierson looked over her body one last quick time. "You don't have any reason to think that I don't want to be with you, please believe that. And you are perfect, physically and mentally. Have you ever thought that might be the reason why I'm taking my time? I told you before, I'm not going to keep starting my relationships the same way I have in the past and have them start and finish in the bed. Theresa, I want you more than you know, more than you can imagine."

Theresa chose to believe him no matter how hard it was. She focused on her ankle, holding the ice in place while he dismantled the massage table and folded the towels. Then he blew out his candles and turned over the music before coming to sit next to her.

"Does it feel better?"

"A little. Help me to the bedroom, and I'll change. Don't want to keep tempting you."

"Hah, hah. I'm glad to see that you haven't lost that sense of humor, although I never knew you had one. Try to put a little pressure on it. If it still hurts, I'll carry you."

"Oww," Theresa said, as soon as she stood. "It hurts worse now. You're going to have to carry me."

"You sure you don't want to go get an X-ray?" he asked, scooping her up easily and heading to the bedroom.

"No. Isn't this funny? I had an image of you carrying me into my bedroom, and I was naked, but I never thought that it would be to do nothing."

"Well, the next time I carry you in here, it will definitely be to do something."

"Promise?" she teased.

"Promise," he concurred, placing her on the bed. "Now, get dressed. I'll go into the living room and pour us some wine."

Theresa threw on a T-shirt and some pajama pants that she used as nightclothes. Sliding into her slippers, she tried to stand again. It didn't hurt until she put her full weight on it, and then she winced and fell back onto the bed.

"Pierson," she called. "I'm ready."

And there he was in the blink of an eye to carry her back into the living room. "So, before I leave, I will carry you to bed. Now, if you're not going to see a doctor tonight, you have to promise me that if you can't put weight on it in the morning that you'll call me or one of your brothers to take you. And don't try to be a hero. Don't go to work if it's hurting. Promise?"

"I promise," she answered, accepting the glass of wine he now offered her. "See, this is why I need an assistant."

"Theresa, we both know that you don't really need an assistant. You've been doing just fine all these years by yourself."

"But an assistant will free up a lot of my time and mind. I won't have to think about every little thing. And I think it will be good for Danielle. For one, it will help to make her more responsible, and second, it will help her to make her own money. It's a win-win situation for both of us."

"Well, we'll see. How much are you planning to pay her?"

"I thought that I would pay her $100 a week cash and put $200 a week into a college fund for her."

"That's $300 a week, more than a high school student should be making, don't you think?"

"Believe me, it will be well earned. She will be working hard for her money. Pierson, she'll be working for one of the presidents of a large corporation. The money has to match the job description, which will include a wide variety of duties. Believe me, she'll be coming home tired every night. If Mikey doesn't talk her to death, running around town sure will. Does she have her driver's license?"

"Yeah, sure, but she doesn't have a car."

"Well, she'll need a car to get back and forth to work. I'll get her a company car."

"A company car? I think that's a bit much," Pierson protested.

"Are you going to bring her to work every morning before you go to the shop?" She watched for a second before continuing. "I didn't think so. I know that you can find her a used car somewhere. Something that is trustworthy, but doesn't cost much."

"I just don't know if she's ready for that much responsibility thrown at her all at once."

"How will you know if you never try it? If you don't give her some responsibility, she'll never be responsible. Okay, then let's make an agreement. I'll pay her the aforementioned amount, and slowly give her responsibility. Before letting her out on her own, I'll have to teach her the ropes anyway, so she'll be following behind me for a while. And I will assign her a driver for any errands away from the office."

"That sounds better. How about if we take it one day at a time on a trial basis? But when school starts, if her grades slip one bit, there's a problem."

"Agreed. I don't need anyone working for me who can't multi-task, and I'll make sure to let that point be known."

"Good, then we're agreed," Pierson said, relaxing back into sofa. He pulled her back into his chest. Kissing her on the top of her head, Pierson ran his hand up and down her arm. "I guess I should be getting home."

"It's still early."

"Theresa, it's almost eleven o'clock. I'm usually in bed by now."

"Well, you could have been in bed by now," she said sarcastically.

"Am I ever going to live this down?"

"No, why should I let you?"

"See, I was going to suggest staying the night and sleeping on the sofa, but I'm afraid you'd try to jump my bones in the middle of the night."

"Oh, please, Mr. Brooks, you are not all that."

"I'm not?"

"Hardly. And I have a spare bedroom, but you trust Danielle by herself?"

"Are you kidding? As soon as she got to the shop with all those bags, she had to call her girlfriend and start contriving a way for her to get over there so everybody can see her new clothes. I thought you would have picked up outfits for her to wear to work for you."

"I did, but she can't wear suits and dress pants all day, every day. We had to get jeans and shirts, and of course, shoes and sandals."

"Oh, of course. You can't have one without the other."

"Then Victoria's Secret was right up the block, so we had to get underclothes and some smell good."

"Smell good?"

"Yes, man. All the things that make you smell good."

"Right. Well, I don't think Danielle needs to smell as good as that big bag would indicate."

"You can never have enough smell good."

"You don't say. And how much do you have?"

"You'll be surprised when I show you. But I'll save that for another time. I don't want to scare you away. So, are you going to stay or not?"

"Only if you promise to keep your hands to yourself," he said laughingly.

"You can walk me to my room, and I'll show you which room is yours. With this bum ankle, I doubt if you have to worry about being raped tonight. Come on and help me up."

They laughed their way down the hallway, past the first room, which was her office. It was cluttered with material and patterns used for doing some of her interior decorating. The next room was the one Pierson was to stay in. It was furnished with a full-size bed, two dressers and a large plasma television. He nodded his approval when he looked into the room.

He knew that the next room was Mikey's because they had played video games in there. And Mikey had showed Pierson his telescope. Theresa's room was the last, at the end of the hallway, and he had been in there once already tonight, but failed to look around. In his distress, he had taken her to the bed as quickly as possible and left. Pierson had missed the sitting area to the side and the massive master bathroom.

"This is nice," he said, moving from her bed to stand in front of the television in her sitting area. He sat down on the sofa. "I didn't even see it the first time I came in here."

"That's because you were in too much of a hurry to get out. I really only watch the news on that television. I'm only in here in the morning, and of course, I watch the stock prices and the news."

"Of course. You didn't strike me as the soap opera type."

"I don't have time for too much television. The only time I really make time for television is basketball season."

"Right, the Celtics."

"Of course, but I watch most of the games, or at least listen to them."

"Well, is there anything you need before I go off to bed? You want something to drink? Or a book or something?"

"No, thank you. I'm all right. I'll see you in the morning, Pierson."

"All right," he said, bending over the bed to kiss her. He stayed on her lips longer than he intended before pulling away slowly. "Good night, Theresa," he said.

Theresa watched Pierson walk out of the room after turning off her light, and hoped for a second that he would turn around. He didn't.

CHAPTER 10

Tuesday morning, Theresa was working steadily, in a good mood after her evening with Pierson. She reminisced over practically everything that had happened that night, from the conversation to the massage to the tender kiss he gave her at the end of the evening. Honestly, she couldn't remember the last time she'd enjoyed herself so much.

Earlier, she had wakened to toast and coffee in bed and the sight of a beautifully built ebony sculpture of maleness serving her with a smile. Theresa wished she'd asked him into her bed, but knew his answer would have been no. She had to respect him for trying to respect her, even when she didn't want him to. Was she being too forward? No, she mused, she was horny.

Being the perfect gentleman, Pierson checked her ankle. After he was satisfied that it wasn't swollen and Theresa double-promised that she wasn't in pain, he helped her to the bathroom so she could get dressed for work. Her ankle was sore, but she wasn't in tremendous pain.

Right before lunch, she received a call from Stephanie asking her to come out to the reception area. There was a man there who said he was an officer of the court and needed to speak to her.

Although her stomach roiled at the thought of what awaited her in the corridor, Theresa left her office. What she deeply dreaded waited patiently for her in the form of a white envelope, which she signed for with quiet resentment. She didn't give the server time to question her identity, simply held out her hand to receive the clipboard. She handed it back, then turned to return to her office. Once the man left, Stephanie followed her boss and friend down the hall.

She noticed Theresa walked with her shoulders a little lower than usual, as if she had been defeated the moment the letter was placed in her hand.

"Theresa," she began, closing the office door, "are you all right?"

"I'm fine, Stephanie," Theresa replied, her earlier happy and hopeful mood suddenly disappearing. She slumped into her chair, throwing the letter in the center of her desk without even opening it. Her eyes were closed, and her demeanor was heavy with depression.

"Is there anything I can do?"

"Only if you know where I can hire an assassin."

Stephanie threw up her arms, as she was prone to do when trying to emphasize her point or call on the Lord, whichever suited her need at the moment. "Lord, she did not mean to say that," she said. Then to Theresa, she said, "Ms. Lady, you are not going to let that man put you into this mood. I won't let you. Theresa, do you realize who you are? You are Theresa Philips. Why are you walking around with your head down? You haven't even read the letter yet." Stephanie pushed the envelope closer to her, beckoning her to open it.

"I don't have to open it. I already know what it says. Ryan is trying to take my son."

"Listen to yourself. Do you really think he could do that? Worst-case scenario, he wants to spend time with his son. So, stop exaggerating."

"And why do you think that is? So he can work his way into taking my son. I'm not going to let that happen. He can't have Mikey." Theresa sat up and slammed her fist on the top of her desk.

"Now that's what I'm talking about. We're going to fight this, just like we do everything else. Now, open the letter."

Theresa did as she was told, her employee giving her the orders. She read the words twice, and then threw it back down. "We're going to court for visitation. Ryan states that he wants to get to know his son better and that I have prevented that for the past years by having Mikey enrolled in a boarding school outside of the state. He's asking that I not be allowed to send Mikey back out of state for another semester. Well, he doesn't have to worry about that, does he? Mikey and I have an appointment at the private school across town."

"Call Joshua right now, and let him know."

Again, Theresa did as Stephanie said without question. These were the times when the employee/boss relationship went right out the window. That was why she had asked Stephanie to be her secretary in the first place. She trusted her more than anyone else. Stephanie had been her friend ever since they met at the hospital while giving birth to their first sons. Even in the hospital, it had been Stephanie teaching her to change Mikey's diaper, not the nurse.

Theresa called Joshua's cellphone and explained the letter she had just received to him. He told her that there was no way the judge would deny Ryan visitation rights, but he would petition the court that afternoon to make the visitations supervised as Mikey did not have a relationship with his father.

The one thing that Joshua said Ryan had on his side was that he never tried to seek visitation rights before. This would help support Ryan's love and true want for a relationship with his son because Mikey was worth over $25 million in his own right. But he planned to bring up Ryan's financial situation so that the court knew he was in desperate need of money and might be seeking Mikey's wealth to resolve his own problems.

"How did he get a hearing so fast?" Theresa wondered aloud.

"That's a good question," Joshua replied. "I can't honestly say that it's hard to do, but you have to know the right people in most situations. Obviously, Ryan has a friend or two working in the courthouse."

"Probably a dark-skinned beauty with a fat ass. Ryan has always had a preference for one or the other, but if he could find the two together, he'd be in heaven." She continued to talk over Joshua's laughter. "This man is going to be the death of me, Joshua."

"Theresa, this is not as serious as you think. I know it's hard to believe, but everything will work out."

"Okay." Theresa noticed Stephanie standing observantly on the other side of her desk. She smiled to herself, knowing that Joshua and Stephanie had been pussyfooting around the obvious for months. "Do you want to speak to Stephanie?"

"No," Joshua replied easily. "I'll see her tonight."

He encouraged Theresa to stay calm and let him handle it, and she agreed that she would trust him to handle it.

When Theresa hung up the phone and smiled in her direction, Stephanie realized she knew. "No, don't start. It's nothing but dinner with a friend."

"Yeah, right. Then why didn't you tell me?" Theresa asked, smiling brightly. She was glad that Stephanie was showing interest in someone decent and who would actually be good to her and for her. Her friend, for all the advice she gave, had a bad habit of attracting the wrong men. Fortunately, she had been smart enough not to marry any of them.

"Because you came out and started going all nervous breakdowny on me before I had a chance to. Now that you're all right and you know about my date, I'm going back to work. You need to relax and concentrate on yours. Mikey will be up from the mailroom in about an hour for lunch with you. I ordered his favorite, a large pizza loaded with pepperoni, sausage, onions, and green pepper, and they'll be delivering it soon."

Stephanie turned and walked out of the office. Theresa tried to focus on her work until she heard a ruckus in the hallway.

"Sir, excuse me. . . I said she wasn't seeing anyone at the moment. Ryan. Ryan! I'm going to call security."

When Theresa looked up, she saw Stephanie rushing into the room with her arms spread wide as if trying to prevent the man behind her from entering. Theresa stood as she watched Ryan practically lift her secretary out of the way and walk into the room. Despite Stephanie's efforts, Ryan briskly walked to Theresa's desk as she scrambled around to the front of it. There was a discomfort in her ankle, but she ignored it.

"What the hell are you doing here?" Theresa yelled.

"I tried to stop him," Stephanie said. Theresa acknowledged her with a wave.

"I asked you a question," she said, trying to stand firm and hoping that he wouldn't see her nervousness.

"I'm here to talk to you about our son."

"We don't have a son. I do." Theresa crossed her arms.

"Look, I'm not here to argue. I just wanted you to know that I have petitioned the courts for visitation."

"You could have said that over the phone."

Stephanie moved over to Theresa's desk and picked up the phone. She dialed security, telling them to come to Theresa's office.

"I was hoping to see my son today. Is that possible?"

"Hell, no. Ryan, get the hell out of here. You think you're just going to walk into my son's life and pick up where you never left off? He doesn't even know you."

Ryan suddenly became upset. It wasn't as if he'd had a choice in that matter, he told himself. She had taken his son from him, and he was the one who had missed out on opportunities. He and the boy could have formed some kind of relationship by now if Theresa hadn't taken him away. He didn't have to be living day-to-day. They could still be married if she had just accepted him for who he was. It wasn't as if he hadn't loved her, he had just been young. Damn, *he* could be living in a mansion with millions of dollars in the bank right now if *she* hadn't overreacted.

"I have every right to see my son, Theresa. And nobody is going to take that from me. You, your brothers, none of you."

"We'll just see about that," Thorne said from the office doorway. He stormed into the room with Michael on his heels. "You must be the dumbest man on Earth, Ryan. But I am so glad to see you." Thorne had his sleeves rolled up, his tie was missing, and the top button of his shirt was undone.

Ryan moved quickly, turning so that instead of facing Theresa, he was standing beside her trying to brace himself for the impact that was coming. He hadn't seen Thorne in years, and the man seemed to have grown substantially since their last encounter.

Theresa moved back behind her desk, the look in Thorne's eyes unnerving her enough to force her to move out of the way. She knew what was coming.

"I warned you Saturday, Ryan, not to come around my sister," Michael said, standing next to Thorne. "What did you think would happen to you if you came here?"

Stephanie ran next to Theresa after shutting the office doors. She was so glad that Thorne and Michael had been in their offices when she buzzed their phones.

Ryan's anger mounted. He had let Thorne and Michael bully him into letting his son go once before, but it was not going to happen again. He had too much at stake this time. This was his second chance at getting the millions of dollars that should have been his when he married Theresa. He'd thought that getting her pregnant would ensure his future, but instead it had contributed to his doom. Ryan saw Michael and Thorne in the newspapers on the society pages, flashing their money, dating their socialites, doing their good deeds and knew that should have been his life. He should be making moves and living better than in the dirty apartment on the wrong side of town.

"I don't care what happens," Ryan replied. "You and Michael jumping on me will only help my cause." Ryan stood his ground although he honestly didn't believe that Thorne would heed his warning. He'd known when he walked into the building that he would get pummeled if Thorne was anywhere around.

"I'm not going to put my hands on you just now," Thorne answered, even though he wanted to do nothing more. "I'm not going to help you take my nephew away. Instead, I'm going to call the police and have you arrested for trespassing. I'm sure that won't help your cause."

Ryan stepped forward, thinking that he should leave.

Thorne shook his head. "Oh, no you don't. Have a seat. The police are already on their way. You might as well make yourself comfortable, because you're not going anywhere."

Michael stood in front of the closed door with his arms crossed, a snide smile on his face.

"So, why are you so interested in your son all of a sudden?" Michael asked from his position.

"Because he's my son. Why don't you two leave and let Theresa and me handle this on our own? Mikey's not any of your business."

"See," Thorne answered, "that's where you're wrong. Mikey is our business. He's always been, always will be."

"I'm still trying to figure out what you want, Ryan," Theresa said.

"It's simple. I want my son. I want to get to know him, and I want to spend time with him. Is that too much for a father to ask? If he was your son," Ryan said, turning his attention back to Thorne, "wouldn't you want to know him? Would you let anyone stop you from doing just that?"

When Thorne stepped closer to him, Ryan visibly flinched.

"No, I wouldn't. But then again, I wouldn't have been absent from my son's life for six years, either."

"Hey, don't put that on me. That was your grand-mother's doing. Ms. Abbie made sure that I stayed away from Theresa and Mikey."

"As I recall, the check that she gave you insured that," Theresa added. "You didn't have to take it, but you decided to take the money and run. That showed exactly how much you wanted to be in our lives."

"Either way, you were going to divorce me. I had to make sure that I was able to take care of myself."

"And I think you're doing the same thing again," Thorne said. "We know that you're broke and that you're in debt up to your ass. You really expect us to believe that money isn't a factor here?"

"Look, this is getting us nowhere. You're not going to change the way you think of me, and I'm not going to stop until I get visitation with my son. So, I'll wait right here and let the police escort me out. Then I'll see you in court, and we'll get this all settled."

By the time Ryan finished his spew, Michael was letting in the security officers who had been waiting by the door.

"The police are being escorted up now, Mr. Philips," one of the guards commented.

"Excellent," Michael replied. "I'm sure that trespassing and posing a threat to Theresa will help our lawyer move these proceedings along quickly."

Ryan looked at him. "But I'm not posing a threat. I'm sitting here peacefully, waiting for the police."

"Are you kidding me? It's obvious that Theresa is traumatized and scared out of her wits. If Thorne and I hadn't come in here, God only knows what you would have done."

"Oh, please. Do you really think that is going to work?" Ryan stood up, but noticed Thorne flex in response. "It won't work. All I want is to spend time with my son. I'm desperate."

"No," Theresa interjected, "you're full of it. And there is not a judge in the world who isn't going to see right through your fake-ass façade."

The police arrived and walked to Ryan after Thorne pointed him out. He didn't resist until one of the officers pulled out handcuffs. He hated to be handcuffed and stuffed into the back of a squad car.

"It's not as fake as yours, Theresa," he yelled. "Playing the victim doesn't suit you well. You think you're so innocent. You've done a lot of things in your life that I'm sure you don't want your brothers to know about. Hell, you didn't even want to have Mikey. I was the one who convinced you to have him."

No one saw Mikey standing in the hallway, watching his mother and father yell at each other. No one saw him until Ryan was pulled out of the office, followed by Thorne and Michael. That was when Theresa noticed him quietly standing off to the side.

And though she prayed that he hadn't heard what Ryan had just said, she could tell he had by the pout of his lips and the sorrowful question expressed in his eyes.

"Baby, come here," she said, expecting him to listen as he always did. Instead, for the first time, Mikey didn't obey. He ran away down the hall.

Stephanie followed closely behind him. He was confused and didn't understand his father's manipulative ways.

Before Ryan was out of sight, he flashed Theresa a devilish smile that made a chill run up her spine. She knew that Ryan had done that on purpose.

Theresa might have once questioned whether she should go through with the pregnancy because she knew that her relationship with Ryan was headed down the wrong road, but she as soon as Mikey was born she wanted her baby. Just then, her fear increased, and she knew that the possibility of losing her son was very real.

"Did you find him?" Theresa asked as soon as Stephanie came back into the office.

"No," she replied. "He was too fast, but he has to be around here somewhere. The elevator wasn't used until the police got in it. I asked if anyone in the reception area saw him. They said no."

"We have to find him. What if—" Theresa's hand flew to her mouth.

"Stop. Right now. Sit down and calm down. Mikey is around here somewhere. We just have to find him." Stephanie handed Theresa a tissue. "I'll be right back." A few minutes later, she returned with a cup of tea. "I think you should stay home tonight instead of going to class. Maybe you and Mikey can spend some time together tonight. That would make both of you feel better."

"Yeah, you're right. I need to talk to him."

Thorne went back to his desk, satisfied that the police were taking Ryan to the station to be booked for trespassing after being told how he barged into the CEO's office and pushed his way past the secretary. He honestly didn't think that it would help Theresa in the custody case, but at the least, it might show that Ryan was unpredictable and easily angered.

He was about to sit down when he heard muffled cries coming from under his desk. Looking down, he found Mikey bundled into a ball under the desk as if he were hiding from someone.

"Young man, why are you under there crying?"

Mikey had always looked up to his uncles, and he tried desperately to wipe the tears from his face, but they just wouldn't stop. He didn't reply.

"Mikey, come out from under there and talk to me like a young man." Thorne wanted to pick the boy up, place him on his legs, and comfort him, but he couldn't do it. He and Michael had never babied their nephew in an effort to teach him that you had to face your disappointments rather than run from them, which was what he was doing right now. Thorne didn't like it.

"Mikey," he repeated, his voice harsher than before.

Mikey came from under the desk with his mouth set in a pout.

"Fix that lip," Thorne said, pulling another chair around for his nephew.

Mikey did as he was told and sat down in the chair.

"Okay, buddy, now talk to me."

Mikey didn't say anything for a second, and then he began. Looking down at his lap, he mumbled, "My mom didn't want to have me."

"No," Thorne said. "This is not how we have a conversation. I have told you before that a young man does not hold his head down when he is speaking. Now, look me in the eye and tell me what the problem is."

Mikey did as he was told. Looking at his uncle, whom he respected a great deal, he said, "My mother did not want to have me."

Thorne was surprised to hear that from Mikey's mouth, and he knew instantly where he had heard it. Obviously, Mikey was somewhere close when Ryan began yelling the nonsense.

Mikey was looking at Thorne closely now, and Thorne knew he was waiting for any reaction. "That is not true," Thorne replied, honestly. His gaze on Mikey was intense. "You listen to me, Mikey, and you listen good. First of all, your mother loves you very much. You have to be blind not to see everything that she has done for you. I know that we have kept a lot of things from you that you're probably old enough to know about now, but it was a decision that your mother, your uncle, and I made for your best interest. Now, I'm only going to tell you this one time. Never let anyone make you question the love your mother shows you every day."

"But my father said—"

"I said no one. You have eyes, don't you? You can see, right? See this stapler."

"Yes," Mikey replied.

"It's not there."

"Yes, it is."

"No, it's not. Now, how much sense am I making? You see your mother's love, right?"

"Yes."

"She spends time with you. So that you can be close to her, she's letting you move back here instead of staying at one of the best schools in the country. I know she cheered her head off at your basketball game, right?"

"Yes."

"Then how can you think that she doesn't love you or didn't want you when she proves it and shows it to you every day."

"You're right."

"Mikey, here's another lesson. People, grown-ups, too, will say things and do things if they think it will turn you against someone else. You have to be a leader, not a follower, and make decisions for yourself. Now, I'm sure that your mother is worried sick about you."

"I think that I made her cry."

Thorne just looked at him.

"I owe her an apology," Mikey admitted.

"Yes, I think that you do," Thorne concurred.

Mikey was about to leave, but he hesitated.

"Is there something else?" Thorne asked.

"Uncle Thorne, do you think that I should get to know my father better?"

Thorne had to stop himself from saying how he truly felt. Hadn't he just told Mikey not to let others dictate your feelings? If he told Mikey how he really felt, Mikey would most definitely follow his lead. The boy was only nine. Instead, he asked a simple question.

"Mikey, what do you think you should do? What do you want to do?" It was an important question that Thorne was sure no one had asked the boy. He felt that Mikey should know that he did have a small say in his own life.

Mikey thought long and hard as he always did when his uncle asked him a question. Both men had told him a long time ago to think before speaking. "I guess I would like to know him. He's my father, and I never had one. Shouldn't every boy know his father?"

"Honestly, I think that every boy should get a chance to know his father. Maybe you should talk to your mother about this."

Mikey looked at him. "Maybe you should talk to my mother for me, if you don't mind. I don't want to upset her any more."

Thorne was about to tell him that as a young man he couldn't run from his problems nor be afraid to express his feelings, but when Thorne looked at him, all he saw was his nine-year-old nephew who wanted his help.

"I'll have a talk with her, but you must talk to her, too. You can't be afraid of the one person who is always behind you. Does that make any sense?" Thorne knew that was how children were with their parents. He had been the same way with his grandmother, who had raised him, Michael and Theresa.

"Okay."

"Now, are you feeling better?" Thorne asked.

"Yes," Mikey answered.

"Good. Now, go away. I have work to do." Thorne laughed with Mikey as he pushed his rolling chair away.

"Uncle Thorne, can I stay with you and Ms. Natalie tonight? Mom has class."

"Where were you supposed to go?"

"With Uncle Michael, but since Ms. Tamia is pregnant, he is always rubbing her stomach and stuff. He doesn't act the same way anymore."

"Well, you have to understand that Michael is about to be a father. After he gets used to the idea, he'll gradually start acting like his old self again. Give him time. And the answer to your question is yes. Go tell your mother."

Mikey didn't waste any time running out of Thorne's office and heading for his mother.

CHAPTER 11

"Theresa," Stephanie said, walking back into the office. It saddened her to see Theresa in such a depressed state. Theresa was a strong woman whose independence, confidence, and strength usually shone brightly. When she saw Theresa with her head in her hands, Stephanie decided to give her time to get herself together. "Theresa, security is bringing Danielle up now. They just finished processing her. I'm going to give her a quick tour of the floor while you get yourself together. It shouldn't take more than fifteen minutes. Get yourself together while I'm gone."

Theresa didn't raise her head fully, but she did nod her head in acknowledgment. "Thanks, Stephanie."

As soon as Stephanie shut the office door, Mikey opened it and strolled into his mother's office as if nothing had ever happened. He sat down in the chair across from her like a little man.

Theresa quietly watched him enter and wondered what was going to come out of his mouth. Did he believe what Ryan had shouted out in an effort to gain their son's loyalty? Did he hate her? Did he think that she didn't love him? Theresa realized that this was one of the scariest moments of her life.

"Mom," he began before looking her in the eye. "I'm sorry."

"No, baby," Theresa quickly interjected. "I'm sorry. I should have never let your father get me so upset." Tears began to fall from her eyes. She wanted to ask him what he had heard, but was afraid to bring up the subject.

"I know that you love me, Mom. And I don't believe what he said." Mikey went around the desk and gave his mother a hug.

Theresa hugged him back. "Thank you, baby. You don't know how worried I was that you might take what he said the wrong way. Mikey, I love you more than anything in this world."

"I know."

"You don't have to be around him if you don't want to. I'll do everything in my power to fight him for custody."

Mikey looked at his mother. He knew that this was the moment that his uncle was talking about. And he should tell her that he felt he should get to know his father, but when he looked in her eyes and saw how hurt she was, he couldn't. He didn't want to upset her any further.

Instead, he changed the subject. "Mom, don't you have class tonight?"

"Yes, but I wasn't going to go. I wanted to stay and spend some time with you. I already told your Uncle Michael that you wouldn't be coming with him tonight."

"I asked Uncle Thorne if I could come to his house. Did you know that Uncle Michael would start acting funny around Ms. Tamia now that she is pregnant?"

Mikey asked it so innocently that Theresa had to smile. "Well, that is what some men do when they are about to become a father."

"It's just weird. She can't hurt herself just by walking from the living room to the kitchen, but he's trying to hold her hand every time she moves and stuff."

"Mikey, I hope you remember that we had this conversation. When you get older, you might act exactly the same way."

"No I won't. I'll never act like Uncle Michael."

Just then Stephanie came back into the office with Danielle on her heels. She showed Danielle into the office, obviously pleased with the smile spread across her friend's face.

"Danielle, thank you so much for coming in today," Theresa said, noticing how fast Mikey moved out of her arms. He stood next to her, the little man returning again.

"No," Danielle started, "I wanted to start working as soon as possible." Her old attitude was slowly disappearing. "Hi, little man," she said to Mikey. They hadn't met yet, but she had heard plenty about him when she and Theresa went on their shopping spree. And Danielle knew that part of her duties as Theresa's assistant was watching Mikey. He was a cute kid, but didn't seem like the little boys she knew. As she watched him in his shirt and tie, it was hard to imagine him running up and down a basketball court the way her brother described.

"Hi," Mikey replied shyly.

Theresa looked in his direction.

"So, I suppose we'll be hanging together tonight while your mother goes to school," Danielle said, squatting down to Mikey's level.

"Okay," Mikey replied to Theresa's astonishment.

Didn't she just tell him that she was staying home tonight? She smiled to herself. He was more like his Uncle Michael than he thought.

Just then Thorne walked into the office. It was almost two o'clock, and he was trying to make the work day end as quickly as possible.

"Oh, Thorne," Theresa said, "I want to introduce you to my new assistant. This is Danielle. Danielle will be helping me with errands, filing, light office work, and some personal things. Kind of like an internship, except she'll be getting paid, a cut check and a savings established for her college fund."

Thorne nodded and extended his hand in greeting. "Welcome aboard, Danielle," he said, noticing the small blush that swept over her face. Not to be conceited, but he had seen the same expression many times before. Young girls were often flustered around him.

Danielle smiled brightly.

"Um, Danielle, this is my older brother, Thorne. You'll see him around often as he is in charge around here."

"Nonsense, the three of us work together and pull equal loads. I just came to grab Mikey. I'm about to leave for the day, and he said—"

"Uncle Thorne," Mikey quickly interjected, "Danielle is going to watch me tonight while Mom is in school, so I'll just see you tomorrow, okay?"

Thorne looked at him briefly, then shared a quick glance with Theresa and Danielle. He looked at Mikey again before realizing what was going on. "Okay, little man. I guess I'll see you later. Enjoy your evening. Matter fact, why don't you treat your new friend to pizza tonight for dinner? Here, it's on me." He pulled twenty dollars out of his pocket and placed it in his nephew's hand.

"Thorne," Theresa said, watching the grin spread across her brother's face. He was really enjoying his nephew, who now seemed to have another crush.

"Good night, ladies," Thorne said before walking out of the room.

"Well, I guess it's settled then. I'm going to class. Now, Danielle, we need to walk down to the garage and put you on the chauffeur's list."

Danielle smiled, "Chauffeur's list?"

"Yes. Some of your tasks involve you leaving the building. You'll need a car and driver in order to run errands for me, and when school starts, one of your after-noon errands will be to pick Mikey up from his school. Since you will only be in school half a day, it will work out perfectly.

"We have a car pool, with a few drivers, and I need to make sure that you will have one at your disposal. Your brother wasn't too keen on the idea of you being assigned your own company car since you haven't had your license that long. And because of your age, I'm unable to add you to our company's insurance policy. Therefore, you will need a driver. But hopefully, we can work on getting you your own car in the near future."

Danielle's eyes lit up like a Christmas tree, and Theresa hesitated for a second. Maybe she shouldn't have volunteered that information. "Um, Ms. Theresa, I want to thank you for saving me from the shop. Not that I didn't appreciate working for my brother, but . . ."

"You don't have to explain anything to me. I understand completely," Theresa replied, walking out of the office. "Let's see, you got your badge for the building. You filled out your work papers, your tax forms, and now, the chauffeur's list. I'd say that you're just about all set. Stephanie gave you a short tour of the building and explained the company to you a little, correct?"

"Yes," Danielle replied, keeping up with Theresa's quick steps. Mikey was trailing behind them.

"Good. Basically, by the time you get here, I'll have a list of errands that need to be done for that day, and occasionally I might call you if something pops up while you're out, but I'll try to keep it to a minimum. I don't want you to become overwhelmed, especially when your three main objectives will be to pick up Mikey daily, keep your grades up and your schoolwork completed, and learn as much as you can about the business. Keep your eyes and ears open and try to remember, as much as you can, people, places, and things."

A young man came around the corner and almost ran into both ladies because the large book he was reading seemed too interesting to put down.

"Oh, excuse me, um, Mrs. Philips. I am sorry, ma'am," he said, then turned to Danielle and stuttered, "Um, I-I-I'm sorry."

Danielle smiled up at the tall, lanky young man with glasses that slid down his nose when he lifted his head out of the book. He looked Italian, nerdy Italian, but he was cute in his own way.

"Danielle, this is Christopher Gamio. Christopher works with my brother Michael. He's sort of an intern also. Christopher, this is Danielle Brooks. She's starting here today as my assistant."

The two young people smiled at each other, then Christopher excused himself as his nerves got the best of him. He spoke to Mikey who, although he liked Christopher very much, was glad to see him leave.

"So, each of you has an intern?" Danielle asked.

"No, not Thorne. He's still in the mindset that he can do everything himself."

"And he looks like he can," Danielle said, half under her breath.

Theresa laughed. That was the way most women saw Thorne.

Theresa sat silently in class Tuesday night. She shouldn't have come. Her mind wasn't on the lesson being taught, and she barely heard a word that was being said. Instead, she was running through her unbelievable day. Not only was she about to be in for the fight of her life, but Ryan seemed to have some serious connections within the court system. How had he managed to get their custody hearing scheduled so soon? She would have thought that it took a judge or lawyer to do such things, but as simple as Ryan was, the culprit was probably the clerk who scheduled the hearings. At any rate, he seemed to have one up on her. It wouldn't happen again.

When she left class, Theresa noticed that she had a message on her cellphone. She knew immediately that it was Pierson. She had tried to call him before she went to school, but he'd said he was on a run and couldn't talk. Theresa wished that Danielle were older so that she could have issued her a car from the garage, but instead she'd had to talk the manager of the car pool into practically hiring another part-time driver just for Danielle. With it being the second half of the season, drivers were busy transporting presidents, managers, and sales personnel, who traveled frequently back and forth to meetings or the airport.

Logically, Danielle would need a means of transportation if she were going to be her assistant. Assistant didn't mean sitting next to her all day and watching her work; it meant taking care of some of the things that Theresa couldn't.

She grimaced as she listened to the message, and wondered if she had overstepped her bounds. Pierson didn't hide the anger in his voice. Theresa called him. She didn't want him thinking that she was trying to go behind his back or be deceptive. The driver was a necessity.

"Hello, Pierson," she started, "I'm on my way to pick up Mikey now."

"Good," he replied, " 'cause we need to talk."

"How was your day?"

"Just fine, Theresa. How long before you get here?"

"Not long. Look, I know that you're mad, but you don't have to be rude."

Pierson was quiet for a moment, then said, "You're right. I apologize, but Theresa, you should not have told that girl she was going to get a car. She thinks that your 'near future' is in a couple of weeks."

"And I didn't mean to, but we were just moving along with the orientation and then I realized that in order for her to be my assistant she would need a driver and eventually her own car once she gets older. I was not trying to go behind your back; I was just talking. I apologize."

"I don't think that you were doing it to spite me, but didn't you think there was a reason why I never gave her one of the cars at the shop? She has to show other responsibility before I give her that kind of heavy responsibility."

"Pierson, I am not trying to intrude on your family business," Theresa said.

Pierson interrupted her. "Theresa, I didn't say that."

"I know, but I'm trying to make you understand. I am not trying to get into your family business or ignore any rules that you have put down for her. I realize that you are trying to raise your teenage sister the best you can to be the best that she can, but what I have found in my experience is that to get someone to be responsible, you have you have to show them that you trust them."

Pierson remained quiet.

"Danielle knows that this is a company car. She can't just tell the driver to take her wherever she wants to go.

Just because she has a vehicle at her disposal doesn't mean it's for her personal use. I've explained all of that to her, and the driver also knows his job. On top of that, the driver has to log in his mileage. But Pierson, you have to show her that she is trusted. If she violates the rules, she will be penalized not only with you but her job will be jeopardized. In teaching her responsibility, we have to show her trust."

Pierson simply responded, "I'll see you when you get here."

"Okay," she said, wondering if she had mistakenly overstepped her bounds anyway.

Pierson put the phone down and sat down at the dining room table. He listened to Danielle and Mikey playing the new Wii game that he had just run out and bought on the spur of the moment when Danielle told him that Mikey was coming to the house with her. He had never had any intention of buying one before, but he wanted Mikey to be comfortable in his home. But it honestly looked as if the boy would have been happy in a trash dumpster as long as Danielle was in there with him.

He knew that Theresa was right; Pierson just wasn't ready to admit that he was wrong. It wasn't as if she wouldn't be under supervision. The driver would be with her, but he worried. When he brought Danielle to New Orleans, he had taken the responsibility seriously, and he was adamant about not letting her get out of control or think that she could act like she had with their father. The more he thought about it, the more he had to agree with Theresa. Danielle hadn't done anything but what he'd said since she had come there, and it had put a slight strain on their relationship. She really hadn't given him any reason not to trust her, and she was always in the shop sitting around, bored to death. Maybe exposing her to new challenges and responsibilities would be good. And it wasn't as if he couldn't keep a tab on her throughout the day.

Pierson snapped out of his deep thoughts when lights from Theresa's car flashed through the window curtains. He walked to the door and held the screen open until she was inside.

At the door, Theresa was unsure of whether she should greet him with a kiss or not, but decided to as an affirmation as to where they stood at the moment. She lifted her face and immediately Pierson bent down and planted a kiss on her cheek.

"So, you ready for that talk?" Theresa asked.

"No, I think we've talked enough," he replied, looking at Danielle, who was looking at him. "You made your point. We'll see how it goes."

Danielle smiled as she once again focused on playing tennis against Mikey. "All right, Mikey. This looks like our last game. Your mom's here. So, I'm going to have to hurry up and beat you."

"Oh, no you're not. I already beat you twice, Danielle."

"But that's because I was tired. I got my second wind now."

"I'm not going to let a girl beat me. What if my uncles find out?"

"Girls can beat boys at things."

Pierson led Theresa into the kitchen as they listened to the banter between Danielle and Mikey. He pulled her into his arms.

"So, how was your day?" he asked, letting his hands move up and down her back.

Theresa loved the feel of his hands as he applied just enough pressure to almost make her forget about the day's dreadful events. *That's right, she'd never had a chance to tell him.* She took a step back and looked at him.

"That bad?"

"Worse. First of all, I was served with papers. Seems that Ryan has found a way to wrangle a custody hearing for Wednesday morning. We have an appointment with a mediator first, and then in front of a judge if we can't come to some common agreement, which we won't." Theresa sat down in one of the chairs at the table.

"Wednesday. That's kind of soon, isn't it? He must have filed the papers a while ago." Pierson took the seat opposite her.

"Or know someone who moved the appointment up for him."

"Damn, I didn't know people could do that."

"You can do anything if you screw the right person," she said bitterly.

Pierson watched her closely. He doubted very seriously if she held any feeling other than hatred for the man, but if he wasn't personally involved with her, he would have thought she still cared for him. He wouldn't address it either way because he knew the truth. Instead, he said, "All it used to take was money."

"Well, now it takes whatever a person wants." Theresa knew how Ryan operated. "He doesn't have money, so he would use the next best thing." She felt Pierson tense as soon as she said it. And even though she didn't mean it as it sounded, Theresa was aware of how it sounded. "I didn't—"

"I know you didn't. Let it go."

She was quiet for another moment, and then took his suggestion. There was no way she could fix it. "Right after that, Ryan had the audacity to walk right into my office." She lowered her voice for Mikey's sake. "Stephanie was trying to stop him, but she couldn't. Came into the office saying that he was going to have visits with Mikey and that there was nothing we could do, regardless of all our money, to stop him. Thorne and Michael ran into the room in the middle of our argument. And he was taunting Thorne. He was hoping that Thorne would jump on him, said it would better his case against me. Then he started throwing out a bunch of accusations." Theresa paused and put her head down. "And Mikey overheard Ryan claim that I didn't want to have him when I found out I was pregnant. I swear, Pierson, I have never wanted to kill someone so much in my life."

"He was only trying to turn Mikey against you. I doubt very seriously if that could ever happen. Theresa, you know that this is going to get a lot worse before it gets any better. You have to do two things. You gotta stay strong, and you have to have faith in your son's love. Even if—"

"Don't even say it."

"God forbid, but if he has to spend time with his father, it will not threaten his love for you. Mikey loves you, you know that."

Theresa exhaled deeply. "I know that." She glanced down at her watch. "I guess I had better get on my way. I can't afford to sleep in all day." She stood, and so did Pierson.

"What do you have planned for tomorrow? School work?"

"Yeah, we have an essay due from a short reading in W. E. B. Dubois's book, *The Souls of Black Folk*. I already read my story. Now I just have to figure out what I want to write. It will come to me sometime around lunch, and I'll type up a quick rough draft. Do we have a date on Friday night?"

"Maybe. Do you want another massage?" Pierson came up behind her, whispered into her ear. "I'd like to give you another massage."

Theresa's legs quivered slightly. She was immediately aroused by his words. A smile came to her face as she leaned back against his strong frame.

"I would like that, but Mikey might be around. That massage might have to wait."

"No problem. You know that I'm a patient man. And I know that it will be well worth the wait." He kissed her neck softly, sending a shiver down her back.

Theresa turned around in his arms. If this was going to be the kiss, she wanted to be fully focused on the moment. And she refused to close her eyes as his head moved closer to hers. She watched his lips move in to lightly brush hers. His lips were full and firm compared to her thinner softness, and just like opposites attracting, Theresa felt sparks of an electrical charge.

Pierson pulled her closer, taking her lower lip between his and nibbling on it until she gasped with pleasure. His hands caressed her hips when he fitted her flush against him.

Theresa raised her arms to his broad shoulders and neck. She wanted him closer, brought him closer, as she greedily fed her hunger and desire with his lips. Moments later, she felt pressure on her arms. He was lifting his head, pushing her away from him.

"If you don't stop," he said on a whisper, "I'm going to embarrass both of us by lifting you up and carrying you to the bedroom now. So," he patted her on the behind, "be a good girl and back up off me."

"You're the one who started this."

"But you're trying to really get me started, and that could be very dangerous . . . tonight."

Danielle and Mikey gave a loud cheer when he barely beat her at the game they played.

Theresa looked quickly in their direction. "I suppose you're right, but now I'm more curious than ever."

"Good."

CHAPTER 12

Theresa left work early on Wednesday to take Mikey to visit the school she had secretly already decided on. Danielle rode with them so that she could become familiar with the routes to the school, as well as give the school some personal information. For the safety of the students, all drivers, nannies, babysitters, and any other people who would be on school property were given a background check. Without it, they were not allowed through the high iron gates.

The grades ranged from first through twelfth. Security was strict at the school as many of the students were children of wealthy people. Originally, that was the reason Theresa had decided on this school. But as they walked through the high-ceilinged corridors, Theresa realized she wasn't particularly thrilled about it. It didn't feel as much like a school as it did a museum.

Mikey, on the other hand, loved it. From the first moment they walked in and Danielle exclaimed over the "cool" marble statues displayed in the foyer, he was hooked. He wanted to go to the school because Danielle liked the statues. Theresa shook her head. Her poor son. He was going to get his poor little heart hurt.

The fact that they had a basketball team for each couple of school grades was also a plus. The academic curriculum met Theresa's approval, so she allowed Mikey to have his way and agreed that he would attend school there in the fall. He was so happy that he wanted to celebrate. And where else should he celebrate but Chuck E. Cheese.

Instead of moaning at his request, Theresa did the motherly thing and called Pierson. She asked him to meet them there as soon as he could because she didn't want Danielle to carry the burden of playing all of the games she knew he would want to play, and she most certainly wasn't going to do it.

By the time she had ordered pizza for them and a salad for herself, Pierson was walking through the door. He was still dressed in his work clothes. Theresa and Danielle just looked at him questioningly.

"Hey, baby," he said, bending over Theresa for a peck on her cheek.

To her credit, Theresa didn't crouch back so that he wouldn't get his soiled uniform near her white Gucci sweater. He didn't get it dirty, but what would she have said if he had? Probably nothing. Pierson was waiting for a response from her, but he got none.

"Why did you come here with that on?" Danielle asked. "You know better than that. If you were my dad, I would be so embarrassed. Your clothes are filthy. Pierson, you've been under cars all day."

Pierson glanced at Theresa. He was testing her, and she knew it. "Well, my girl wanted me here, so I came."

Danielle shook her head and snapped her eyes at her brother. "I'm going to find Mikey. If you really want her to be your girl, you need to rethink a few things. I'm telling you this for your own good, big brother."

"Thank you," he said, sliding into her empty seat. "I guess she told me."

"Well, I get the feeling that you were expecting her reaction to be mine."

He smiled.

"I thought we weren't playing games. Granted, anyone in their right mind would have, should have, stopped and changed clothes before coming here in their work clothes after working on cars all day. But I'm not your judge or jury. That's Danielle's job, I suppose. She is right, though. I would have been embarrassed, too."

"I brought a change of clothes, Theresa. I just wanted to shock you. Do you think I would have dressed like this on purpose?"

She looked at him pointedly. "You did dress like that on purpose."

"You know what I mean. I'm going to change into jeans and a T-shirt. They're out in the car."

"Where are you going to change?"

"In the bathroom," he said nonchalantly.

Theresa just shook her head. "Why didn't you just change at the shop?"

"I wanted to shock you," he replied.

"Well, I'm honestly more shocked by what you just said than I was by the way you came in here."

Just then Mikey ran over to the table.

"Hey, Mr. Pierson."

"My man. What you up to, Mikey?"

"Nothing. Are you ready to play? Danielle doesn't know how to play right. Her man keeps dying."

"That's because she's a girl." Pierson laughed, receiving a punch in the arm from his kid sister. He raised his arms to Theresa in defeat. "Duty calls." Pierson got up and left with Mikey. Soon, they were trailed by two, five, then seven other little boys, all vying for a chance to beat Pierson at one game or another.

"Has he always been this good with kids?" Theresa asked.

"From what I can remember. But what do you expect, he's a big kid himself," Danielle said.

"Yeah, I've noticed that."

"Theresa, can I ask you a question? Not employee to boss, but as Pierson's sister."

Theresa focused her attention on the young lady. She'd never had a conversation like this before, with a concerned family member. Ryan didn't have a sister and his parents had died when he was young. Theresa was shocked that it was with someone much younger than herself, but Danielle did have a right to ask questions just the same.

"It's pretty obvious that you like my brother. And he likes you, too. I don't want you to think that I'm prejudiced or anything like that, but why do you like him?"

"I'm going to be as honest with you as I can, Danielle. First, I don't think that you're prejudiced. I think you're concerned and you don't want your brother hurt. I'm not going to hurt Pierson. Hell, I'm trying not to get hurt myself. I've been lonely for a long time because I thought

177

that I had to be for my son's sake. And just when I told God that I had come to terms with past issues and was ready for a good man to come into my life, I met Pierson."

"But?"

"Listen, don't let the expensive clothes, cars, and such fool you. Danielle, I'm a regular person. I am a multi-racial, single mother and businesswoman interested in your brother for his intelligence, manner, and wit. I see him as a potential life partner. Now, does that explain my position enough to you?"

"You said multi-racial? What does that mean? You're white and something?"

"Yes, I'm white and black."

Danielle laughed, caught momentarily between shock and disbelief. She quickly pulled herself together. "I'm sorry. Have you looked at yourself lately?"

"Don't worry. I get that a lot. But it's true. My grandfather was half black."

"You'd never know it to look at you."

"That's why I'm taking my classes. It's all about learning more about my history and myself. See, it doesn't matter who else knows it. I know it."

"I understand. You make my brother happy. I haven't seen that since I've been down here. I just don't want to see him hurt."

"I understand that," Theresa said. "I'm glad that we've had this talk. Danielle, you and your brother love each other very much. Just as you don't want to see him hurt, he doesn't want to see you make the same mistakes that many other girls, including me, have made by falling in love with the wrong guy and believing that he loves you, too. That's why he's so hard on you."

"I know. Sometimes I just wish he would be my brother, not my father."

Theresa smiled. She knew that feeling well. "Maybe he just doesn't want to lose another sibling unnecessarily. And the age difference between you two probably doesn't help much either."

"Yeah, I guess you're right. I wish my parents hadn't waited so long, but I get the feeling that they thought they were done."

"Surprise babies are special gifts from God."

"I've been told that a million times."

"It's true." Suddenly Theresa laughed and pointed toward the play area. "Would you look at him."

Pierson and Mikey were playing foosball against two teenagers. They were arguing back and forth about who was going to win, who was making the right moves, and who knew what they were doing. Mikey was making as much noise as Pierson was.

Theresa had never seen Mikey have as much fun in her life. Thorne and Michael had taught him to be tough with their wrestling and how to help one uncle beat up the other uncle. But Theresa had never seen him having so much fun with other kids.

"Theresa, Mikey and I can rent some movies and chill at the house if you and Pierson want to hang out tonight."

"Thank you, Danielle. You know what? I think that I might want to take Pierson to Michael's girlfriend's restaurant tonight. Usually, every Wednesday night everyone meets there to talk about his or her week. I've never been. I'll bet they'll be surprised to see me show up."

"Everyone in your family?"

"Well, extended family. Thorne, his fiancée Natalie; Michael, his girlfriend Tamia; her sister Tamya and her boyfriend; and their brother Stephen and his girlfriend. Just a relaxing night of unwinding. Like I said, I've never been."

"Well, before you go, make sure Pierson changes, please."

They both laughed.

"I will. In fact, if it's all right with Pierson, you can take my car to your house, and I'll take him to my house to change. And I'll be there to pick up Mikey afterward."

"No need. Mikey can just stay over, and we'll come to the office in the morning. That way you can sleep in if you want to." The look in Danielle's eye told more than her mouth did.

"I'm not sure about that. We'll have to see what your brother thinks of that."

"We'll be fine. It is my job to take care of Mikey. I will. I bet he'll like the idea."

"Yeah, he'll like it a little too much. That's what I'm worried about. My son seems to be smitten with you."

"Mikey's a little sweetheart. Now his uncle Thorne, wow."

"Calm it down, sweetie."

"I'm just saying. I haven't seen the other one yet."

180

"And you don't need to be acting like that. What about someone your own age, like Christopher?"

Danielle blushed a little when she thought about the nerd they'd seen in the hallway. She had told herself that she was going to make an effort to get to know him.

Theresa saw her blush and said, "Ah, so it's like that, is it?"

"He's okay, I guess."

"I can arrange another meeting if you wish."

Danielle wanted to say yeah, but she knew that Christopher was so probably so shy that in order for him to let her into his world they would have to build a friendship, not be set up.

"No, that's okay. I think that would scare him to death. You know, my brother doesn't want me dating at all."

Theresa smiled. "Mine, either. I think it's just a brother thing."

They watched the guys play for a while longer. When she couldn't take it any longer, Theresa signaled for Pierson to wrap it up. She wanted to have enough time to get home and shower before they went to the restaurant.

As soon as they came to the table, Theresa told them Danielle's idea. The smile on his Pierson's matched Mikey's. For different reasons, both males were happy with their plans for the evening.

"Danielle, are you sure?" Pierson asked.

"We'll be fine. You two go on and enjoy yourselves. We'll see you in the morning," Danielle said.

"Oh," Pierson interrupted. "Mikey asked if he could work with me tomorrow. I said it was okay with me if it's okay with you."

"At the garage? I don't know. There are so many dangerous tools and heavy equipment." Theresa's imagination ran wild as she thought of her baby standing under a car that teetered on a lift.

"I'll keep a close eye on him. Come on, let the little guy get his hands dirty," Pierson encouraged.

"Please, Mom. I want to spend the day at Mr. Pierson's *garage*." Mikey said the word as if the garage were Disney World.

Theresa looked at Pierson.

"Theresa, I'll keep a close eye on him. I promise."

"Don't let anything happen to my son, Pierson."

"He'll be fine. All I have tomorrow is light work anyway. I won't let him near anything dangerous. I promise."

"And Mikey, you listen to Mr. Pierson. Don't give him a hard time."

"I won't, Mom. Thank you." Mikey wanted to give her a hug, but Danielle was sitting right there.

Theresa could see his dilemma. He just kissed her on the cheek. She understood that he was growing up, and she was going to have to let him. But Theresa wondered if she would be so blasé about it when he grew older and the girls weren't ten years older and it wasn't just a schoolboy crush. How would she react when Mikey and the girl were the same age, and she was less than desirable in Theresa's opinion? Theresa pushed the thought aside, knowing that the answer wasn't a positive one.

"You're welcome. Just be careful. Now, you and Danielle are going to go bug out at their house, and Mr. Pierson and I are going to Noah's Ark. You be good for Danielle."

Theresa quickly pulled him close against his will and planted a kiss on his cheek.

$\partial\!\!\!/\!\!\!\ell$

"You can take a shower in there," Theresa said, pointing to her bedroom.

"Are you going to join me?" Pierson asked, walking toward the room.

Theresa would have thought he was joking, except he didn't laugh. Still, she couldn't believe that he was serious. For the past couple of weeks, he had been playing the strict and straight-laced guy. Was he suddenly changing his role? First, he had shown her more passion than she could ever remember at his house, and now, he was asking her to join him in a shower. She didn't know whether to be ecstatic or afraid.

Theresa glanced at her watch, wishing there was enough time. "No. We have to hurry. I'm going to throw on something more comfortable," she said, looking down at the business suit she was wearing.

A half hour later, Theresa stood in the living room waiting for Pierson to come out of the bedroom. She looked at her watch again, then walked to the kitchen. There were a few dishes in the sink, which she quickly put in the dishwasher. When she walked back into the living room, they were both pleasantly surprised.

Pierson had shaved and changed into pair of dark blue jeans and a pale pink button-up shirt. The top button was unfastened and his sleeves were cuffed and showed a large silver watch. He was so handsome that Theresa's breath caught when she first saw him.

Pierson had a similar reaction to seeing Theresa in her tight jeans, baby doll tank top and matching sandals. Her hair was pulled up high on her head and curly strands hung around her forehead. She was breathtaking, and he was shocked at how she could change from a serious businesswoman to a sexy siren so quickly. Suddenly, Pierson didn't want to go anywhere.

"You are beautiful, Theresa," he said, strolling forward until his arms were around her. He bent down and claimed her lips with his own. "And you taste so good," he whispered.

Theresa couldn't move, didn't want to move, from his arms. She returned his kiss, pressed her body against his.

Pierson's lips blazed a trail from her lips to her neck to her shoulder as his hands moved over her hips and behind, pulling her closer.

They were both beginning to slip past their self-control when her cellphone rang, bringing them to their senses. They pulled away from each other slowly, shocked that their control had slipped away so easily.

"Um, hello," Theresa said, still a little dazed.

"Hey, girl," Michael said. "I'm on my way to the restaurant. Do you want to go hang out?"

"I'll be there," she simply answered.

"I'm about to leave now. You want me to come up?" The three siblings each owned a floor at the top of the Philips Corporation building. Michael's floor was under Theresa's. Thorne had the penthouse.

"No, I'm fine. I'll meet you there."

"Okay. I'll see you later," Michael said, hanging up the phone.

"I'm sorry about that," Pierson said as soon as she hung up the phone.

"You don't have to apologize to me, Pierson. I was enjoying myself. I'm not weak or helpless. And you didn't and won't hurt me."

"I would never hurt you, Theresa."

"I know, but you act as if I'm fragile."

"I don't think you are, but this relationship is, and I don't want to do anything that might break it." Pierson held her hands in his. "This is precious to me, and I don't want to mess up."

"Being unsure of yourself is not good for anyone. If I don't like what you're doing, I'll let you know." She quickly kissed him again. "Now, let's go. Michael's on his way to the restaurant."

"So, this is the big introduction to the rest of the people in your life."

"Well, it's actually just extended family. The only person in my family that you haven't met yet is Thorne. You met Michael and his girlfriend last weekend at the basketball game. You met my mother there, too. These are actually potential in-laws, Thorne and Michael's. You know their girlfriends are sisters."

"Gotcha. The twins at Noah's Ark?"

"No, Michael goes with one of the twins, Tamia, and Thorne is engaged to their older sister Natalie."

"Well, let's go meet your folks, shall we?" He put her arm in his and led her to the elevator.

◈

Noah's Ark was a popular restaurant/sports bar that most nights was filled to capacity. Tamia and her twin sister Tamya had put their hearts and souls into the business. Tonight was no different. With Tamia's reputation growing as one of New Orleans' best up-and-coming chefs and Tamya's display of bartending tricks and delicious array of drinks, Noah's Ark was quickly becoming the place to be.

Theresa and Pierson walked in hand in hand, laughing at a joke that Pierson had made in the parking lot. He was flirting outrageously with her, and Theresa's face had blushed slightly at his comment. Pierson's hand slid to her waist as they walked through the restaurant toward the bar area. He was conscious of the eyes turning their way, but he didn't care. The door opened again after they entered, and everyone's eyes turned to that intruder, too.

"Hey, guys," Theresa said, as she led him to a tall, muscular man with olive skin and dark curly hair.

Pierson had to admit two things about the man at the bar who turned toward them and focused all of his attention on him, a man he assumed was the famous Thorne.

He could see why he easily intimidated so many people. It wasn't just the fact that he was tall, handsome, and muscular. The man exuded authority, assuredness, and confidence.

Pierson wasn't intimidated; he was impressed. He and Thorne looked to be about the same age, yet this man was carrying the large weight of corporate management on his shoulders and seemed to be doing it fairly easily. Pierson was impressed with the whole family. In any other circle, you would be hard pressed to find millionaires making good friends and building relationships with everyday blue-collar workers.

"Ah, here she is," Thorne said, his hand resting on the leg of the attractive black woman seated next to him. He stood up authoritatively and came forward to hug his sister. "And your friend?" Thorne said, waiting for introductions.

Before Theresa could introduce him, Pierson stepped forward. "Pierson Brooks," he said, extending his hand.

"Pierson," Thorne said, accepting his handshake. "Why don't you come have a seat? You've already met my brother Michael, yes?"

"Sure. Uh, yes. Michael. What's up?" Pierson acknowledged him as Thorne led him to a table away from the women. Michael and another man followed. Theresa was walking with him until Thorne turned around.

"We don't need you for this, Theresa. Go with Natalie and them," he said.

She didn't want to leave Pierson alone. It was as if she were in high school all over again. It had been so long since she'd brought a man to meet her family that Theresa was beginning to regret this moment. She wanted to say something. After all, she wasn't in high school anymore, which was exactly what she had been telling them for years.

Pierson could tell that she was torn. Confusion was written all over her face. But Pierson understood what was going on. He was a brother, and he expected to be doing it himself in the coming years.

"Theresa, go ahead, baby," he said, taking her hands in his. "I'm fine." He gave her a kiss on the cheek and turned around in time to see a look being exchanged between Thorne and Michael.

"Damn, you'd think we were going to take you out back and jump on you or something," Michael said.

Pierson laughs. "She just worries about me."

"So we see. Pierson," Thorne said, "I haven't see my sister act so concerned about a man in a long time."

"Well, I'm concerned about her, too. We're good friends."

"Good friends," Thorne repeated. "I'm sorry, we didn't introduce you to Stephen. He is Natalie's brother."

Pierson shook Stephen's hand.

"So, Pierson, you're a mechanic, right?" Thorne began the questioning. He didn't say the word mechanic like it was a bad thing, but simply a question.

"Yes, I own a repair shop and towing service not far from here. It started off kind of slow, but now I get a fair share of business. I have two shops, and I'm actually thinking of opening another soon."

"Theresa's considering making his shop our designated maintenance shop for the car port and offering discounts to employees who begin visiting his shop. She's waiting for our current contract to expire," Michael informed.

"Smart girl," Thorne said. "It would be smart to help friends and family and our employees, plus, I guess it's kind of like keeping the money in the family. Is that correct, Pierson?"

All eyes turned to him, waiting for his answer. "Is that a slick way of asking me how I feel about your sister, Thorne?" Preston asked.

"Yes. Are you trying to build a future with her or are you just, uh, having fun?" Thorne actually put his fingers up and made quotation marks when he said "having fun."

Pierson had to laugh. "First off, I have not 'had fun' with your sister yet." Pierson used his own quotation marks. He felt this was important to Thorne, but he had to make sure that they understood that his and Theresa's business going forward would be just that. "But when we do start 'having fun,' I assure you that it will be with the utmost respect and with the intention of building a future together. I care for your sister, and I am getting to know her slowly but surely. Theresa has told me about the past and what is going on right now with Ryan."

Michael leaned forward. "What about Mikey?"

"Mikey is not even a question. I love him already. We get along very well."

"Do you realize that you're the first man Theresa has had in her life since she got rid of Mikey's father?" Thorne asked. "We don't want to see her hurt."

"I don't want to see her hurt, either. Hell, I don't want to get hurt myself. Listen, guys, I have a sister so I know what this is. I will treat your sister exactly how I expect my sister to be treated. And if I don't, I expect you to address me."

"You can be sure that we will, but for now, I'm glad that my sister has met you," Michael said. Thorne remained silent. "Now, I've got this beautiful '57 Chevy, but I'm having a little problem with—"

"Not now, Michael," Thorne interrupted. "Tonight is for celebrating. It's the first time our sister has come to family night. Plus, she's sitting over there giving me the evil eye. We better head back to the family."

As the four men walked back to the bar area where the women waited, Theresa was relieved to find that they all had pleasant looks on their faces. She knew both Thorne and Michael tended to be overprotective of her. She also knew that neither knew how to hold his tongue. Her worst fear was that they would insult Pierson, who was not quite as cocky as her brothers, but just as confident and sure of himself as they were.

Once Pierson placed his hand on her shoulder, reassuring her that everything was okay, Theresa began introducing him to Natalie, Tamya, and Sandra.

"Theresa, he's as good looking as Tamia said," Natalie teased.

Michael sat up and looked at Tamia. "When did you say that?"

"Oh, after we saw them at the basketball game, I told them about Theresa's beau. You know, girl talk," Tamia answered.

"No, I don't know," he replied.

Tamia's eyes rolled up in her head. *Here we go again.* Tamia knew that Michael loved her, and she loved him. But she refused to marry him because she knew that he had asked her only because of the baby.

"Okay, since we're all here, does anyone have anything they want to talk about?" Thorne asked, stepping in before Michael put his foot in his mouth. "Anybody have any announcements?"

Michael put his hand up quickly. "I've got something to say." He looked at Tamia. "Stephen, I don't know if Tamia has told any of you or not, but I asked her to marry me."

Stephen was about to clap his hands and stand up until he saw the look on Natalie's face. He eased back down in his seat. Nothing surprised him when it came to Tamia or Michael. Their obvious love for each other was overshadowed only by the uncompromising desire each had to remain independent.

Michael continued, "Of course, she turned me down. I was hoping that you would talk some sense into the girl."

"Michael Philips, don't you ask my brother to talk sense into me. I have a mind of my own, dammit." Tamia slammed the drying cloth she was holding into Michael's chest. She was so mad that she could have screamed, but instead she walked to the office in the back of the restaurant. Michael got up to follow her.

"I'm giving my baby a name," he said, leaving the room.

Theresa and Pierson looked at each other, but remained silent.

"Don't worry about them," Natalie said. "This happens every week. They'll get into the back room and make up." Her eyebrows lifted. "That's probably why she's pregnant now."

"Natalie," Tamya said. "That's not nice. So, when are we going to start making wedding plans?"

"Soon. Thorne and I have decided that we want to marry in the fall. Maybe the middle of next October. Fall is our favorite time of the year. I'll tell all of you soon. I've been looking at dresses, trying to decide on colors and such, but it's a lot of work. I've decided to finish refurbishing this last house so that I can dedicate all of my time to the wedding. As soon as I put it on the market, I'll be ready to settle down and start planning. Give me a couple more months, then I'll be able to focus."

Theresa looked at Pierson. "Natalie has sold about fifteen houses that she has fixed up. She's very good, and has an excellent eye for details. Stephen is an artist, a famous sculptor, and Sandra is member of the NOPD."

Pierson didn't miss the look that she gave him. Pierson didn't feel it necessary to divulge details of his past life. And he didn't. "Interesting," he replied.

They stayed for another hour and talked about the news, politics, and sports. When Theresa decided she was ready to leave, Pierson observed that Michael and Tamia had yet to come out of the back room. He said his good-byes to the group and was surprised to hear Thorne express a hope to see him again soon.

On his way out the door, Pierson was stopped by his friend Mark, who frequently visited the bar. Pierson quickly introduced him to Theresa, then said a word or two before heading out the door. He knew that Mark would be at the shop first thing in the morning with a million and one questions because he had kept Theresa a secret from everyone except Danielle and one or two of his employees. It wasn't that he was ashamed or embarrassed. He just wanted to be sure that he had something to brag about before talking about her. After tonight he hoped that he did.

CHAPTER 13

Pierson and Theresa held hands in the elevator all the way up to her apartment. They were silent, each wondering how the rest of the evening would play itself out. Each wanted the evening to end the same way, wrapped in the other's arms, completely sated and satisfied. But neither would admit to the real reason they were a little hesitant to go that route.

Theresa hadn't been with a man in a long time. Although she couldn't imagine a better way to top off the evening than to lie in Pierson's arms, Theresa was unsure of herself and her ability to please him. Her nerves would probably prevent her from being able to relax and fully give herself to him even though she wanted him, had wanted him since the first time she had seen him.

Pierson had told himself that this relationship was going to be different. And it was different. He had taken his time and gotten to know her and her son very well, but still he was afraid that it might be too soon to take their relationship to the next level. There was no doubt in his mind that Theresa could handle it, but could he? He was already falling faster for her than he wanted to. If they made love, would he be able to control his feelings for her? The last thing Pierson wanted was to be hurt again.

As soon as they stepped into her apartment, they separated. Theresa walked into the kitchen, and Pierson headed to the living room.

"Hey, you want something to drink?" Theresa asked.

"Please," Pierson replied, letting out a long breath. "I think I need one. Theresa?"

"Yes?" she said, leaning over the countertop, her arms crossed and her head bent down. She was trying to get herself together. There was no sensible reason for her to be this nervous.

"You, too, huh?" Pierson said from directly behind her. He put his hands on her arms and massaged them. "Nervous?"

Theresa leaned back against him. "Yeah, I guess I am. It's surprising. I've imagined being with you since the moment I saw you get out of that tow truck, and now I'm acting like a schoolgirl, unsure of myself."

"That's normal for most people the first time, if it's something meaningful. I'd be offended if you weren't nervous because that would mean that you didn't care."

Pierson turned her around to face him. He lifted her head so that she looked directly at him. And then he bent down to kiss her lightly on her lips.

Theresa began to relax as the kiss deepened. She let everything slip from her mind except the feel of his lips against her own. And she responded to him, moving closer to him until their bodies were flush against one another. Her arms wrapped around his neck as she lost herself in the magic of the kiss.

"I've been telling you that I want to take this slow, but keeping my hands off you has been the hardest thing I've ever done, Theresa. I just didn't want to take the chance of messing up something that I knew could be very special."

"Are you saying that you won't be touching me tonight?" Theresa asked disappointedly.

"No, I'm not saying that at all." Pierson lifted her into his arms.

Theresa squealed and giggled at the surprise and pleasure of Pierson's strength as he quickly walked through the living room and into her bedroom.

He placed her gently down in the middle of the king-size bed. As he stood back and looked down at her, Pierson thought that the bed was too big a bed for Theresa to have been sleeping in it alone for all those years. He wanted to change that.

Theresa looked beautiful. Her hair fanned out around her, and Pierson could see her chest rise and fall as her excitement caused her breathing to become heavier. And her eyes were on him. He didn't know what excited him more. He removed his shirt and tossed it onto a nearby chair. Then did the same with his under-shirt.

Pierson was handsome. Her breath caught as she watched him remove the layers. Theresa loved this display of manliness: his broad shoulders, the expanse of his back, his muscles working under his skin as he turned one way or the other. Her eyes moved down to his solid chest and stomach, and then rested on his hands, which were working the button and zipper of his jeans. Her anticipation grew.

Theresa began to take off her own clothes, but he stopped her.

"No," Pierson said. "I want to do that. Just relax." He removed his jeans.

"Oh, so you get to undress me, but I don't get to undress you?" Theresa asked, her eyes moving from his face to the boxers he wore. The bulge that was hidden by the cloth had her mesmerized.

"You want to undress me? Please, be my guest," Pierson said, more than happy to oblige her. He stood back, lifted his strong arms, and waited for her.

Theresa was even more nervous now. She should have just kept her mouth shut. But she couldn't let her nervousness show. Instead, she moved towards the end of the bed until his pelvis was directly in front of her. Theresa forced her hands to stop shaking long enough for her to reach the band of his boxers. She took a deep breath and pulled them down. And she smiled.

Pierson watched her closely, watching for any reaction from her. He was glad to see her smile. But that smile only made matters worse for him because it intensified his need to have her. She watched him grow harder with desire.

"I think we had better get you undressed, now," he said softly.

Theresa was speechless when he pulled her to her feet and ravished her lips and face with kisses. She didn't realize that her shirt was unbuttoned until she felt his hand cover her breast. Pierson squeezed her nipple. Theresa gasped at the pain, but she loved the pleasure it gave her.

He had her shirt and her bra off in a matter of seconds, then spent time kissing her neck and shoulder before he moved on. He kneaded her breasts and then blazed a wet trail across them as well.

Theresa thought she would pass out from the pleasure. Her knees almost gave out when he took a tightly drawn nipple between his teeth and lightly bit down on it. She couldn't suppress the moans that escaped her. Theresa kept telling herself to calm down, *calm down*, but Pierson was taking her further and further into a bliss she had long forgotten.

Working his way further down, Pierson allowed Theresa's loud moans to feed his greed. He placed kisses across her stomach as he worked her pants down her legs. Pierson stopped briefly to look at her standing there in just the black satin bikini-cut panties.

"Damn, Theresa, you are beautiful," he whispered just before placing kisses on her hips. Pierson pulled her panties down to the floor and stood before her. "Are you sure you're ready for this, Theresa?" he asked sincerely.

"Baby, I've been ready for this. I want you, Pierson," she replied, thinking this was an awkward time to ask that question, with both of them standing next to the bed completely nude. Standing on her toes, Theresa kissed him passionately, urging him to continue.

Pierson didn't hesitate any longer. Instead of second-guessing whether he was moving too fast or how their relationship might change after this night, he stopped worrying about everything except pleasing her. Eagerly returning her kisses, Pierson laid her back on the bed. He positioned himself between her legs, but continued to kiss her until he felt she was relaxed.

Theresa opened herself to him. She braced for his entrance, believing that it could possibly be painful.

Pierson entered her quickly and smoothly in one thrust. She had told him that it had been a few years since her last time, and he didn't want to linger. Once he was completely inside her, Pierson didn't move.

Theresa's gasp was mixed with pleasure and pain as she tried to quickly adjust to his size, but she was pleased with the look of pleasure on Pierson's face.

"I'm sorry," he whispered, trying to quell his own rising ecstasy. She felt so good tightly surrounding him that Pierson realized if he didn't calm down that this wouldn't be as pleasing to her as he wanted it to be. He wanted to make their first experience one that she would never forget or get enough of.

"I'm fine," she mumbled. Pierson was proving to be everything that she had imagined he would be. Theresa closed her eyes and forced herself to relax as he began moving slowly inside her.

"Damn, you feel so good," he whispered near her ear. The warm wetness he felt drove him crazy, made him want to lose control, but he didn't want to hurt her.

It didn't matter how slowly Pierson moved. Theresa's pleasure built higher and higher until she was yelling out her pleasure and letting Pierson know that she was approaching the end of her journey to paradise. He didn't want it to end and while she went through her climax, he concentrated on pleasing her even more. As close as he was, he had to make this first experience special.

Pierson waited for her breathing to become steady once again, waited for her to join him on a lower plane, and then built her passion back up. This time he joined her. He placed pressure on her hips to keep her still as he plunged into her repeatedly. Not one part of her body was left untouched when he was through with her. He suckled her nipples, rubbed her bottom, even took the time to massage her legs and feet as he made love to her.

Theresa was thoroughly sated by the time they finished. She couldn't begin to express her feelings to him. She wanted to say something, but as she lay on her side and he came up behind her, tears fell from her eyes. He whispered his enjoyment to her, but stopped when he heard her whimper.

"Hey, are you okay?" he asked, his arm around her waist holding her tightly.

"I'm fine. I've just realized that I've never been made love to before. This is the first time I've ever been completely made love to. I'm in my thirties, for God's sake. That is so sad."

"Baby, I'll make up for all of those times if you give me a chance. You can forget about the past now. We're going to work on the future, together. I'm not going anywhere."

"I don't want to put a damper on the moment, but I've heard that before. And I think that's one reason why it's taken me so long to think of the possibility of a relationship. I don't want to be hurt again, Pierson."

"And I have no intentions of hurting you. Let's make a pact. You don't judge me by what Ryan did to you, and I won't judge you based on what has happened in my past."

"Okay. It's just that there are two kinds of guys, those who are relationship types and those who get into relationships but are the single types."

"I tried to tell you before, Theresa. I'm a relationship type of guy. I've made mistakes in the past because I'm human, but I've learned from those mistakes. I am a good man, a marrying type of man when I find the right woman. You might find this hard to believe, but some men want the same thing as women do. A steady mate, a trusted companion, a friend and lover. I don't want you to think that I waited to make love to you just to say I did it."

"Well, what are you doing it to say?" Theresa asked.

"I want to say, 'Let's do it again and again and again.' " They laughed together as Theresa felt Pierson's fingers span her thigh. She followed the pressure placed on her hip and willingly turned toward him.

Early in the morning, Theresa stretched leisurely and smiled exuberantly. She reached over to Pierson before opening her eyes and realized that his side of the bed was empty. She looked around the room, wondering where he had gotten off too. Sitting up in bed, Theresa felt disappointment begin to consume her. She couldn't believe that he would leave without saying a word.

"Wake up, sleepyhead," Pierson said, walking into the room wearing only his boxers. He carried a tray holding toast, coffee, butter and jam. "It's almost seven. I know you have to get ready for work, but you probably should eat something real quick. Good morning."

"I'm sorry. Good morning," she replied, a bright smile on her face.

"What are you sorry for?" Pierson asked.

"I'm just sorry," Theresa said. "Why don't you come back to bed so I can show you how sorry I am?"

"Aren't you hungry?"

"Not for what's on that tray."

Pierson smiled back down at her. He'd be a fool to say no. "Okay, but if you're late to work, don't blame it on me."

"I don't think I'll get into too much trouble. My boss is pretty lenient with me. What about you? Don't you have to open the shop at a certain time?"

"Nah, I already called Carter. He has a key," Pierson answered, smiling brightly.

"So you were already working on a plan?"

"Well, I knew that I wasn't going to leave this morning without making sure you thought about me all day." He pulled off his boxers and reached for the box of condoms on the nightstand. "Now, scoot over and let me in."

Theresa was an hour late to work, but she was in a very good mood. She had called Danielle before leaving her house to check on her son, who seemed to be having the time of his life and had bugged Danielle to death with questions about the garage. Danielle said he was up and waiting for Pierson to pick him up, and Theresa heard the excitement in his voice when he took the phone and she told him that Pierson was on his way. She told Danielle to come into the office around lunchtime. That would give her time to get a list of errands together.

Theresa was sitting back in her office chair, her eyes closed, and a smile plastered on her face as she relived the events of the night before. She didn't know that she was being watched until she heard the distinct clearing of Thorne's throat.

"Good morning, Thorne," she said without opening her eyes. She knew what was coming, but wanted to hold onto her images for just a moment longer.

"Good morning, sis. How are you doing this morning?" He moved into the room and took a seat across from her.

"I'm actually doing very well. Thanks for asking." Theresa looked at him and waited.

"So, Pierson . . . he stay the night at your place last night?"

Theresa rolled her eyes. Just as direct as ever, Thorne quietly waited for her answer. She didn't think that he deserved one.

"Thorne, don't you dare come in here with that big brother mess. I'm well over twenty-one, and I don't have to answer that. You should not be asking me that. Do I ask you or Michael about your dates?"

Thorne didn't say anything. He simply watched her. She was answering the question whether she knew it or not.

"I just want you to be careful. I worry. I'm not trying to run your life, Theresa. I like the guy. He seems to be a good fella and not easily intimidated. That's good. But I don't want to see you hurt. You're my little sister regardless of how old you are."

"Thank you, Thorne, but I'm okay. Pierson is a good man, and I know that he wouldn't intentionally hurt me. Stop worrying so much. You need to be worried about your impending nuptials, not me. I know you and Natalie want to pull out all the stops."

"Actually, we were talking last night, and we decided that we wanted a small, intimate affair with just our family and friends. Neither of us wants a big fancy to-do when all we really care about is that you guys are there."

"Well, you know that you are expected to put the engagement announcement in the society page."

"People have always expected a lot from me. I don't always follow suit. They should know that by now."

"Is it that or all of those socialite hearts who still think they have a chance at you that you're worried about?"

Thorne joined in the laughter at her joke. "Michael said the same thing to me."

"Well, he's got a nerve. I haven't seen any long-legged beauties on his arm since we found Tamia in the elevator crying her eyes out that night."

Theresa remembered that night vividly. It was the night that she first met Tamia. She hadn't known that Tamia and Michael had spent time together or that he truly had feelings for anyone in particular until he saw the compassion in his eyes when the found her in the elevator and the anger that consumed him once he knew she was okay. She, Michael, Thorne, and Natalie were coming back to the building. As soon as Michael saw her crumpled in the corner, he possessively scooped her into his arms and held her in his arms all the way to the penthouse. He demanded that she tell him who had hit her and argued when she wouldn't tell him. But Natalie told him, which prompted Michael to leave in a rage, determined to find the man. They came back with Stephen, who had been looking for the man too, lightly injured and heavily drunk.

"I think finding that her ex-boyfriend was putting his hands on her made him realize how much he really did care for her," Thorne said.

"Against his wishes or not, huh?" Theresa laughed.

"Exactly. You know there comes a time when we men realize that life isn't all about how many skirts you can stroke your ego with. What matters most is finding that one woman who has your back in good and bad times, the one who is with you because she loves you, not because of your money, your power, or your charms."

"Well, I'm glad to see that the both of you have found that one because I was honestly beginning to lose track of the parade of women passing through the lines of you two."

"Okay, but let's keep all that really low key. There's no need to keep bringing it up."

"Oh, I know you're not afraid that Natalie might find out just how much of a playboy you used to be."

He stood up. "First of all, I'm not afraid of anything. Now, this conversation is over. But seriously," he leaned over the desk and looked directly into her face, "you are beautiful today, Theresa. And if Pierson had anything to do with it, I owe him a great deal of gratitude. I'll see you later."

She watched him leave. Theresa could see that he still carried the self-imposed weight of this company, this family, on his shoulders. Thorne had always tried to be her protector, even when she fought him tooth and nail. He'd never hidden his feelings or held his tongue, but this was the first time that he had given her such a wonderful compliment. Her older brother never ceased to amaze her.

Ryan parked his car across the street from Brooks Repair and Towing Service. He wanted to find out more about this man, Pierson Brooks, that he had seen at the game last week with Theresa. He hadn't yet found out as much as he wanted to, but he still had more information coming from a contact in Philadelphia. Apparently, the man had just moved to New Orleans a few years earlier. Ryan had been sitting across the street since the shop opened, but he had yet to see the man he was looking for.

Suddenly, he sat at attention and watched as the tall, muscular black man got out of his pickup. Ryan watched as he went to the other side of the truck and opened the door. He wondered what the man was getting out of the truck since his vision was blocked. His mouth dropped open when he realized that the little boy walking next to his nemesis was his own son.

The anger that bubbled up inside Ryan was quick. He banged his hand against the steering wheel repeatedly, wishing that he could start his car and smash right through the front windows of the shop. Only if his son wasn't there. Obviously, Theresa and this man were a lot closer than he had thought. Ryan couldn't let his anger ruin his plans. Once everything was in place, he would make his move and have all the money that he needed.

He watched a while longer, saw how well his son and this man got along. Ryan saw Pierson stop at different pieces of equipment in the shop and point them out to Mikey and watched as he let Mikey roll a tire to him so they could fix it. Ryan realized this was a father and son moment that he wasn't a part of. He wanted to take the car in for a tune-up just to get a little more information, but he couldn't do it with Mikey there and he wasn't sure whether Pierson would remember him from the game or not.

It didn't matter. All of the garage stall doors were up, and by using his binoculars, Ryan could see everything that was going on. He didn't like it, but he made himself sit and watch the camaraderie between the two. Ryan had no association or relationship with his son, and he had really never cared before, but seeing his son interact with another man didn't settle well with him.

❦

"Mr. Pierson, why did you want to be a mechanic?" Mikey asked once they took their lunch break.

Of course Pierson had been forced to order pizza. He didn't think he had eaten so much pizza in his life as he had since he meeting Mikey. "I guess I like working with my hands and working up a sweat. This is hard work, and you've done a good job today. When you get home, make sure you tell your mom that you changed a tire, tuned up a car, and replaced the battery for an electric window. She won't even know how you did it."

Mikey smiled. "I want to be a mechanic when I grow up."

Oh, Lord. The last thing he needed was for Mikey to go to his mother and tell her that he wanted to be a mechanic. Theresa would bite his head off. Pierson was sure that Mikey was being groomed to head the Philips Corporation one day. "Well, being a mechanic isn't for everybody. As smart as you are, I think you would be a great doctor or an accountant. You're good with numbers. I think you'll probably help your mother and your uncles run the business. That's a real important job, too."

"I know, but I want a fun job. This job is fun."

"Are you kidding me? It's fun now because you've only done it one day. Believe me, it's not that much fun, and by the time you grow up there will be a dozen other jobs that you will find interesting. Now, let's finish this pizza. We have to fix that muffler for Mr. Palmer. And remember what I said. You have to stay behind that line when I lift the car off the ground."

The smile on Mikey's face disappeared. Pierson had told him the same thing three other times that morning.

"I promised your mother."

Mikey had heard that before, too. He couldn't do anything about it so there wasn't any point to fighting it. "Okay. Mr. Pierson, can I come back with you tomorrow?"

"Tomorrow is Saturday. We don't have to work tomorrow. As a matter of fact, don't you have a game tomorrow?"

"That's right, I do. Can we go to lunch after the game?"

"Let me guess. Chuck E. Cheese?"

Mikey smiled.

"You know, your mother is going to get tired of Chuck E. Cheese real soon. She doesn't like it the way we do. Maybe we should give her a break and go somewhere that she will like."

"But Mom goes to the ritzy restaurants."

"Well, maybe we can talk her into going to McDonald's."

"Yeah, I like McDonald's." Mikey's arms went into the air in triumph.

Pierson smiled as he watched him walk out of the office and into the garage. Pierson quickly got up and followed him. They worked the rest of the day with a system. He taught Mikey the names of the small tools he used, and it was Mikey's job to hand him the tool he called out. Mikey was a quick learner, and he took his job seriously, taking his time to make sure he picked the right item.

CHAPTER 14

Danielle made sure she was at work on time. She dressed professionally, copying Theresa's business style. After all, she wanted to make a good impression on her boss, not the woman dating her brother.

Theresa had to admit that she was pleasantly surprised when Danielle walked into the office. She almost didn't know who she was, but to her credit, Theresa acted as if she didn't notice and got right to work.

By the time she was finished, Danielle had a long list of items that needed to be completed by the end of the day. For the most part, it was running from one floor of the building to another to retrieve items or follow-up on previous requests. It took her three trips to different floors for Danielle to look at the list and choreograph her movements by floor. Afterward, she found that her tasks were completed much quicker.

She was making record time when she got into the elevator to make a return trip to Theresa. It shocked her to find Thorne standing in the elevator alone. He held the door open and moved to the side for her to enter. Danielle nodded her head in thanks, but didn't say a word. Thorne made her nervous.

"Hi. Danielle, right? Theresa's assistant." He extended his hand to her. Danielle took it. "Nice to see you again."

Sometimes, Thorne found that no matter how personable he tried to be, he still tended to make people uneasy.

"Hi," she said shyly, wanting to kick herself in the butt. *What a high schooler,* she thought. Thorne was even better looking than Theresa's brother Michael, who she had bumped into a couple of days ago and thought was gorgeous. And just like a young girl, she was tongue-tied and afraid to say anything more.

"You don't have to be scared of me," Thorne joked. "I'm not a bad person."

"Um, no, you're not," Danielle stammered as the elevator doors opened. She had never been so happy to see elevator doors open. She practically ran out of the elevator. But when she had gotten to Theresa's office and calmed herself down, she saw Thorne was coming into the office after her. Suddenly, she wished that she had stopped at her own desk, which was in the hallway next to Stephanie's area. She loved having her own space, now matter how small. It was complete with a phone, tape, stapler, and other desk items. She had not yet had a chance to organize it. No time like the present, she thought, trying to finish her business with Theresa so she could leave.

"Hey, sis," Thorne said cheerfully as he walked to Theresa's desk.

"Hi, Thorne. I thought you would be out of the office all day."

"I was at Natalie's, but she kicked me out. She said that I kept bothering her and she couldn't get anything done."

"And I bet she wasn't lying."

"No, she wasn't. She said that I was trying to catch up with Michael."

Theresa just shook her head, then glanced at Danielle. "Danielle, my brother likes attention at home as well as work."

"Please don't tell her that. I think I already put a fright in her. She practically ran away from me."

"Ah, so she's smarter than I thought. I knew there was a good reason why I hired her."

They both laughed.

"Very funny," he said. "Hey, where's the little man?"

"He went to work with Pierson this morning," Theresa said, glancing at her watch. She couldn't wait until they left so she could hear all about his work day. "They're going to meet me later."

"He's at the garage? Good for him. He needs to get outside of these four walls every once in a while. There is nothing like working outside."

Danielle giggled.

"What?" Thorne asked.

"It's just that I couldn't wait to get out of that place. I'd rather work here than in that dirty garage any day."

"Well, girls are different," Thorne said.

"Oh, wait a minute," Theresa chimed in. "Are you saying that a garage is no place for a woman?"

Thorne began backing out of the room. He knew where this was going. "I didn't say that, Danielle did." Then he quickly turned and walked out of the room.

Theresa and Danielle looked at each other.

"Don't pay him any attention," Theresa said. "We go through our little spats every now and then. Thorne's a good guy, good older brother, until he begins to think he's your father." Theresa shuffled a few papers on her desk and picked up a folder. "I need this to go down to the financial department. Salary. Have it signed off on and make sure that the adjustments are made. It's the increases for four recent promotions."

"Will do," Danielle said, reaching for the folder. She really didn't care too much about the information inside. After carrying folders from floor to floor all day long, interest in the contents didn't carry as much weight as the pain in the soles of her feet. She would definitely be wearing flats from now on.

The financial department, she found, was only one floor down. And to her surprise, Danielle also found Christopher, the guy she had met a couple of days before, sitting at one of the desks. They both looked at each other for an instant. Then she forced herself to walk by the awkward young man, regardless of how attractive she found him.

Danielle couldn't imagine herself going on a date with him, or taking him around her friends. She would never hear the end of it. But still, there was something about him that she liked.

When she returned to the office, Pierson and Mikey were there, both filthy from their work in the garage.

Pierson let out a long whistle when he saw her. "Wow, Danielle, I don't think I've ever seen you so dressed up before."

She cut her eyes at him.

"Doesn't she look beautiful? All professional and whatnot," Theresa added. "But I bet next time she won't be wearing those shoes, will you?"

"You are absolutely right," Danielle said, sitting down at her desk and kicking the heels off again. "Monday, I'll have on some sensible flats."

"What are you two doing here?" Danielle asked.

"Well, since Theresa has class tonight, I thought Mikey and I would hang out. We decided to have a man's night. Right, Mikey?"

"Yep. We're going to go to mall and hang out for a while. Get a bite to eat, you know, guy stuff."

"That actually sounds like something women do," Danielle replied.

"Well, its guy stuff when we do it. Right, Mikey?" Pierson put his hand up for a high five, which Mikey quickly supplied.

Danielle rolled her eyes in her head. "Whatever."

"So, we need the key to the apartment so we can change, and then we'll be out of your hair. We'll see you when you get out of class."

"Okay," Theresa said, passing the key to Pierson, who walked around the desk to give her a kiss. "Uh-uh." Theresa leaned back in the chair. "Don't touch me, Pierson. You'll mess up my clothes."

"How quickly we change our tune," he said under his breath. "Tonight, you just remember you said that."

Theresa blushed. "Just don't touch me. Here, lean in," she said, standing up. They bent forward until their lips touched briefly, then Theresa quickly moved away. "You too, little man," she said to Mikey after sitting back in her seat.

Mikey came around and did the same thing he'd seen Pierson do and kissed his mom's cheek.

"See how women treat you when you're dirty, Mikey? That's why your uncles are always so impressively dressed," Pierson said, having seen Thorne walk into the office.

He laughed.

"That is true, Mikey," Thorne agreed. "But when you clean up well, they will want you to be dirty all the time."

He and Pierson shared a quick nod. Mikey was confused, but instead of questioning it, he just stood there waiting for Pierson to leave.

"Mikey, you staying with me and Natalie tonight?" Thorne prodded.

"Sorry, Uncle Thorne, Mr. Pierson and I are going to have a guys' night. Do you want to hang out with us?"

"Um," Thorne said, a little speechless. He had never had to vie for his nephew's attention from anyone but Michael before, and he usually won out. This was a new experience for him, and he shamefully admitted to himself that he was having a little trouble with it.

"Yeah, Thorne, you should come with us. Maybe Michael would like to hang out, too." Pierson waited for him to agree. The last thing he wanted was for Thorne to feel that he was trying to move into his territory. Pierson had felt the same way when Danielle first wanted to call Theresa. Even though it was about girl stuff, he felt that he had always done enough for his sister. But Danielle did need Theresa's help, more than he would admit. If he hadn't let them build their own small relationship, Danielle would have eventually begun sneaking behind his back.

Understanding a compromise when he saw one, Thorne agreed that it was a good idea. "Okay, that sounds like a plan. I'll call Michael. As a matter of fact, we could stop by the football field. I hear some of the boys are out there practicing."

Theresa rolled her eyes in her head. "Pierson, just so you know, he's not talking about little leaguers. Thorne used to practice with the Saints. He still has a lot of friends in the organization."

Pierson's eyes grew wide.

"You ruin everything," Thorne teased.

" 'Cause I wasn't going to have him out there looking awestruck. I knew you weren't going to tell him," Theresa argued.

"Well, thanks for the heads-up, baby, but honestly, I'll still be awestruck. Come on, lil' man, let's go get dressed." Pierson winked at Theresa before walking out of the office.

"So you really like this guy, huh?" Thorne questioned.

"Is that so hard for you to believe?"

"Not at all. I can see why you would like him. And Mikey obviously likes him."

"Don't worry, Thorne. You'll always be one of his favorite uncles."

"Yeah, I know, but it's still hard to share him with another man, a father figure."

"So, what are you going to do when you start having your own kids? At some point, Mikey will begin to miss not having a father figure in his life."

"I just want to make sure that you and Pierson are serious, especially with him spending so much time with Mikey."

"Didn't we already have this conversation once? I wouldn't have Mikey around him if I didn't think he was a good man. Can't you trust me with my own child?"

"You know it's not like that. I'm gonna go and call Natalie to let her know that I'm hanging with the fellas tonight."

"Thank you for that, Thorne."

"Hey," he said, leaning in to plant a kiss on her cheek, "I'm open to anything when it comes to you and my nephew."

&

When Theresa returned to the house after class, she was surprised to find Pierson standing in the living room holding a glass of wine he had just poured for her. Her frustration from the long day seemed to fall right off her shoulders.

"How was class?" he asked quietly.

"Interesting, as usual. We discussed family this week and the male role, if and how it has changed and why. This week's assignment is to discuss our father's role in the family and how his role affected our lives."

"That doesn't seem as if it's as easy as it sounds."

"No, not at all. Some of the students didn't have a father figure, some had substitutes, and some, like myself, can't remember their fathers that well."

"But you had a substitute, correct? Your grandfather?"

"Yes, he was the closest to a father that I ever had." Theresa took a deep breath as she sat down on the sofa. "Where is Mikey?"

"He's sound asleep. Michael, Thorne and I had so much fun with him tonight. Between the excitement of the football game and the trip to the arcade, he's not waking anytime soon." Pierson sat down next to her. He placed his hand on her knee. The look on her face worried him. "Is everything all right?"

"You know, sometimes I wonder if I'm doing the right thing by him."

"Now don't you start that again. Theresa, you have done a great job with Mikey. I don't understand why you constantly second-guess yourself."

"It's just that in class today we talked about how important it is to have a male figure in your life. And Mikey hasn't had a father figure."

"I'll bet that Thorne and Michael will have a serious problem with that statement. They've been excellent role models for Mikey, excellent father figures. And what am I? Chopped beef?"

"You know what I mean. With him away at military school for the majority of his life—"

"Just stop it, Theresa. You can't change the past. Mikey is a fine boy. I'll be the first to agree that a boy should probably know his father, but not every circumstance is the same. You did what you did for a reason, a good reason. And I understand why you don't trust Ryan now. Look, I don't want to see you worrying yourself sick over this. Mikey loves you, and he doesn't feel as if he's missed out on anything. And he won't feel that way, unless you begin to make him." Pierson kissed her on her cheek. "Now, I have to get on home. I told Danielle to be home by twelve, and I'm definitely going to be there to make sure she is. I'll call you soon as I get in."

Theresa walked him to the door. "Thanks, Pierson. You're right. The bottom line here is protecting my son, and I know deep in my heart that Ryan is up to no good. I'll see you tomorrow at the game." They kissed at the door and Pierson left.

CHAPTER 15

The gymnasium was crowded as usual when Theresa, Mikey, and Pierson walked in. She wasn't at all surprised to see that Thorne and the others were already there. Thorne sat between his mother and Natalie, and Michael sat on the next bleacher with Tamia and Tamya. There was another game being played, but they were halfway through the fourth quarter. Mikey's team was playing next.

"Hey, guys," Theresa said as she walked up the bleachers. "Looks like the gang's all here."

"Not yet," Natalie said. "Stephen and Sandra are on their way."

"Really?" Mikey said. "Wow, the whole family will be together."

"And don't forget Danielle is coming," Pierson said, a smile spreading across his face when Mikey's eyes lit up.

"Yeah, Mikey," Thorne chimed in. "We're all here to see how good a player you are. And I also have a surprise for you."

"We're all going to Chuck E. Cheese after this?" Mikey questioned.

Theresa and Pierson looked at each other. "Pierson got him started on that," Theresa said.

"No, but I've invited your entire team and the team that you're playing and their families to a big picnic out at Gladewinds. Tamia and Tamya's crews are setting everything up as we speak. There will be a lot of kids out there and games."

"Cool," Mikey said.

"And a friend of mine is coming to watch you guys play."

"Really, who?"

"You'll see. I'll bring him over to meet you guys as soon as he shows up."

"Okay," Mikey said, seeing that his coach was signaling him to come join the rest of the team.

"Thorne," Theresa said as soon as Mikey walked away, "what have you done?"

"Don't even ask," Natalie said. "You won't believe it if I tell you. Your brother never ceases to amaze me. I guess it's not that surprising how he goes above and beyond for those he loves, but the things he comes up with. . ."

"But that's why you're marrying him, right?" Pierson suggested.

"That's one of the reasons," she replied, rubbing Thorne's knee and leaning into his embrace.

Amanda smiled as she watched her family. Even without their father's presence, they had turned out to be remarkable children. She herself had been missing from Thorne's life until recently, yet he was strong and loving, caring and gentle. Each of her children possessed the same qualities that she'd found in their grandmother so many years ago.

Ms. Abbie had helped Amanda so much after she left her son and moved to Chicago. They stayed in contact, Ms. Abbie sent her money, put her through school, and always kept her updated on Thorne. Ms. Abbie even told her son where to find Amanda in Chicago in hopes of a reunion between the two, but it never happened. Despite finding that they were still sexually attracted, Amanda and Matthew came to the conclusion that they both had valid reasons for not fully reconciling. Amanda stayed in Chicago, and Matthew married his second wife.

"Ms. Amanda, would you like anything from the concession stand? I'm going to run over there real quick. Anybody?" Pierson questioned, pulling Amanda from the past.

"Yes, young man, I would like some Twizzlers if they have any."

"I'll walk with you, Pierson," Thorne said.

"Me, too," Michael chimed in. He was not about to miss out on this conversation, wherever it was headed.

"So, Pierson, everything good between you and Theresa?" Thorne asked.

"We're great. I'm really enjoying myself with her and Mikey."

"Good. I'm glad to hear that because I'm, we're, very happy to see the changes in her, and I can only attribute those changes to you."

As they walked toward the entrance to the gym, Danielle walked through the door holding the hand of a goofy-looking white guy that Pierson had never seen before. The smile on his face quickly disappeared. Not because the guy was white, but because the guy was with Danielle. She was smiling, and there was a glow on her face that Pierson wasn't sure he liked. He stopped in his tracks, catching Michael and Thorne off guard.

Danielle did a double take when she saw his expression. She honestly hadn't thought that her showing up at the game with Christopher would be a problem. He wasn't much older, just a couple of years, and she was going to be a senior this year. She should have already graduated, but after her mom passed away, her grades had suffered a little, and she had been kept back. But no matter what excuse she worked out in her head, Danielle knew that she wasn't prepared for the lashing she was about to take. But it was too late to turn back now.

Christopher must have felt her pause because he turned to her with a worried look on his face. He was about to ask her what was wrong when Pierson approached.

"Hello, Danielle," Pierson said. He bent forward, giving his sister a kiss on the forehead, then turned his attention to Christopher.

"Oh, Pierson, this is Christopher. Christopher, this is my brother Pierson."

"Nice to meet you, sir," Christopher said immediately. He offered his hand and smiled cheerfully at the large man in front of him. When Danielle had said she had a big brother, he hadn't taken her literally.

"Christopher," Pierson said, after giving the young man the once-over. *Harmless,* he decided, shaking Christopher's hand. "Theresa and everyone else is down there. We're going to the concession stand. You want anything?" Christopher looked as if he wasn't quite sure what to do with a girl. He was clearly uncomfortable. Perfect. Danielle could have picked a much worse character.

"No, thank you, sir. We just ate."

"Really? Is that why you were out of the house so early this morning?"

"Yes, we didn't want to miss Mikey's game." Danielle smiled up at her brother, silently thanking him for not doing what he usually did, play daddy. "And look, we made signs for everybody." She gestured at the stack of poster boards Christopher was holding.

"Mr. Philips, how are you today, sir?"

"Good, Christopher, and you two?" Michael replied. "Pierson, Christopher works for me in our financial department, part time. The young man is a wiz with numbers. He's one of the company's rising stars."

Pierson just nodded his head.

"Well, we're going to take our seats," Danielle chimed in, getting out of the situation as fast as she could.

"You handled that quite well, Pierson, considering the shock on your face," Thorne laughed.

"Well, it was hard for me to blow up at the kid when I'm standing here trying to plead my own case to big brothers."

"You're right," Michael said. "But Christopher is a good kid. I'm surprised she managed to get him out here at all. I've never seen the boy without a pocket protector and a book."

"Remind you of anyone?" Thorne laughed, resuming his steps.

"Whatever," Michael answered. "I might have been a nerd, but I was always a cool nerd."

The group had taken only a couple of steps when Ryan walked in. He had a young chocolate beauty on his arm. This week he wasn't dressed like a thug. He had on a pair of tan khaki pants and a short-sleeved three-button polo shirt. His date had on a tank with tight jeans and three-inch heels. She didn't look like a slut, more like a video chick; she looked good. All three men had to admit that.

When he saw them, Ryan simply smiled and walked on by. He hoped that the three men would be drawn to turn around and watch Mollie as she walked by, but to his dissatisfaction none of them did. They walked straight ahead as if she weren't worth a second glance. That pissed Ryan off. He had spent his last bit of money picking out just the right outfit for her to wear. She had turned enough heads in the parking lot and was still turning heads as they walked through the gym, but not the ones he had wanted. At this point, Ryan wanted to cause any extra trouble that he could. He was sure that Mollie could spark at least an interesting conversation amongst the couples that night.

As soon as they hit the concession stand, out of sight of their families, Thorne and Michael looked at each other. Neither of them said a thing. Pierson watched them. He definitely wasn't talking. But Michael, as always, cracked first.

"Did you see the ass on that chick?"

"How could you miss it?" Thorne volunteered. He wasn't impressed, but he was a man.

Pierson still stayed quiet.

"Pierson, don't try to act like you didn't see that."

"I didn't see anything," he lied.

"Look, you're among brothers here," Thorne said. "We know you care for our sister. Hell, I'm about to marry Natalie. Michael has a baby on the way. But you're still a man just like every other man in this building, and you saw that."

Pierson looked at both men. "I didn't see anything. That's my story, and I'm sticking to it. Besides, fellas, you know that what looks good ain't always good for you. Every woman is worth one glance, but for them to get a second one from me, they have to have more than a big tail."

"Good answer." Just then, Thorne was distracted by a loud burst of noise coming from behind him. "That must be my surprise for Mikey. You guys go on back inside with the stuff. I'll meet you in a second."

"What's he up to?" Pierson asked.

"With Thorne you never know," Michael answered. They ordered the food, then walked back to their seats.

Just as they sat down, the first game was ending, and Thorne rushed into the gym. He walked to the announcement table and spoke to the announcer, who then spoke into the mike.

"Ladies and gentlemen, may I have your attention please. We at the PAL League are very honored to announce that we have a special guest of young Mr. Michael Philips and the McDonald's team coming in today to watch the game. Please give a warm welcome to our own Hornets basketball star, Templeton Conquest."

The crowd erupted as Templeton Conquest came out onto the court in a pair of jeans and a Hornets basketball T-shirt. He waved to the crowd and went out onto the floor to meet the players of both teams.

Pierson's mouth fell open.

"Close your mouth, dear," Theresa said.

"I can't believe he got Templeton Conquest to come to a PAL basketball game. That must have cost a pretty penny."

"Actually, Thorne is good friends with the owner and the team. My brother knows a lot of people. He and Michael both. Plus, he's genuinely a nice guy, so people tend to do anything he asks and vice versa."

"I'm beginning to figure that out."

"And I wanted to tell you that I am proud of the way you handled yourself earlier. I thought I was going to have to run down there to protect poor Christopher."

Pierson smiled. "Well, the thought of jumping on him did cross my mind, but I looked at her. It must be the same thing that Thorne and Michael see when they look at you. That must be what's stopping them from jumping on me. But still," he said, looking over at the teenagers, "it's quite odd, isn't it?"

"Some people would say the same about us. About this whole family, really, but that's what makes it so special."

"Did you see—"

"I saw him. Not surprised, and not caring." Theresa looked Pierson in the eyes. "I've got everything I need right here. Ryan and his friend are the least of my worries or concerns."

Their attention returned to the court as Templeton finished meeting the players and walked over to Thorne. Of course a dozen or so fans ran over to him for autographs, which he politely signed. And then there were women that they had to get through before they finally got to the family.

Thorne introduced Templeton Conquest to Amanda first, then Natalie, and eventually made his way around the whole group. "Temp has to go, but—"

"No, no. I think I can stay for a while, if you don't mind," Templeton said.

"Of course, not," Thorne said. "We're going to have a picnic after this with the team if you'd like to come as well."

"Thank you. I just might do that," he replied, looking at Tamya. "I'm going to sit up here, next to Tamya, if you don't mind, that is?"

"Uh, of course not," Tamya smiled. The surprised reaction on everyone's face made Tamya smile even more. She wasn't sure what Templeton was up to, but since she was single and she knew he was single, there wasn't any harm in getting to know an NBA basketball star.

They watched the game, cheering for Mikey every time he made a basket. His confidence was high, and he was so happy that his whole family was there. He had watched his father come in with the other woman and wondered if that was his wife. He'd also seen Danielle come in with Christopher, which he didn't like, but when they pulled out the signs with his name on them, Mikey figured that Christopher wasn't a bad guy. Plus, Danielle was really old, and Samantha Carter wasn't. She was the center on his team.

"Why are we here again?" Mollie asked, for the third time. Basketball really wasn't her thing. She could be lying down somewhere right now doing her nails. This was boring. Ryan wasn't showing her any attention. The only highlights of the game for her were the goo-goo eyes she had gotten from the men as she walked into the building, the new outfit Ryan had bought her, which she had mistakenly thought was because he cared, and seeing Templeton Conquest.

"I told you to watch my kid's game. Now shut up," Ryan said as his eyes moved back over to Theresa and Pierson. The two of them seemed to be having the time of their lives.

"So, that's the ex, huh? She looks exactly like the tattoo. Is that why we're here?" Mollie ventured to ask.

"We're here to get rich. Now do you want a part of the money or not? If so, please shut the hell up and let me think." The game was coming to an end, and once again, Mikey had done an excellent job. His team won. Ryan wondered at the feelings inside of him. He was proud of his son, but he wondered if he should be. Sure, he could gloat that his son was the star of his team and a good kid, but it wasn't as if he had taught him how to play basketball or be a good kid. Everything that Mikey had become was due to Theresa and her family. Maybe that was a good thing. Surely if he had been involved, Mikey would be much different, probably less happy and more demented like his old man. Well, for that Ryan decided to be thankful. But it didn't take away from the necessity of the plan. Ryan needed his son now.

Once the game finally ended, Ryan moved quickly to the floor. He wanted to make sure that he got time with Mikey before the family started crowding in on him.

"Good game, Mikey," he said as he approached him. Ryan was caught off guard when Mikey's arms went around his waist. But isn't that what fathers and sons do? They hug. And by instinct, Ryan lifted him up in the air and tossed him cheerfully before setting him back down. "Man, you are the best player. You get better and better every week."

"Thanks," Mikey smiled. "I'm glad you came."

"Oh, I'll be at all your games."

"Did you see Templeton Conquest?"

"Yes, I did, and I think that one day, you're going to be just as good as him. You could probably play in the pros, too."

"Wow."

"Listen, pretty soon, you and me will start hanging out together. Would you like that?"

"Yes."

"Good. I have to go, but I'll be here next week, okay?"

"We're having a picnic. Don't you want to come to that?"

"Oh, no. I think it's best that I don't. Your uncles and I don't get along too well. But don't you worry. Soon, we'll be—"

"Hello, Ryan," Theresa said from behind him.

Ryan turned and stood to his full height, meaning to intimidate her, but it was all for naught when he had to look up to Pierson's huge presence.

"Mikey, baby, good game. Why don't you go get your stuff? We can stop so you can change before heading over to the picnic if you wish."

Mikey ran off obediently.

Ryan could see Thorne and Michael standing in the background with the rest of the family, waiting for the outcome of this situation. He decided to make the best of it. The ball was still in his court. They would be going to family court Wednesday, and there wasn't any need for him to mess that up. There was probably no way he could hide the hatred in his eyes, but he would hide it from his voice.

"Theresa, how are you doing today?" Then he reluctantly acknowledged Pierson, who could not go ignored. "And you must be Theresa's beau? Man? Husband?" He extended a hand.

Pierson gripped it solidly. He didn't give Ryan the answer that he wanted, just his name, which he could have easily gotten from Mikey had he asked. "Pierson Brooks."

"Well, nice to meet you. I was just telling Mikey what a good player he is. Hopefully, I'll be able to take him to the park and such soon." That was just a final jab thrown at Theresa.

She almost fell for it, too, but Pierson reached up to massage her shoulder. Ryan's eyes darkened slightly as he observed the tenderness. But instead of saying anything, he raised his hand and signaled Mollie to the group. She quickly obliged.

Ryan smiled as she approached and the eyes of every man in the gym, save Pierson's, turned in her direction. "This is my friend Mollie. Mollie, this is Theresa, my first wife, and her friend Pierson. We're going to get on out of here. You have a good evening."

Mollie smiled politely, sure that she wasn't supposed to do more than that. Ryan was using her, plain and simple. That had always been her role.

As they turned to walk away, the crowd practically parted for them. Ryan made sure to move his hand from her small waist down to the top of her wide behind.

Pierson, to his credit, stepped in front of Theresa and turned to her, blocking them from their sight. "You're a marvelous woman, Theresa. That's why I'm falling for you."

Theresa's head swung up and she looked into his face. Ryan was forgotten. "You're falling for me, Mr. Brooks?"

"Is that what I said? What I meant was—"

"Oh, no you don't. I heard you." They hugged before turned back to the family. Mikey was already there clapping hands with his uncles and Templeton Conquest, who had decided to stay for the whole game and go to the picnic.

"So," Thorne said, "I've already given the address to the team coaches to distribute to the families. We're off.

Mom is riding with Natalie and me. Christopher and Danielle can follow us. Tamya, you riding with Michael and Tamia?"

"No," Templeton interjected, "she's going to ride with me. We'll follow Michael."

There was a moment of silence, but when Tamya didn't reject the offer, Stephen said that they would follow also.

"Let's just go," Natalie finally suggested. "Everybody knows where it is."

"Okay," Thorne said, "let's go."

"Oh, Mikey wants to get changed first so instead of heading all the way back to the apartment, I'm going to stop at one of the stores and pick up something and then stop by Pierson's real quick so he can change."

"Okay, we'll see you out there."

234

CHAPTER 16

"Mikey, make sure you wash under your arms and stuff. You've been sweating a lot," Theresa said as she turned on the showerhead in Pierson's bathroom, which was beautifully renovated with a Jacuzzi tub and a glass shower.

"Mom," Mikey said desperately before shutting the bathroom door, "I'm not a baby."

"Sorry," she said, returning to the kitchen to wait.

Pierson came up behind her. "Mom, I'm not a baby," he teased, pushing his pelvis close so that she could feel his quick arousal through the thin material of her capris.

"I know you're not," she replied, moving her hips against him.

"You are so lucky that Mikey's in the next room," Pierson whispered against her ear, "or I would be having you right on this countertop." His hands moved up her sides to cup her breasts and squeeze them gently.

"There's always later," she said, turning around to face him. Her hands went around his back and she tilted her head back for the kiss she was about to receive. As their lips met, Theresa's hands moved down to Pierson's strong buttocks, and she pulled him even closer to her. She could feel his print against her stomach. While the kiss deepened, so did the motion of her hips against him.

"Stop moving before I forget about Mikey, and take you to the bedroom." His breathing was hard on her cheek.

"You can't control yourself, Mr. Brooks?" Theresa teased, not knowing that she was playing with fire.

He was watching her body intently, but Pierson knew that he didn't have a lot of time. He listened to the pattern of the water, making sure that it was off beat as it went from hitting Mikey to the shower floor. Then he realized the water had stopped running.

"Theresa, Mikey's done."

"You're lucky," she said, realizing their situation. "I was just about to jump your bones."

"Yeah, right," Pierson laughed with her.

❧

Pierson couldn't believe what he was seeing. When they pulled up to Thorne's house, he was both surprised and amazed at the beauty of the place. It was a magnificently large house sitting on a slight hill, surrounded by all kinds of greenery. The fields were filled with cars, tents, and game setups.

"Is this were you grew up?" he asked Theresa.

"Yes, it's beautiful, isn't it? Thorne has done a lot to the place, but it was always beautiful."

"Wow."

"Just wait until you see the other places. Michael's place is under reconstruction right now, but when it's done, it will give Gladewinds a run for its money. Of course Michael is not into the country look. His place looks like something out of the future. It's all state-of-the-art and whatnot."

"I'd imagine yours is full of rose bushes and all romantic, right?"

"Whatever," Theresa said as he came around the car and grabbed her into his arms.

Mikey ran past them to get to his friends. He shook his head. They had been doing the googly-eye thing that he had seen Uncle Michael and Tamia doing.

"You know, I owe you one for what you did in the kitchen," Theresa said.

"Oh, you didn't enjoy it?" Pierson raised an eyebrow. " 'Cause it sounded like you were enjoying it a lot."

"I didn't say that I didn't enjoy it, but my son was in the other room."

"And he didn't hear us, and we didn't get caught. Sometimes, that's part of the fun. Weren't you more aroused from the possibility of getting caught doing something naughty? Besides, I was just trying to make a point."

"Which was?"

"I wanted you to know that I know your body, and I do have control over it at times." He said it as plainly and simply as he could.

"We'll talk about this later." Theresa didn't want to start a heated discussion like this in the middle of a picnic. She had plenty of time to prove to him that the situation was vice versa later.

"You know you loved it," he said quickly before they reached the group.

She couldn't deny it as they greeted everyone. Her cheeks were glowing brightly and Natalie and Amanda both looked at her twice during their conversations. Once everyone dispersed, they sat her down.

"Ohh," Natalie said, "you nasty, Ms. Philips."

"What?" Theresa said innocently.

"You heard her," Amanda concurred. "You and that young man of yours done something that you ain't got no business doing. I don't know how you did it with my grandson around, but it's written all over both of your faces, especially yours."

"I don't know what you're talking about," Theresa repeated.

"Ain't no use, Amanda. She's going to deny it to her grave, but we know."

"Know what? He's a good man. I'm enjoying getting to know him better. And Mikey likes him a lot."

"He really likes you and Mikey."

Theresa looked over at the men and boys as they gathered to pick teams for a softball game. Most of the men and boys played that, while the women sat under tents and watched. The food was close to being served.

To everyone's surprise, Templeton had called a few of his teammates and they came out with their families. There was a lot of autograph signing and pictures taking.

When it was time to eat, Mikey found Theresa and Pierson sitting at the far end of a table. He brought his plate over to them.

"Hey, Mikey," Pierson said. "Are you enjoying your day?"

"Yes, but I need a partner," Mikey said.

"For what?"

"The three-legged race. Mr. Pierson, will you be my partner?"

Theresa smiled as she and Pierson looked at each other.

"Sure, Mikey, but are you sure you don't want to ask one of your uncles?"

"I'm sure," he replied.

Theresa could have sworn that she saw Pierson's chest puff out to twice its size, but she didn't comment. She silently ate her food as if this were a normal occurrence. She wondered what Thorne would say.

As the teams lined up for the race, Theresa was surprised by the reactions from both her brothers, who decided to team up together. They were both happy that Mikey had asked Pierson. Right before the whistle blew, Theresa had a photographer take a picture of Pierson and Mikey going over their strategy.

They came in second, but both promised that next time they would win. Thorne and Michael were arguing about who had caused them to fall over and vowed to never team up again.

Around 4 p.m., the picnic began to dwindle down to just the family. They moved inside the house, where Mikey slumped on the sofa. He was so obviously tired that Theresa wanted to get him home.

"Hey, Mikey," Natalie said, "do you want to stay with me and Thorne tonight? You can go shower, put on your nightclothes and relax. Then later, you and Thorne can go play one of those large video games that he has for no other reason but your entertainment."

"Okay," Mikey said. "I'm going to my room."

"He'll be asleep before his head hits the pillow," Thorne said.

"Thank you, Thorne," Theresa said. "He had a wonderful day."

"Hell, I had a wonderful day to be followed by a wonderful night, which I plan to get started while my nephew is asleep." He looked at Natalie, who was watching him just as intently.

"We get the hint," Michael said, far too used to the routine by now. "Let's go, baby," he said to Tamia. "My brother is going to be disgusting to your sister, again."

"The way they act, you'd think that she liked it," Tamia laughed. "Tamya, we'll drop you off on the way."

"Oh, I'm, uh, I got a date," Tamya said. "Um, Templeton is coming back out here for me. I'm going to steal one of Natalie's outfits and change."

"Okay, sis. I see you," Tamia cheered. "Doing big things. Well, have a good time and call me when you get in."

"Will do." She hugged her twin.

"The date thing must be in the air. Danielle said she had a date tonight, too," Pierson said. "Which means that we'll be staying at my house tonight. I need to make sure she's in at a decent time."

"I understand," Theresa said.

Everybody said their good-byes and went their separate ways.

When they got to Pierson's house, it was close to six o'clock. Danielle's car was in the driveway. They were both tired, and Theresa felt dirty from being outside all day. Pierson's stomach was growling.

"Sorry, I'm a growing boy. The picnic was lunch anyway."

"Yeah, I guess you're right. We can order or we can go pick something up and bring it back. I'm not really in the mood for dining out."

"Me, either," Pierson agreed. "We had better decide before we get out of this car, 'cause once we're in, we're in."

"I gotta taste for a sub."

"Well, I could do with a cheesesteak. Let's hit the deli down the street. It's close and convenient."

They went to get their food, then came back to the house. This time Danielle's car was gone.

"She must have seen us pull up the first time and decided to scatter before our return."

"Do you blame her?" Theresa questioned. "She didn't want to hear your thousand questions or you telling her to go change her outfit. Trust her, Pierson. Besides, Christopher doesn't strike me as the first-move type of guy."

"Yeah, you're right."

"This relationship will go only as far as Danielle wants it to."

"That scares me, too." He got out of the car and walked up to the front door.

"I'm going to eat, shower, and get right in the bed," Theresa said. "I am pooped."

"Yeah, it has been a long day. At least tomorrow is Sunday. Nobody has to move."

After she ate, Theresa did as she said and headed for the bathroom, but instead of the shower she decided to get into the oversized tub and turn on the jets. She lounged in the water with her eyes closed and luxuriated in the feel of the jets massaging her back. Then she smelled the scent of jasmine. She opened her eyes to Pierson standing over her with a box of bubble bath that he was pouring into the water. Instantly, thick bubbles floated to the top of the water until she was completely covered.

"I must have dozed off."

"That's okay, enjoy yourself."

"You going to join me?" she asked before he could leave the room.

"You sure?"

"Of course I'm sure. Unless you don't want to," she teased, lifting one leg out of the water for his careful perusal.

"Okay," Pierson agreed, peeling off each layer of clothing under her watchful eye. He was already excited and aroused by the time he pulled off the last item. It was the look in her eye that had him. She was promising him something that he wanted so badly, and it wasn't her body. Theresa was willing to give him her heart.

Once he was in the water, Theresa wasted no time going to him. From watching him undress, she had kindled a thirst inside of herself that she needed to quench. Theresa leaned into him, capturing his lips quickly and forcefully. This time, she wanted to be in control.

Pierson could feel her energy. And he was willing to let her have the lead. That's what a relationship was, a compromise. He wasn't totally surprised because he knew that she had a lot of passion inside of her waiting to be released. Pierson was glad that he was the recipient.

"Oh, now you want control?" he asked, prompting her into her role.

"I have control," she answered, biting him lightly on his lower lip.

Pierson jerked, but not because of the bite. Under the water, Theresa held him firmly in her grasp. He grew a little apprehensive, unsure of her plans, but then she kissed him again roughly and gently massaged away his concerns.

He smiled as he leaned back against the tub and enjoyed himself. Between the massage she was giving him and the feel of the jet action against his back, Pierson was near utopia. All he needed was one thing, he decided, as he picked Theresa up and easily settled her on top of him.

"Pierson," Theresa exclaimed after getting herself comfortable. "I'm supposed to be in control."

"You're on top, aren't you?" he questioned without even opening his eyes. "You're still in control. You were just taking too long, and I didn't have much time left."

Pierson smacked her rear through the water to get her moving. "Come on, baby."

Obediently, Theresa began to move over Pierson as he gripped her thighs under the water. He laid kisses over her breasts and shoulders. Water began to splash over the sides of the tub as her thrusts became wilder.

"Pierson, my knees are hitting against one of these damn holes," Theresa finally protested. She had taken all the punishment she could.

"No problem," he said, lifting her to sit on the end of the tub. He was still inside the tub on his knees when he moved between her legs.

Theresa wrapped her legs around his waist when he entered her. She loved this position, and conceded that he was back in charge, but that was okay with her. Theresa threw back her head and arched her back. But she was surprised when he stood up. His hands were on her bottom, holding her in place as he walked through the house.

Pierson continued to kiss her as he made his way to his bedroom. He didn't want to make love to her on the hard surface of the tub no matter how much she seemed to be enjoying it.

Once they got to the bed, he lowered them slowly. By this time Pierson had calmed himself down, and he was able to make love to her as he wanted to. And Theresa responded, opening herself to him, welcoming him, urging him to take everything she had to give.

Pierson moved inside her as meaningful as he could, making each plunge plant a memory in her mind. He loved to hear her moan and gasp against his ear and whisper his name repeatedly. And whenever he felt each of them was reaching the end, he pulled himself back. He didn't want it to end.

"Don't stop," Theresa pleaded, trying to pull him closer to her.

"I don't ever want to stop loving you, Theresa," he whispered in her ear.

"And I don't want you to," she responded as another wave of ecstasy hit her.

Pierson covered her groan with a kiss as he moved deeper inside her. He shouldn't have done that, he realized too late. Theresa gripped around him tightly and his own orgasm was swift to follow. He collapsed on her, breathing heavily.

"You know what?" Pierson asked as he moved to lay behind her and pull her into his arms.

"What?"

"You definitely had control that time."

Theresa was about to ask him if he was being smart, but she heard the soft rumble of his snoring. She got up and shut his bedroom door. Any minute, she expected to be asleep herself, and she did not want Danielle walking into the house to see them lying across Pierson's bed naked.

Danielle finally came in at eleven. She'd had the time of her life. Christopher had taken her to a poetry reading.

He didn't write it, but he said that he liked to hear the creativeness of the readers. She had never done anything like that before, and it seemed like a grownup type of date to her.

Neither of them was old enough to drink yet, so they had sodas. Both of them loved popcorn, so that was their snack of choice as they walked around downtown.

At the end of the night, he took her back to her car, which was parked at Pierson's shop. They stood in the parking lot for a minute and talked, but she had to initiate the goodnight kiss. And she probably wouldn't have gotten one if she hadn't. Danielle smiled to herself as she thought of Christopher's clumsiness when he first kissed her. She'd actually stopped him.

"You haven't done this much, huh?"

"Is it that obvious?"

She smiled at him. "Here, you let me do it, and just follow my lead when you're comfortable."

Luckily, Christopher was a quick learner. Before she knew it, Danielle was wrapped in his arms, and he was kissing her back softly, not demanding but definitely with a lot of yearning. Danielle couldn't remember how long they stayed out there, but she knew she had to get home before big brother tracked her down.

She and Christopher said their goodbyes, and he suggested going to the mall the following day.

Now, at home, Danielle smiled to herself as she moved through the house. It had been a great first date. She went to the kitchen and grabbed a soda as she turned to the television, she heard the tub running loudly.

At first, she thought that they might be in the bathroom, but as she moved down the hall, she realized that the door was open. Danielle turned on the bathroom light after making a loud noise. She just smiled and shook her head at the sight.

You mean to tell me that they couldn't turn off the tub? There was water all over the bathroom floor. She couldn't help thinking about the way Pierson got on her about wasting electricity. She turned off the tub, but she was not about to stick her hand in the water to let it out. Instead, she took out a few big towels, spread them across the floor and turned the light back off.

CHAPTER 17

After spending a beautiful night and morning with Pierson, Theresa was ready to face the week ahead. And even though Wednesday was quickly approaching, she was looking forward to it. From here on out, she was taking one step at a time and things were going to go her way.

Stephanie came into her office with a bouquet of flowers, and both she and Danielle, who she was giving another list of errands, looked up in surprise.

"Beautiful," Theresa said, thinking they were from Pierson, until Stephanie winked at her and handed them to·Danielle.

"These just came for you, Danielle," Stephanie said, standing nearby as if waiting for an explanation.

"Really?"

"Really," she answered as Theresa watched. "I was going to put them on your desk, but I figured that you would want to see them right away."

"Wow, somebody has been a busy little bee. Who are they from?" Theresa asked.

"I don't know." Danielle was just as stunned as everyone else.

"Here's the card," Stephanie pointed out.

Danielle took out the card, read it, and put it back. She didn't say a word, just smiled to herself.

Stephanie and Theresa looked at each other.

"Oh," Stephanie said, "that's how you're doing things? Well, you sure have learned fast from your boss."

"Who are they from?" Theresa asked, leaning in close.

"They're from Christopher."

"Christopher?" Stephanie asked.

"From accounting," Theresa explained.

"The quiet nerd who works in financial?" Stephanie laughed. "You've got to be kidding me?"

"Apparently, he's not as quiet as we thought he was," Theresa said.

"Apparently. No wonder he looked so different this morning. Like he had a little swagger," Stephanie said, leaving the room, followed by Danielle, who said that she had to get back to work.

Theresa's cellphone rang.

"Yes?"

"Hello, beautiful. How are you today?"

"I'm just fine, thank you, and yourself?"

"I'm good. I was just sitting here at lunch, thinking about you. I figured I'd give you a call. Do you have a lot of work?"

"Not really, but I have to go out of town until tomorrow. I wanted to ask you two questions. One, I was hoping to take Danielle with me. I wanted her to get to see the Dallas office before she started school. And two, can Mikey stay with you tonight while I'm gone?"

"The answer to both questions is yes. Where is Mikey now?"

"He's here, but I'm going to have Danielle bring him to you and pack a bag for herself while I finish some paperwork. Then we'll be leaving around four on the private jet."

"Well, you be very careful and have a safe trip. And call me once you've landed. I was wondering if you were okay with Wednesday approaching so quickly."

"I'll be fine. I've been so busy that I haven't been able to really think about it, and I still have to get my homework done by tomorrow."

"Will you be back in time for class?"

"I should be. But if not, I'm sure I can make the professor understand."

They both laughed.

"Yes, you can be very convincing when you need to be."

"I'll take that as a compliment. Oh, by the way . . . never mind." Theresa stopped herself from gossiping. It was not her place to tell him about the flowers.

"What is it?"

"Just thank you for everything."

"You're welcome. Thank you, too. Don't forget to call me later."

"Okay," Theresa replied, as if she could forget. After she hung up, she called Stephanie's phone. "Stephanie, Danielle is going with me tonight to Dallas." Then, she called Danielle's cell. "Danielle, I need you to find Mikey. I think he's working with Michael today. Then I need you to pack him a bag and take him to Pierson. And pack a bag for yourself. We're going to Dallas tonight."

"Dallas? Really? Flying? I'm a little scared to fly, Theresa, um Ms. Philips."

"Don't worry. So am I. Now, tell Christopher that you'll talk to him later."

Danielle looked from her phone to Christopher. How did she know? Then she explained everything to her friend, gave him a quick kiss, said she would call later, and headed on her way. Everyone in the cafeteria had been surprised to see Christopher sitting with the young beauty, especially the several other workers who had already asked Danielle out.

⁂

"Welcome back, ladies," Stephanie said late Tuesday afternoon when Theresa and Danielle slowly walked past her desk and toward the office.

"Thank you," they both said somberly.

"Theresa, would you like me to call Amanda and let her know that you won't be in class tonight?"

"I called her from the airport and emailed my report. She has it. But thank you for thinking of it. I'm going up to my apartment and sleeping until tomorrow."

"Okay, Pierson is up there with Mikey. Do you need a wake-up call for court tomorrow?"

"Oh, no. I'll be up bright and early for that. Danielle, you go on home. Don't worry about working tomorrow. I'll get Michael or Thorne to keep an eye on Mikey while I go to court."

"You sure?"

"Definitely. We both need a break. Thank you for all your help yesterday and today."

"Thank you for the opportunity, Theresa. Good night. I told Christopher to wait for me. I'll see if he's still here before I go."

"Good night."

"Oh, tell Pierson that I'll be home shortly. I've got to hit my bed. You wouldn't think that sitting on a plane would take so much out of you," Danielle said.

"I think it has something to do with the altitude."

They went their separate ways. When Theresa reached her floor, the elevator doors opened and she heard Mikey hollering at the top of his lungs that he was going to get Pierson. She was alarmed until she heard Pierson hollering right back that he wasn't.

When she found them, they were sitting in front of the floor model television in the spare room with the video game hooked up. The sound was up so high that they didn't even hear her come in. A big box of pizza sat between them. She stood in the doorway until they saw her.

"Mom." Mikey got up and ran to her. He hugged her tightly.

"Hey, love," Pierson said. "Glad you're back. Do you want something to eat?"

"No, we had salads on the plane."

"That can't be good for you."

Theresa looked at the pizza again and lifted her eyebrow. "And that is? No, I'm going to go into my room and get ready for bed. Could y'all turn down that game a little, please?"

"Sure, baby." Pierson signaled for Mikey to turn the volume down and gave him the one-second sign as he followed Theresa out of the room. "Is everything okay?"

"Yeah, I'm just tired, and I've got a big day tomorrow."

"Well, you go ahead and rest. I'll stay until Mikey goes to bed. Want me to call you in the morning?"

"Of course I do. Aren't you going to court with me in the morning?"

"Of course I am. Meet you at the courthouse or here?"

"Um, I'll pick you up on my way." Theresa turned and moved into his arms. She kissed him goodnight and went into her bedroom. "Good night, Mikey," she yelled.

"Good night, Mom."

❧

Ryan sat at his desk Wednesday morning. His eyes were shut as he concentrated on moving into character for the best acting job of his life. He was planning to give the judge an Oscar-worthy performance. It shouldn't be that hard a stretch. It wasn't as if he didn't truly like his son. Under different circumstances, he would have probably genuinely enjoyed being the father of a boy like Mikey. Unfortunately, circumstances weren't different. He needed money to get himself out of this rut and the loan sharks off his back, and the answer to his problems was Mikey.

The help that he needed to beat the Phillipses in court came from the files he had collected on some of the city's most influential people over the years. He wasn't a great investigator, but when it came to finding city officials in compromising positions, he was the best. Nobody had contacts in the dark streets of New Orleans like he did. But instead of using all of his valuable pictures at once, Ryan had saved some for later, which turned out to be the smartest thing he'd ever done in his life. Who ever said that blackmail didn't pay?

Those pictures had ensured him a speedy hearing in family court, and he was certain that the judgment would be in his favor. He planned to start spending time with Mikey that very weekend, if possible. But more importantly, he couldn't wait to see the look on the faces of Thorne and Michael when he had bested them. They thought they had control of this situation, just as they did everything else. But this time Ryan was in charge.

He picked up the magazine that lay on his desk and smiled devilishly at Thorne's picture. The caption on the cover only increased the anger that built inside him every time he thought of the family. "Voted African-American Businessman of the Year." *How in the hell had he done that when he'd found out that he was black only a few months ago?* And although Ryan was white and knew that he would never have had a chance for the award, even if he was black, he hated the fact that Thorne was being embraced by any group of people. He just hated Thorne Phillips. But that was fine, because today was going to be Thorne's turn to get burned.

Ryan slammed the magazine on the floor and stood. Then he placed the heel of his shoe squarely across

Thorne's face and ground into it until the cover separated from the rest. Now he was ready.

ello

"Are you kidding me?" Theresa yelled at the judge.

"Control your client, counselor," Judge Carlson said nonchalantly, as if he had never eaten dinner at their grandmother's house, as if her grandmother hadn't helped him out a million times before and he hadn't hired Thorne to build his last house. "Now, Mrs. Philips, it's obvious that you've kept this man's son from him for the majority of his life. I understand that you think he might not have the boy's best interests at heart, but unfortunately, you have not been able to prove that."

"But, Your Honor," Theresa tried to interrupt.

"I have no choice but to grant the father visitation rights. And because of the obvious concern and sensitive nature surrounding them becoming reacquainted, I order that the visits be supervised." The judge lowered his eyes to avert the murderous look Ryan gave him.

Supervised? That's not what Ryan wanted. Ryan gritted his teeth as plans began to form in his eyes. The first thing he was going to do for sure was send the pictures he had of Judge Carlson's wife having sex with their pool guy to the newspaper.

"However, the visits will start immediately, Sunday afternoons from one to five."

Theresa felt Joshua's hand on her arm right before he spoke into her ear. "Theresa, don't do this. You'll make matters worse for yourself."

"If you think I'm going to stand here and let a man who has never given a damn about my son in his life—"

"Please, Theresa," Joshua said. "Let me handle this. I'll file a petition immediately. I'm not sure what the judge is thinking, but at least they will be supervised."

As tears ran down Theresa's face, Thorne stood and walked out of the courtroom. He didn't know what had possessed Judge Carlson to make such a harsh and clearly ridiculous ruling, but he was certainly going to get to the bottom of it. He called the only person he thought could help him in this situation. His sister was crying, and that didn't sit well with him.

"Hello. I need your help. Meet me at the office in an hour." Thorne stood looking out the big window in the courthouse hallway. He didn't realize the courtroom door had opened until he felt Michael's hand on his shoulder. When he turned around, Ryan was leaving the courtroom. The smug look on Ryan's face made Thorne want to run over to him and punch him in the face.

Ryan kept his eye on Thorne. He knew what would be happening to him if he were anywhere else. Thorne and Michael both would have jumped on him by now. Wisely, he walked past them without a word.

When Theresa walked out, she was silent, but tears continued to roll down her face. She was leaning on Pierson for support. It was as if her whole world had crumbled. She had lost the hardest battle she had ever fought in her life. For years, she had done everything in her power to keep her son out Ryan's grasp because she knew that nothing good would come out of him being in Mikey's life.

Michael looked at Thorne when they were back in his car. They were following Pierson and Theresa to the building.

"So, what are we going to do about this?" Michael asked.

"I've been wondering that since we left the court-house. I honestly don't know. I called Coby. I want him to follow Ryan foot to foot. That snake is up to some-thing. And I can't figure out what he had on the judge. As good a friend as Grandmother was to him, this case should have been open and shut, with Theresa winning. I'm going to get to the bottom of that, too."

"Well, we could always have Ryan dealt with," Michael suggested, only half joking.

"That thought ran through my mind, but it's illegal."

"I don't mean kill him. I just mean take him down, beat him down. It wouldn't be the first time."

"No, but it would help his case. We both know that Ryan doesn't give a damn about Mikey. So why all of the sudden interest? It's not coming from any paternal feelings."

They pulled into the building's garage, and Michael pulled into his parking spot.

Ryan bounced into the confines of his tiny office, almost on cloud nine. He was one step closer to his goal.

As he remembered the look on the faces of the Philipses when the judge announced his ruling, he wondered where Mollie was. He couldn't think of a better way to finish his afternoon off than inside her.

Out of nowhere, a fist connected with Ryan's jaw. He was hit so hard that only one thought ran through his mind. Death was coming. Before he heard the voice in his head, his gut told him that it was Harp's heavy hand that was lifting him off the floor.

"I need that money, Ryan," he said.

"I'll have it this weekend. Tell Johnny D that I got it. I'll have it delivered to him by Monday."

"I'm sorry to hear you say that. Johnny D said that if you didn't have it to break something."

"Whoa, whoa, man." Ryan's arms went up into the air in surrender. "Look, let me just go into the bedroom and get it out of my safe."

"Don't try nothing crazy, Ryan. I'm watching you."

But Harp let Ryan go into the bedroom alone. If he'd had half a brain, Ryan thought, he would have checked the layout before Ryan came in. Once he was in the room he used for sleep and sex, Ryan opened the window and leaped out onto the fire escape. He wondered how long Harp would sit there waiting for him this time. He would have to call Johnny D and explain what he was doing so he would call Harp off. The last thing he needed was that nuthead trying to follow him around while he visited with Mikey.

Tears were still running down Theresa face when they got off the elevator and walked into the penthouse. Pierson tried to console her the best he could, but it didn't help. After a while, he just held her in his arms. He led her to the sofa, and they sat there for a minute quietly.

Pierson rubbed her shoulder, hoping to offer her a little comfort. "Theresa, do you want something to eat?" he asked, glancing at his watch. They had been sitting there for two hours.

"No, I'm not hungry. I'm mad. Pierson, this is my worst nightmare come true."

"Theresa, baby, I understand that you're upset. But maybe it's not as bad as you're making it out to be."

Theresa sat up on the sofa and looked at him disbelievingly. How could he say that it wasn't bad? "I'm not some kind of drama queen, Pierson."

"I know. Please don't take this the wrong way, but you're not used to not getting your way."

"So now I'm only upset because I didn't get my way, not because Mikey's father is a selfish and manipulating man who doesn't give a damn about his son?"

"Theresa, I know that I'm new on this scene, and I don't know anything about your past with Ryan or Ryan himself besides what you're telling me. But I think that it's possible that the man might truly want to get to know his son better. If I had a son and his mother refused to let me see him for over five years, it would be a big problem. All hell would have probably broken loose. And you didn't just stop him from seeing Mikey.

You made sure that Mikey was in a whole other state until recently."

"Because I was protecting my son."

"Baby, I'm not saying that you weren't. All I'm saying is that you should give this a chance. One chance isn't too much to ask."

"And I say it is, after he took money to stay out of his son's life in the first place."

Pierson realized that what he'd thought would be a simple conversation had quickly escalated. He reached over and grabbed her hand, but she snatched it away from him. He watched as she stood and stalked toward the door. Immediately, he stood up to follow. Pierson knew what was coming next, and although he didn't want to leave her in this negative state, Pierson understood that now was not a good time to force the issue.

"Theresa," Pierson said once he reached the door. "I'm sorry, and I didn't mean to upset you. I just thought that maybe you should see things from the other side. Maybe I overstepped my boundaries."

"Yes, you did. Pierson, I know what's best for my son. And I don't need to hear that I am raising him wrong from a—"

"A what?" Pierson asked. He knew what she was going to say.

Theresa bit her tongue.

"A complete stranger," Pierson finished her thought. "Is that what I am to you, Theresa? As long as I have been trying to show you that I care for you and Mikey?"

Theresa couldn't do anything but look at him guiltily. She had let her emotions get the best of her, and she had hurt him. A look of disappointment crossed his face as he took a deep breath and exhaled. Theresa wished that she could take everything back, but Pierson didn't understand what she was going through. How could he know?

Pierson looked at her one last time, then stepped into the elevator. He didn't say a word, just left.

Now she was alone. Mikey was with Danielle, Thorne and Michael were at the office, and Amanda was working at the school. Instead of giving in to panic, Theresa called Stephanie and asked her friend to come up to her apartment.

When Thorne got to his office, Coby was sitting in the waiting area. As soon as he saw Michael and Thorne walk past him, the older gentleman immediately stood up and followed them without a word.

Both men wore faces filled with stone-cold anger. It didn't take Coby long to figure out the problem or the assignment. He had heard that Ryan, his ex-partner, was going for custody of his son. Coby and Thorne had always been good friends, even before he took a wet-behind-the-ears Ryan under his wing and tried to teach him how to be as good a detective as he was. At one time, Coby had thought that Ryan had a lot of potential. It might have even been his fault that Ryan and Theresa met in the first place. Thorne had sent Theresa to Coby with important documents for a case he was working, and Ryan was at the office. Both were young and innocent at the time, and Coby had thought they would make a suitable couple. How wrong he had been.

"Coby, I need an eye on this guy at all times," Thorne stated. "He's about to have my nephew for hours at a time, and we can't be near. I know that there will be a chaperone, but that's not good enough for me. Just have someone close by."

"That won't be a problem."

"And we need somebody to start digging a little deeper into his personal life," Michael added. "From what we know so far, there really isn't any valid reason for him to want to be back in Mikey's life. We figure that the bottom line is money."

"Well," Coby started, "we know for sure that Ryan owes Johnny D a substantial amount, around seventy thousand, that he doesn't appear to have handy. The girl, Mollie, who works for him is just an occasional lay, nothing serious between them. Besides that, he's only got one or two clients right now. One's an older black woman, the other's a white man."

"And what did they hire him to do?" Michael asked.

"We don't know that yet," Coby replied.

"Maybe it would be wise to find out," Thorne said. "We'll pay you extra for this, Coby, and any additional manpower that you need. Our nephew is very important to us."

"I understand, Thorne. I'll get right on it and give you a call tomorrow morning with an update." Coby shook the hands of both men before leaving.

Thorne and Michael looked at each other, but neither said a word.

CHAPTER 18

Mikey was up early Sunday morning. He was excited about spending time with his father. He just knew they were going to have fun because when he was away at school, he used to watch all of the other boys with their fathers. His classmates would talk about all of the fun things they did with their fathers whenever they went home on vacation. And he was finally going to hang out with his own father. His uncles were cool and fun, but his father . . . he just couldn't wait. Whenever Ryan came to the basketball games, Mikey could hear him cheering in the stands. He tried to play well because he wanted his father to be proud of him.

He moved quietly through the house, careful not to wake his mom, who he knew was in a bad mood. Mikey wondered if she and Mr. Pierson had had an argument because Mr. Pierson didn't stay after his basketball game. And they didn't sit together like they usually did. Mikey liked Mr. Pierson. They had fun together.

Mikey knew that his mother didn't like his father, but he didn't really know why. In fact, nobody in his family liked his father. His mother had told him that he would be spending five hours today with his father so that he could get to know him better. Mikey was confused because even though she smiled at him, he could tell that she had been crying and was about to cry more. He didn't know whether to be happy or not.

After making himself a bowl of cereal, Mikey went into the den, sat in front of the television and played video games until his mother got up. He had forgotten all about his father until he saw her face.

Theresa had tried her hardest to hide her feelings from him, but she was so upset. Every time she thought about Mikey being around Ryan for more than ten minutes, her heart broke. She knew deep down inside that her ex-husband cared nothing for his son. Ryan was a struggling, barely capable private investigator who had a son worth more than he would ever see. If she had given him the opportunity, he would have tried this years ago. She was actually surprised that he hadn't, and wondered why he'd waited until now. If he was really concerned with spending time with his son, he could have taken her to court for custody a long time ago. Something or someone was pushing him to make a desperate move.

And what was he going to do with Mikey for five hours? Ryan didn't know the first thing about kids or how to talk to one. To her knowledge, he didn't care for them at all. Luckily, he would have a chaperone, but she didn't trust her son's well-being with Ryan or the stranger.

She looked down at Mikey again. He was staring at her.

"Mom, are you okay?"

"I'm fine, baby," she replied.

"You look like you're sick or sad. Your eyes are all red and puffy."

"I'm okay. Don't worry about me. I'm going to hop in the shower. I want you to get dressed soon, okay?"

"Okay," he answered. Mikey's clothes for the day were already laid out on his bed. Everything he would need, right down to his socks and underwear. All he had to do was shower and dress, and he was ready to spend the day with his father.

Theresa went into her room and lay across the bed. Before her head hit the mattress, the fresh tears were rolling down her face. How was she going to make it through the day? She had already pushed Pierson away because of her idiotic statement. A statement that she wished with all her might she could take back. But she didn't need him around her if all he was going to do was offer reasons for her to believe Ryan was genuine. He didn't know Ryan.

It was 8:30 in the morning, and she was supposed to have Mikey downstairs by 11:30 to meet the chaperone, whom she had met the day before at Joshua's office. The chaperone and Mikey would meet with Ryan and then she would meet them back downstairs at 5:30 that evening. Theresa had asked if she could send Mikey's nanny along, but they had refused. She trusted Danielle and would have gladly paid her extra for working on Sundays.

Her cellphone rang, causing her to jump. She looked at the caller ID and saw Amanda's name.

"Hello," she answered.

"Hello, dear," Amanda said cheerfully. "How are you feeling this morning?"

"Not any better, I'm afraid. Regardless of how I want to believe with all my heart that this will be a good experience for Mikey, I know that this is setting him up for disappointment. And there isn't a damn thing I can do about it."

"Theresa, listen to me. Your father passed away before you were old enough to really enjoy the small amount of time you had with him. And you know that he was a good man because of the stories your grandmother told you. He was a wonderful man. I loved him with all my heart. But ask yourself this question. Even if you had never been told anything about him, and even if he wasn't so good a person, wouldn't you have wanted to have some kind of relationship with him?"

Theresa remained silent.

"Ryan might not be a good person. He might have been a horrible husband, but the only one who can show Mikey that he is a terrible father is Ryan. Sometimes in life, we have to let the ones we love experience disappointment. It's the only way for them to learn. Mikey's not a dumb kid, not by a long shot. He will know sooner or later whether a relationship with Ryan is what he thought it would be."

"I hope that you're right, because I will kill Ryan before I let him hurt my son."

"Don't talk like that. We need to keep this positive. We will pray for the best. People do change. You're living proof of that."

"But he's not people. Ryan's the devil," Theresa commented.

"Well, I'm sure that at one time, right after I left, your father probably thought the same of me."

"Oh, no. That was different," Theresa said, trying to comfort Amanda. "You were trying to protect him and your son. You thought that Thorne and Daddy would have a better life without you around. And who knows if the marriage could have survived. Most interracial marriages didn't back then."

"It's okay. I came to terms with what I did a long time ago. And he forgave me a long time ago. The only thing I would have done differently was find my son, my children, sooner. Baby, you can't let this consume you. For Mikey's sake, you really have to pull it together. I'll come over and sit with you once Mikey leaves."

"Okay. Thanks, Mom."

"Have you talked to Pierson yet?"

"No."

"You need to. I think you owe him an apology. I don't know about you, but it was very uncomfortable for the rest of us to have him sitting so far away from the group."

"I'm not ready to deal with that right now."

"Well, you'd better think real hard on this. I personally believe he has proven himself to be a trustworthy, honorable man who loves your son. You're going to lose the perfect man for driving yourself sick over one you already know is not."

Theresa let out a long breath. "What are you talking about?"

"Pierson. A good man. I don't know too many men who would have come to watch Mikey play, even though the two of you were mad at and not speaking to each other."

"Well, did you notice that Mikey's father wasn't there at all? He finally got what he wanted and doesn't need to show outward support to his son any longer."

"Maybe the man was busy."

"No, he wasn't."

"Theresa, aside from all of that. I just told you the same thing that Pierson told you before you put him out of the house and stopped whatever was building between you. Why was it so easy to hear the same from me just a minute ago?"

"I don't know. I guess because it wasn't fresh. I've had a couple of days to think about what's going on."

"Let me tell you something. You cover chitterlings with vinegar, not gravy."

Theresa looked at the phone. *What?* She hated when older people used metaphors that she didn't understand.

"Are you going to explain that?"

"You think about it, and I'll see what you come up with later. I love you. Kiss my grandson for me."

"Love you, too," Theresa replied as she hung up the phone.

No matter how slowly Theresa moved around her house she couldn't make time move any slower. Before she knew it, she was looking at her watch, and it was 10 o'clock. Mikey hadn't wasted any time getting dressed when she told him to do so. And although his excitement was nauseating to Theresa, she forced herself to remain positive even when she thought she would break down and cry.

His excitement beamed in his eyes as the elevator moved downward until it reached the garage level of the building. When they got to the garage, Mrs. Tallons was already waiting, to Theresa's dismay. She had informed the security officers of Mrs. Tallons's impending arrival, but had hoped that the woman wouldn't show.

The older, gray-haired woman got out of the car with a smile on her face and greeted them cheerfully. Theresa wasn't wearing a smile at all, not until it was time for her to say goodbye to her son. For his sake, she plastered a fake smile across her face and wished him a good day. Once he was securely in the back seat of the car, Mrs. Tallons turned to Theresa.

"Don't worry, Mrs. Philips. I know it's hard the first time, but it will get easier. I'll meet you back here at 5:30."

Theresa didn't respond, not even when Mrs. Tallons gently squeezed her elbow for comfort. She just kept watching her son. His excitement was growing, and in that moment, Theresa realized that Amanda had been right. Try as she might, there was no way for her to shield him from the world or the pain in it. There were some things that he would have to find out on his own. She just hoped that Ryan was sincere about wanting to know his son.

As soon as Mrs. Tallons pulled off, a familiar blue Nissan Altima pulled into the parking lot and stopped in front of her. Theresa let out a sigh of relief when she saw that it was Amanda. She had dreaded having to go back upstairs by herself.

"Perfect timing," Theresa said, after bending down to the window.

"I tried to get here sooner. Let me park in my spot, and I'll be right over," Amanda replied. Amanda was over at the Philips Corporation Building often with her son living in the penthouse. If it were up to Thorne, she'd be living with him, but although they had just found each other about six months ago, Amanda realized that her son was a grown man with a life. No matter what Thorne thought, the last thing he needed was his mother sharing his quarters. She was quite content in her small rancher.

But this time, her daughter needed her; "adopted" daughter, but there was no difference. Theresa and Michael had been her heart and joy just as her son was over the past months, and she was proud that they had taken her as their mother, too.

Ryan had to admit that he was a little excited about having his son to himself, except for the chaperone. He had sat up all night making plans about how to spend the day with his son. It wasn't going to be hard to rid himself of the older lady that served as chaperone. A frown crossed his brow. A chaperone. The notion was ridiculous in itself. He was a grown-ass man. He didn't need a chaperone to watch him spend time with his own child.

The irony of the situation didn't escape him. Ryan might not need a chaperone, but Mikey did. Wasn't he planning to use his son to extort money from a family he despised? If he couldn't get it just by being Mikey's father, he would get it another way. He was tired of struggling to pay bills and staving off men wanting to break his body parts while the Philips family lived like royalty.

Lying on his back and looking up at the ceiling, Ryan wondered how different his life might have been if he had tried a little harder in his marriage to Theresa. Maybe he should have showed her that he loved her instead of thinking that telling her so was enough. She had probably never believed a word he said because every time Ryan said that he loved her, she would almost catch him in the act of adultery. And it wasn't even that she didn't satisfy him. He just knew how much she loved him and figured that he had her and she would never leave him.

He had to admit that Theresa was a good woman. She was loyal, and she had stood beside him even against her own family. He tried to figure out when everything between them went wrong. He loved her, but he had resented her for some reason. No matter how hard she'd tried to be a regular person, Ryan could see through to her high-breeding, her higher education, and her larger bank account, which she was unable to touch because of him.

Getting out of his bed, Ryan stretched, kicked Mollie's jeans out of his way, and walked to the bathroom. He glanced back at her nude body as she turned in her sleep and decided that once he relieved himself, he would wake her. But then he looked out his window to the street below and what he saw disturbed him.

At first, he thought his eyes were playing tricks on him, but they weren't. His old mentor was walking down the street carrying a newspaper and a cup of coffee. What was he doing out there? Was it just a coincidence? Or had Thorne hired him to follow Ryan, and if so, how long had he been watching him? The man must be getting old, Ryan thought as he slowly shut the blind, then opened it only slightly to peer out. He would have never put himself in the position of being seen before, but it was early in the morning, and Coby probably thought Ryan was still asleep.

This was something that Ryan was going to have to handle right away. He was too close to the prize to let it fall apart now. Ryan watched him for a few more minutes, then went to the bathroom and dressed. He went into his office and removed the small handgun from his desk and went outside.

When he came back inside, he slid into bed, gently tapping Mollie on her shoulder.

Ryan was at the park an hour early. He wanted to have a look around and make sure that his plans couldn't be interrupted. He found the perfect place in the park that would take him out of the chaperone's vision for a minute, providing she stayed a few steps away to give them minimal privacy. Just far enough away for him to get his son out of there. He moved his car closer to that area and waited. Today was going to have to be the day. Because of Coby, he probably wasn't going to get another chance. He had removed the files and pictures of himself and Mikey from Coby's car, but it wouldn't take long for the police to put two and two together.

When Mikey and Mrs. Tallons arrived, Ryan was sitting on the park bench. He rose and smiled, mustering up all the fatherly love he could. And to his surprise, Ryan found that it wasn't that hard. Mikey walked towards him with love in his eyes for a man that he didn't know. But it wasn't the man that he was seeing, it was the idea.

Ryan realized that Mikey didn't know him at all. He was happy just to have a father, not that Ryan was his father. Something tugged at Ryan's heart. Theresa had been able to give Mikey everything in the world, except his father. And the boy needed his father. At that moment, Ryan decided that he was going to take Mikey with him. He was going to get the jewels, and he was going to have his son.

"Mikey," he said, outstretching his arms for a big hug, which Mikey willingly provided. "How you been, my man?"

"I'm fine," Mikey said. He was with his father. "This is Mrs. Tallons. She said that she has to stay with us."

"Yeah, I know. But that's okay. We're still going to have lots of fun." Ryan stood and greeted Mrs. Tallons. "Thank you so much. I really appreciate you taking time out to do this."

"It's my job. So I'll just be a few feet away. I'll try to give you as much privacy as possible, but you do realize that I have to keep a watchful eye. In any case, I'll probably be coming with you only for a month or two. Then when I report back to the court, they will decide if I'm still needed or not. So, you two, go about your business. The park isn't that crowded, so this should be simple."

"Thanks. We'll be right around here first. I want to talk to my son and get to know him better. Then I thought we'd walk to the aquarium, if that's okay?"

"That will be fine."

Ryan and Mikey walked away from Mrs. Tallons, not far, but far enough that she didn't hear their conversation. They sat on another bench.

"So Mikey, tell me about yourself. What do you like to do?"

"Um, I like basketball and video games, but my mom only lets me play them a little bit."

"That's smart. You know too many video games dull your brain."

"That's what she says. I'm good at math, too. Really good. Uncle Michael says that I'm almost smarter than him. And he's really smart."

"Good. So when you get older, what do you want to be?" Ryan thought that he would say a policeman, fireman, even a cowboy, like most young boys his age.

"I'm hoping to become an environmental economist or a forensic scientist, but I think Uncle Thorne has hopes of me running the corporation one day."

Ryan just looked at him. He said it so nonchalantly that Ryan knew he was serious. What were they doing to his kid? Who says things like that when they're nine years old?

"Well, it's good that you have thought that far ahead. You're a smart kid, Mikey, and I know that you can be anything that you want to be." Wow, Ryan thought, that sounded fatherly. But why shouldn't it? He was the boy's father. "And I heard that you got great grades in school."

"Yeah, Mom is going to let me go to Welshire Academy this year so I can be closer to home. I didn't like being all the way in Texas."

"Texas?"

"That's where my school was last year, but now I'm staying in Louisiana."

"Good, then we can spend a lot of time together." Ryan didn't want to pry, but he had been dying to ask this question. "So, what about your mom's boyfriend? Do you like him?" Kids tended to be the best source of information. If you asked the right question, you usually got all the answers you needed.

"They don't go together anymore, I don't think. Mr. Pierson hasn't been to the house in a couple of days. And he was at my game, but they didn't sit together. I like Mr. Pierson, and I know she likes him a lot."

She liked him a lot. Ryan felt a twitch start in his left eye, but he remained quiet and let Mikey finish.

"He took me to work with him and showed me how to take off a tire and do an oil change. It was fun. I think I'd like to be a mechanic."

Now there was the nine-year-old that Ryan had been looking for.

"That's not a bad job to have."

"What do you do for a living?"

Ryan smiled. Nothing, he wanted to say, but instead he said, "I'm a private investigator. Do you know what that is?"

"Yeah, you find stuff for people."

"Exactly. As a matter of fact, I'm working on a big case right now. I'm trying to help a lady find her jewelry."

"She lost it? She should have a safe, like my mom does."

"I know your mom has a lot of jewelry. She always did."

"Yep," Mikey agreed. He heard the sound of the ice cream cart, and his ears perked right up.

Ryan smiled. There must be something about an ice cream cart's music that kids instantly associate with. "Would you like some ice cream, Mikey?"

"Yes, please."

"Come on, let's get it." He signaled to Mrs. Tallons that they were walking to the cart. She nodded, but didn't get up to follow because she could see the cart from where she sat. This is good, Ryan thought.

They got the ice cream and returned to their spot.

"Hey, Mikey, what if you helped me with my investigation?"

Immediately, Mikey was intrigued. "You mean be your partner?"

"Exactly. It would be fun, father and son working together to solve a mystery."

"Okay."

"Okay. But we have to lose Mrs. Tallons because she won't understand private eye business. For some reason, girls aren't good at that kind of stuff."

"I bet my mom could be a private eye. She always finds out what I'm doing, even when I try to hide it."

"Well, moms are different, especially when it comes to their own kids. But when we go to the aquarium, we'll go out the side door and start working, okay? I don't have pictures of the jewels that I'm looking for, but I have a sketch of what they're supposed to look like. You might even have seen them before."

"Okay, but I haven't seen any jewels."

"Well, you just said that your mother had jewelry."

"Yeah, but she doesn't have that lady's jewelry." Mikey licked his ice cream cone innocently.

"You're right, but you've been around jewelry before so you can help me." Ryan had to be more careful. Mikey was a kid, but he wasn't a dumb kid. Ryan decided to change the subject while they waited for the aquarium to open. The aquarium usually attracted a lot of families on Sundays, and Ryan was hoping that the same held true today.

"So, you going to sit in the house for the rest of your life looking like a sour-patch kid? All you have to do is call, you know."

Danielle got no reply.

"I'm sure she's not in the best of moods right now. You know that Mikey goes to spend the day with Ryan soon?"

Pierson sat in the chair with his arms and legs crossed. He might have appeared to be ignoring the world, but Danielle knew he heard every word she said.

"Well, you can sit there and be stubborn all you want, but you're letting the best thing that ever happened to you run right out of your life. Me, I got a picnic date with Christopher. So, I'll see you later. I'm going to call Theresa and see how she's doing. Do you want me to tell her anything?"

He stayed quiet. If Theresa wanted to see him, she was damn sure going to call him first. There was no need for her to react the way she had. Pierson had done nothing over the last few weeks but show her support, encouragement, and maybe even love, and just because he said something that she didn't like or want to hear, she was able to push him away. Well, maybe that was how it should be.

He stood and watched his sister pull out of the driveway. One thing Theresa had done, he had to admit, was transform his sister into the woman she had become. Danielle had all but blossomed overnight under Theresa's wing. She was more confident, less angry, and eagerly approached her future.

Pierson had been doing the same thing, until he met Theresa alongside the roadway. Over the past few days, he couldn't count the number of times he had wished that he hadn't made that run and left it up to one of the workers instead. Maybe then he wouldn't be in this predicament.

CHAPTER 19

"What do you think of the class so far?" Amanda asked Theresa. She had finally gotten her off the subject of Mikey and Ryan. And as she glanced at her watch, Amanda realized it had only taken a little over two hours.

"I love it. Sorry I missed the last class."

"That's not a problem. I don't really have to do attendance. Most of my students can't wait to get into the class. If someone isn't there, I know there's a valid reason, and you had one."

"I just—"

"Michael has decided to take the class, too," Amanda quickly added, determined not to let the conversation veer back to Mikey and Ryan.

"He has? He didn't tell me that."

"Yes, I think with the baby coming he feels he needs to get better acquainted with his African-American ancestry. Said that he was going to talk Tamia into going with him. He thinks it will make them better parents. Maybe I shouldn't be telling you this. He didn't say it was confidential, but I got the feeling that it's one of the first times he has really opened up about his feelings. I don't want him to think that I would betray him in any way."

"Oh, I'm sure he wouldn't think that. I think it's good that he wants to attend the class. Maybe Thorne will, too, if he ever slows down enough. Of course, you could just make him come."

Amanda laughed. "Yes, I suppose he would do it if I asked, but then he wouldn't be learning for himself, would he?"

Just then, the elevator bell rant, indicating someone was coming. They were not surprised to see Thorne, Natalie, Michael and Tamia exit the elevator. Theresa was so glad to see her family. She had figured that they would be by sometime during the day. She got up and ran to Thorne, who held her close as she slowly began to break down again.

"Shhh, it's going to be all right, Theresa. He'll be back in a couple of hours."

"I know, but I just hate the idea of him even being around Ryan."

"Come on, let's sit down. Natalie, see what she has in the kitchen."

"I'll come with you," Tamia said. "We'll whip up a meal."

Michael and Thorne sat down next to Theresa after giving their mother a kiss.

"Theresa, have you spoken to Pierson, yet?" Michael asked. "Don't you think he'd want to be here?"

"He probably would, but no, I haven't called him and he hasn't called me," she answered.

"You do realize that you were wrong, right?" Thorne asked. "You need to call him and apologize."

"I know."

"And you need to do it sooner rather than later."

"I know."

Natalie and Tamia came back into the living room with a platter filled with sandwiches, chips, and drinks for everyone.

"Here, Theresa," Natalie said, passing her a plate. "You need to eat something. You've been so worried this past week that your face looks pale. You haven't been taking care of yourself." She passed one to Amanda, then to Thorne as she sat down next to him.

"Thanks, Natalie. You're right. I'm worrying myself sick for no reason. Y'all are starting to make me feel like a fool."

"Oh, baby," Amanda said, pulling Theresa into her arms. "You're a mother. Worrying is what we do best." She looked at Thorne. "Be it right or wrong, you love your son, and the decisions you make are based on that love. Now let's eat so that you'll be in a good mood when he gets home. And remember to listen to his new adventure with open ears and a smile."

"You're right. I will."

They were almost finished with their meal when Theresa's phone rang. She looked at Michael and asked him to answer it for her. He quickly ran to the kitchen.

"Thorne, come here," Michael yelled from the kitchen.

Just as Thorne stood, his cellphone rang. He looked down at the number, but continued to walk out of the room.

"What's up?" Theresa called as he walked away.

"I don't know. Michael, what are you up to now?" Thorne asked as he walked into the kitchen. But they stayed in there for a moment, never talking above a whisper.

"Have you heard from Coby?" Michael asked.

"No. And I'm wondering why not." They both walked into the living room with serious looks on their faces.

"What is it?" Theresa said, worried confusion flashing across her face.

"Um, Theresa," Thorne started. "That was security. The police are on their way up. It seems that—"

"Oh, my God. I knew it. I knew it." Tears flooded her eyes as her worst thoughts flooded her mind.

"Now, you need to stay calm. The chaperone called in and reported that she lost Ryan and Michael at the aquarium. She tried to find them, then got the security at the aquarium to help her, but they couldn't. Security reported that an unauthorized side door had been opened. The chaperone called the police. She is with them now."

"Where's Mikey?" Theresa asked.

Thorne was quiet.

Theresa stood, followed by Amanda, Natalie, and Tamia.

"Where is he, Thorne?"

"They don't know."

"Oh," Theresa said, collapsing to the sofa in a fit of tears. All of the women gathered around her for support.

Thorne ran his hand through his thick mane of hair. He and Michael looked at each other for a brief moment before Michael began to pace helplessly. Thorne stood by the elevator with his arms crossed, waiting for the police to arrive.

"Hello, Mr. Philips," Detective Miller said. He was very familiar with the Philips family from past dealings and knew of the family's extensive philanthropy and business dealings. He extended his hand. "It's unfortunate that we meet again under such circumstances. I want you to know that we are doing everything we can to find your nephew. Detective Cassell also insisted on coming along. She states that she knows the family."

"Yes," Throne agreed, hugging Sandra, who was in a relationship with Natalie's brother. Then Sandra went over to Theresa and the others. "She's part of the family. Listen, Detective," Thorne said, leading the rest of the officers to the kitchen, along with Michael. "I know that it might have been against some rule or another, but I hired—"

"We both did," Michael interjected. He wasn't going to let his brother take all the blame, as Thorne was so apt to doing.

"Right. We hired a local private investigator to keep an eye on our nephew. We thought it would be good to have another pair of eyes on him besides the chaperone. Our nephew is worth quite a bit of money."

Detective Miller looked at both men for a brief moment. "That explains a lot," he said. "A private investigator named Cobierius Donovan was found dead today around 12:30 p.m."

"Damn, that's him," Thorne said.

The officer continued. "He was found in his car with a gunshot through his chest. Close range, small caliber handgun. Bullet went straight through."

"Ryan must have seen him and realized he was being followed."

"So you think that your ex-brother-in-law is a murderer as well as a kidnapper?"

"Wouldn't be surprised," Michael said. "We know that he owes some pretty mean people a lot of money. Maybe he's trying to use Mikey to get it. He knows that we'll do anything for Mikey. He'll probably be calling soon."

"Well, we've already contacted the FBI. They should be here soon. They'll take over the investigation. It's usually policy to wait twenty-four hours before declaring a kidnapping, but because this is a sensitive matter in the eyes of the captain and the mayor, we're not taking any chances, Mr. Philips."

"I appreciate that," Thorne replied, knowing that what Detective Miller meant to say was 'because you are the Philipses and you donate large sums of money to the mayor's campaign and the policeman's fund, we're going to get right on it.'

Two hours later, the FBI had arrived, along with Joshua and Stephanie, who had been called at Theresa's request.

"Theresa, I am so sorry. I should have tried harder," Joshua said as soon as he saw his cousin's disheveled appearance.

"It's not your fault, Josh. There was nothing you could have done. Ryan had something to do with that, too. And if it's the last thing I do, I'm going to find out what and have that judge removed from the bench for putting my son in this situation."

"Well, please count me in." He kissed her cheek and went into the kitchen to where the FBI set up and where Thorne and Michael were.

Thorne was on his cellphone when the house phone rang a little before 8 p.m. The room went silent.

"I'll see you when you get here," Thorne said into his cell. "I'll answer it." He moved into the living room to sit next to Theresa, who gladly gave him control.

She knew that she wouldn't be able to answer, let alone talk, her nerves were so unraveled.

"Ryan," Thorne began, "where is my nephew?"

"My son is right here with me. We're having a good time together."

"Why are you doing this?"

"Where is my wife?"

"Your wife?" Thorne questioned.

Everyone else in the room was listening to the speakerphone. They looked at Theresa.

"Ryan, how about we stop playing games and you tell me why you're doing this? What do you want?"

"Okay, let's do that. I know that Theresa is listening. You should have never kept my son away from me,

Theresa. He's such a good kid. I would have loved watching him grow. But since you did, I really can't feel as fatherly towards him as I should. Maybe that's why I'm able to use him like this. If you hadn't divorced me, we wouldn't be going through this right now."

"So it's her fault that you were a no-good husband, a cheat, an abuser, and now a murderer?"

Theresa's hand reached for Thorne's arm. She didn't want him to push Ryan too far. God only knew what he would do to her son. And Thorne's anger was visibly growing.

"Oh, so they've found Coby already, huh? Now that does change things, doesn't it?"

"You do realize that you're not going to get away with this, don't you? We know it's you. Let's make this simple," Thorne said. "I don't care about anything except getting my nephew home to his mother. If you give Mikey back, I won't do anything, but if you don't, you know that we'll track you down like the dog you are, right?"

"I know that you will, but once I have what I want, you'll never have to worry about me again."

"Good. So what is it that you want this time, Ryan? Money to pay off Johnny D? Enough to get you out of the country?"

"I want the one thing that might be hardest for you to part with," Ryan answered.

Thorne and Michael both looked at their sister. She was the only thing that he could be talking about. He wanted to trade Mikey for Theresa. It didn't make sense, but then again, it did. Having Theresa back would probably validate whatever sick fantasy was in his mind, but what he would do to her was unimaginable.

"You think that having my sister will make things easier on you?" Thorne asked. "You hurt her once before. Do you think we'll let you do that again?"

"I'll go," Theresa whispered. "Anything for Mikey."

"What I want from you are the Umergodia jewels. They're worth more than any amount of money you'd give me and less trouble than your sister would be. And I want them tonight or Mikey and me are hitting the road tomorrow. And you'll never see him again."

"The Umergodia jewels?"

"I'll call you back in one hour to tell you where to drop them off," Ryan said and hung up the phone.

"Did you get a trace?" Detective Miller asked.

The FBI agent shook his head. "He must have been using some kind of block. I couldn't pinpoint a location."

"So, what are these jewels that he's talking about?" Detective Miller asked.

"Joshua, get your father on the phone, please," Theresa said.

"The Umergodia jewels are family heirlooms that were passed down to us," Thorne simply told the detective without going into details about the family's past. The fact that they were received through the family of their real African-American grandfather, Michael Morris, who was his grandmother's gardener, was left out. The jewels were still being held at Joshua's father's office. Howard Connor was their grandmother's first cousin and their most trusted lawyer.

"He's on his way with the jewels, Thorne," Joshua answered after a few minutes. "Thomas is bringing him in. I wonder how Ryan even knew about the jewels."

"Fortunately, he believes that they mean as much to us as they do to him," Theresa commented. "As far as I'm concerned, Mikey is the only jewel that I have, and that bastard has stolen him."

"Don't worry. We'll get Mikey back. I doubt very seriously if Ryan is stupid enough to hurt him."

"I know that Mikey is worried and wondering why he hasn't come back home yet. He knew that he was supposed to be back home at 5:30." Tears started to fall from Theresa's eyes again. "I swear, if he does anything to my baby—"

Just then the elevator chimed. When the doors opened, Pierson stepped out. He searched the room frantically until his eyes rested on Theresa. Danielle was right beside him, and Christopher was standing next to her, looking slightly uncomfortable.

Pierson's face was solemn, devoid of emotion, until he saw the pain in Theresa's eyes. The activity around him seemed to fade away as she stood and rushed into his arms.

Theresa didn't care who else was in the crowded apartment. All that mattered once she saw Pierson was the fact that he was there. She somehow felt a huge burden come off her shoulders, a sense that everything was going to be all right.

"Pierson, I'm so sorry. Please forgive me," she said half into his shirt as she buried her face deep into his chest.

Pierson bent down to kiss her forehead. "It's okay, everything's going to be okay. Let's walk into the bedroom real quick." He led the way, speaking as he passed Amanda and the others. Theresa followed willingly, hoping that he would come up with an idea to get her son back.

"How are you doing?" he asked as soon as they got into the bedroom. "Have you eaten?"

"Um, yeah, I had a bite earlier," she replied, wiping at her eyes.

"Listen, I owe you an apology. I shouldn't have downplayed this whole thing the way I did. You were concerned from the beginning, and I thought you were just being overprotective. What I should have done was be supportive, regardless of what I thought. But we can forget all of that."

"I just want Mikey back. I shouldn't have let him go."

"Then you would have been in contempt of court and in jail. And Ryan would still have Mikey." He hugged her again. "It's going to be fine. You have all of those officers working for you. Mikey will be home before you know it."

"I hope you're right."

"Theresa," he said, pushing her back and looking straight into her eyes, "you have to believe it."

"I do," she whispered. "I do."

"Okay, let's get back out there," Pierson said. Taking hold of her hand, he led her to the living room. "Excuse me, Natalie," he said, once he went back into the room. "Could you, Danielle, and Tamia figure out how many people we have in here and order some pizza, subs, and drinks? I think this might be a long night, and Theresa needs to eat something."

"Sure, Pierson," Natalie replied. She'd had the same idea.

Pierson passed her his credit card, and she accepted it although she had no intention of using it. She knew that the order was going to be large. Instead, she would use Thorne's card. But she took his because she understood the way a man's mind worked, and she not going to disrespect him.

Once they went into the bedroom to order the food, she gave his card to Danielle. "I'll use Thorne's card. This is going to be a pretty large order."

Danielle took it. "Should we order a sandwich platter instead of subs? Different kinds of sandwiches and have the toppings put on the side because we don't know what people like?"

"Smart," Tamia agreed.

In the living room, Pierson kissed Theresa on her cheek after she sat back down next to Amanda. He then walked into the kitchen to find out what the latest information was.

"Thorne," he said, reaching his hand out, "thanks for calling me."

"Well, I knew that you would want to be here, and honestly, Michael and I both thought that you should be."

"So, what do we have?" Pierson looked directly at the detective in charge.

"And you are?"

"I am former detective Pierson Brooks of the Philadelphia Police. I am also Mrs. Philips's—"

"Yeah, he's Theresa's man and a member of the family," Thorne interrupted, "so tell him what's going on." This was not a time to be sizing each other up. It was time to get his nephew back, and Thorne was quickly losing his patience.

The house phone rang again. This time Theresa was the one who answered it.

"Ryan?"

"Hey, love. How are you doing?"

"Not too well, Ryan. Where is Mikey?" she asked, her strength growing when Pierson came into the living room and sat down next to her.

"He's fine."

"Can I speak to him, please?"

"You know that I won't hurt him."

"I know. I just want to hear his voice."

"Theresa, I explained to him that you wanted him to stay the night with me so that we could spend more time together. We've been playing video games and eating pizza. The boy has a monster appetite. He must get that from me."

"Ryan, can I please speak to him?"

"No, not right now. Theresa, I loved you. You know that?"

"Whatever you say, Ryan."

"No," he screamed. "Not whatever I say. I said that I loved you. You have no idea how much. You just weren't willing to let me be my own man. You wanted to control everything, just like that grandmother of yours."

"Okay, Ryan. You're right. When can I get my son back?" She had no idea where he was going with his conversation, but needed him to stay focused. She wanted to know where her son was. That was all that mattered, not his feelings for her or vice versa.

"Is your new boyfriend nearby? He's probably listening with everyone else in the room. I know that he was a policeman and had an interesting military career, too. So, that's who you want to be with?"

"Yes," Theresa answered without hesitation. "Now, can I speak to Mikey?"

"No. Mr. Brooks, it seems that you are taking the only things that I've ever cared about in my life. My wife and my boy."

Pierson didn't answer. He, along with everyone else, wondered where Ryan's conversation was headed.

"Theresa, have you readied the jewels yet? It's time for me to be going on my way. I want the jewels delivered to me at the abandoned pier, building number seventeen. Once I have the jewels, I will give Mikey back to you. But please don't make me do anything foolish. I don't want anything to happen to my son. Make sure that the police stay outside the gate, or something crazy might happen. That wouldn't be good for any of us, would it?"

His voice was raspy, scary. He sounded as if on the verge of a breakdown.

"Detective Brooks, I know you can hear me. Since you want to be involved with my family, let's just put you in the middle of everything. I want you to bring the jewels to me. It would be useless for me to tell you to come alone, wouldn't it? So you don't have to, but you better be the only one coming onto the premises. The building is close enough to the gate, but far enough for me to track any movement on the outside."

Ryan had started looking for the perfect place to play out the last leg of his plan as soon as he knew he was going to leave town with the jewels himself. But he still had two goals that he was determined to meet. He was already wanted for murder, and one more wouldn't make too much of a difference.

"Ryan?" Theresa asked.

"Be here in two hours, Brooks."

"Ryan?"

The phone disconnected.

"Pierson, you can't go in there alone," Theresa said. "He's going to try to kill you. I know it."

"The operative word is try. If this is what we have to do to get Mikey back, then that's what we'll do."

"Pierson," Thorne said. "You know that he's not working with a full deck right now. This is dangerous. He's already killed one man today."

"Once a policeman, always a policeman, huh?" Detective Miller asked, coming forward with a bullet-proof vest and a gun belt complete with an automatic firearm.

Pierson stood and pulled off his shirt without question. He pulled the vest over his head until it rested on his shoulders. "Apparently so." He put on his shirt and then strapped the gun belt around his waist.

"I have orders to get you sworn in as a New Orleans policeman immediately. Come into the kitchen. I have the captain and the mayor both on the line. They want to speak with you."

Pierson followed them.

Howard and his son arrived with the jewels at the same time that the food came. He walked into the back room with Michael, Thorne, Pierson, Detective Miller, two FBI agents and his sons.

"Gentlemen, please shut the door."

"Howard," Thorne started, "we don't care about the jewels. This is all about Mikey."

"I understand, Thorne. I've brought all three pieces," he stated laying all three out. The room grew silent as Howard laid out all three pieces of the beautifully crafted solid gold jewelry encrusted with rubies, emeralds, and diamonds.

"Wow," one of the FBI agents said. "This is what he wants? I can understand why. They must be worth a fortune."

"Mikey is our fortune," Michael answered.

"I'll try to come out of there with Mikey and the jewels, Thorne, but if Ryan is as unstable as he sounds, I doubt very seriously if he's going to let me go with both easily."

"Pierson, I appreciate you doing this. And when you come out, you know you have approval from both of us to marry our sister."

"Well, if I come back, I'd appreciate that."

"You know that we wouldn't be too upset if he doesn't come out of there, right?" Michael asked.

Thorne looked at Michael.

"I mean, do whatever you have to," Michael said, hunching his shoulders. He looked back at Thorne. "What?"

Thorne just shook his head. Sometimes, what's in your head shouldn't come out of your mouth.

CHAPTER 20

Ryan was not sure how he was going to pull off getting out of the city with both the jewels and his son, but that was his intent. He and Ryan had spent a wonderful day together, and he found himself liking his son very much. But this realization only made his anger multiply. He would have been a good father to Mikey if he had been given the chance. Over the last six years, he'd missed out on a lifetime of Mikey's growth. And now he was a virtual stranger to his own kid, and to add insult to injury, he had been told that he needed to be babysat in order for them to get to know each other again.

Once they got back to the warehouse, Ryan took him up to the apartment on the top level that he had prepared weeks before. He lied and told Michael that it was his apartment. He had it fully stocked with food, a television, bed, bathroom, and all types of video games in preparation for this moment. He used the money that he owed to Johnny D, thinking that he had time to steal the jewels and rebuild the money before Johnny D sent Harp after him. He had been wrong, but the money he had spent was nothing compared to what he would get back once the exchange was done.

He had an unmarked vehicle parked at the other end of the warehouse and a golf cart hidden to take him to it.

All he had to do was keep them at bay long enough to get to his car. He could do that by staying on the phone with Theresa and leading her to the wrong place to pick up Mikey. Having Pierson drop off the jewels was a bonus. He was not going to let Pierson and Theresa build a life together. If he couldn't have Theresa, why would he willingly let another man have her?

He glanced at his watch.

"Mikey? Time to get in the tub. I put some pajamas in there for you. Do you need me to help you?"

"No. I can do it myself. My mom doesn't help me. Can I have some ice cream after I bathe?"

"Sure, but that's it. You've been eating all day. I don't want you to get sick. And I don't want your mother to be mad at me."

"I should call her and say good night," Mikey said. He had wondered earlier why his mother had decided to let him stay the night. Mikey knew that she hadn't been thrilled about him seeing his father at all. What had changed her mind?

"That might not be a good idea. She said that Mr. Pierson had asked her out on a date. I think they are going to make up."

The smile that came to Mikey's face made Ryan instantly mad, but he hid it well. Instead of throwing something across the room, he gripped the back of the chair in front of him tightly until he had put a cap on his anger and Mikey was out of sight.

Ryan glanced at his watch again. Soon.

Theresa hugged and kissed Pierson one more time after they put the wire under his shirt. Then he went to talk to the FBI agents one last time. They were outside the gates at the abandoned pier where Ryan had said to meet him. There were so many police cars that it looked just like a scene out of a *Die Hard* movie. Police lights reflected off the surroundings, and officers ran around hectically to get to their positions.

Helplessly, she stood next to her brothers and the rest of her family and waited. Everybody seemed to jump when her cellphone rang. Theresa nearly dropped the phone in trying to get to it so fast.

"Hello," she said.

"Theresa, pass the phone to your boyfriend," Ryan said. She did as she was told. They had expected him to call Thorne's phone, which was the number they'd given him. Walking over to Pierson, she gave him the phone.

"Pierson, it's Ryan," she said.

"Ryan," Pierson said into the phone, "I'm ready."

"Good. Come on in. Walk into the left end of the building. Slowly. I'm watching you. And make sure that you're not followed. My son's life depends on it." Pierson slowly lowered the phone from his ear.

"What did he say?" Theresa asked.

"Nothing. He wants me to walk into the building. Nobody follow me," he said. Then looking at Theresa, he continued, "I'll see you when we get back."

She reached up and hugged him again, "Thank you, Pierson."

"Thank me when I get back," he replied, and then began to walk the hundred feet to the large building. He saw Danielle move closer to Theresa out of the corner of his eye. Both women were crying.

"Mr. Brooks. Come on in," Ryan said from the top of the stairwell. He walked down slowly as Pierson entered the building with his hands in the air. A small black duffle bag dangled from one hand. Although the lighting in the warehouse was low, he could see the tall, bulky man clearly from the lights in the background. "It seems as if you brought the whole neighborhood with you."

"Everybody's interested in seeing you in handcuffs."

"And you're going to arrest me, huh? You know, you got a lot of balls, Pierson Brooks. First, you try to take my wife from me, then my son, and now you think you're going to take me to jail. But I have a gun pointed at your head. I could shoot you now and put an end to all of my misery."

"Do you think that killing me is going to solve your problems? I didn't take your wife. You pushed her aside years ago, remember?"

"Theresa Philips will always be my wife!" Ryan yelled.

Until she's my wife, Pierson wanted to say, but he knew better than to antagonize Ryan. The man was already standing on very unstable ground. "Ryan, I only came in here to exchange the jewels for Mikey. So, where is he?"

Pierson looked around the room, hoping Ryan would think he was looking for Mikey. But Pierson was looking for cover. He had a strong feeling that this was going to get serious real soon, and he needed to make sure he had a place to fend Ryan off, just in case it got ugly.

"Mikey's not going anywhere. I've decided that I like having my son around. He's a pretty special kid. I guess I could say that he took after his old man, but you wouldn't believe me, would you?"

"Not by your actions of late, no. Why do you want to hurt Theresa so much?"

"I don't want to hurt Theresa. I love Theresa."

"But you want to take her child, kill the man she loves." Pierson knew he shouldn't have said that.

Ryan practically ran down the next few steps. The look in his eyes turned instantly murderous. "The man she loves, huh?"

"Isn't that why you wanted me to bring the jewels? You want to kill me so that Theresa and I can't be together."

"Just shut up and throw the bag over here. I'll deal with you in a minute."

Pierson didn't drop the bag.

"How did you even know about the jewels, Ryan? They were kept a close family secret."

Ryan hunched his shoulders. "I guess I could lie and say that I was that good of a private investigator, but we both know that's not true. I was hired by a distant cousin of the Philips family who felt that the jewels should have gone to her son, not Thorne."

"So, you decided to steal the jewels for yourself? What an honorable guy," Pierson said, looking at him disapprovingly.

"Don't look at me like that. Like you're judging me. You don't know a damn thing about me."

"I know that you're a thief and a murderer, who is trying to use his own son to extort money."

"Money that should have been mine in the first place. I was married to Theresa, and she just pushed me to the side like I was nothing, cut me off without a dime."

"Didn't her grandmother give you money? Didn't you take it? I think that shows right there just how much you loved her."

"I didn't have any choice. If I hadn't taken that money, I wouldn't have gotten anything."

"Look, Ryan, I really don't give a damn about all of that. I'm only here to do one thing, and that's to get Mikey. So where is he? I'm not leaving here without him."

"You won't be leaving here at all if you don't throw that damn bag."

"Not without seeing Mikey first." Just then, Pierson heard a sound behind him. He turned around and saw a big, brawny guy running up from behind.

"Harp, no!" Ryan called out.

But it was too late. Harp dove on Pierson, and the two men tumbled across the ground. The duffle bag was thrown across the floor. Harp threw two hard punches that landed on Pierson's chin. Pierson threw hard hits back, but they didn't seem to affect Harp at all. Both men scrambled to their feet. Harp swung again, but Pierson managed to duck and connect with Harp's kidneys. Then he came back down with a quick left into Harp's throat. Harp fell to his knees, and Pierson kneed him in his head to knock the big fellow out.

Ryan had the duffle bag in his hand. He was about fifteen feet away from Pierson and about to run out the back of the warehouse. The golf cart wasn't far. He would have to leave Mikey there, but that was fine. With the money that he held in his hands, he could hire a hundred mercenaries to come back for Mikey if need be.

"Freeze!" Pierson yelled. "Ryan! Don't move."

"You going to shoot me, Pierson? Shoot Mikey's father? How much do you think he'll like you after that?"

"I don't want to shoot you, Ryan, but I want Mikey now. I can't let you leave without you giving him to me. Now!"

"Mr. Pierson?" Mikey said, coming down the steps. He had obviously been awakened by the noise. "What's going on?"

"Stay right there, Mikey," Pierson said calmly, pointing his finger at Mikey.

"Are you here with my mom?" Mikey asked. He had yet to notice that both men were carrying guns.

"Mikey, do me a favor and go back upstairs," Pierson said. He didn't take his eyes off Ryan who was inching his way back to the staircase. "Mikey, your mother's right outside. Please, go back upstairs for me."

"No, Mikey. Come here," Ryan said.

Mikey was confused. Not wanting to make either man upset, he decided not to move at all.

Ryan moved closer to his son. Pierson moved closer to Ryan. Both men still had their guns pointed at the other.

"Ryan, don't do it," Pierson pleaded. Ryan's best way out was to use his son as a shield. As he moved quickly toward Mikey, Ryan fired. Pierson felt the bullet pierce his upper arm.

Mikey ran up the stairs just in time to be out of his father's reach.

"Damn it, Mikey. You come back here," Ryan yelled.

Mikey kept running until he was back in the room. He locked the door behind him.

"Mikey!" Ryan yelled again. He didn't have time for this. He had to get to the other side of the pier. But if he couldn't have his son, neither would Pierson, he decided. "Well, I guess I might as well get some pleasure out of this. What do you think, Mr. Brooks? Are you ready to see that brother of yours again?"

Pierson lay completely still. He listened for Ryan's footsteps, waited until he heard him move closer.

Ryan stood over Pierson. He pointed the gun at him, and as he tightened his finger on the trigger, he heard a gunshot and felt a hot heat run through his stomach and up into his chest. As Ryan dropped to his knees, he fired his gun and then fell forward, dead.

Pierson laid still and tried to catch his breath. Just a few inches higher and more to the left and he would be dead. Instead he had taken another bullet in the same arm he'd already been shot in. He had used it to steady his aim at Ryan. He was losing blood fast and felt his eyes drifting close.

"Mikey?" he yelled. "Mikey!"

EPILOGUE

When his eyes opened, Pierson tried to moisten his dry mouth. His vision was still blurry, but he welcomed the straw that was placed between his lips. He strongly sipped at the cold apple juice to quench his thirst.

"He's getting better. He's still greedy."

"Danielle?" Pierson asked, trying to focus in on the voice he heard.

"Yeah, big brother. It's me. Stop acting like a baby. Wake up," she said.

He struggled to open his eyes and sit up, but the pain that shot through his left side stopped him cold.

"Ughhh," he whined.

"Lie still, Pierson," Theresa said. "You've been through a lot."

He turned his head to his left side, towards Theresa's voice. "Where's Mikey?" he asked, focusing on her face.

"I'm right here, Mr. Pierson," Mikey said cheerfully. Then more curiously, "Does it really hurt?"

Pierson looked down at his arm. It was tightly bandaged up and hanging high from some contraption attached to his hospital bed. "It hurts as bad as it looks, little man."

Theresa began to rub his head and cheek.

"I mean it really, really hurts," Pierson said.

Theresa bent down to place a kiss on his cheek. He smiled up at her.

"Oh, please," Danielle said. "Come on, Mikey. Let's go tell the others that he's up."

Once Mikey and Danielle left the room, Theresa moved to the other side of the bed. She held his right hand.

"Pierson, thank you so much for getting Mikey back for me."

"I'm not quite sure I can take the credit. Last thing I remember is lying on the floor, losing blood. And I remember Ryan saying something about a distant cousin of yours hiring him to get the jewels. That's how he knew about them."

"Yeah, well, don't worry about that right now. We'll have a meeting once you feel up to it and handle that business later."

"But if they think they should be the rightful owners of the jewels, they might try to come for them again."

"I'm just grateful for your help. Mikey said that you called his name so loud that he came out of the room. He saw that you, Ryan, and some other guy were lying on the floor. He saw the police lights outside and ran toward the cop cars."

"He's a smart kid, Theresa."

"I'm glad. I can't tell you how glad I was to see his little body sprint across that lot. I was fighting the cops to get to him. Of course, they couldn't hold Thorne back, so they ran after him. He grabbed Mikey up and ran him back to us. Then Mikey told us that he thought you and Ryan were dead. My heart just dropped."

Theresa kissed his hand.

"I was afraid that I had lost you. I don't ever want to feel that way again."

"You'll never lose me, Theresa. I'm not going anywhere."

Theresa bent forward and kissed him again. "Good. I was hoping that you would say that. Listen, the police have a couple of detectives outside that want to speak to you."

"I don't want to talk to anyone but you and my family."

"I think they want to offer you a permanent position at the station," Theresa teased.

"Then I definitely don't want to talk to them. Now I remember why I quit the force in the first place. I gotta ask you something."

Theresa paid close attention to him.

"Is Mikey all right? I mean, really?"

"He'll be fine. I am going to make an appointment with a child psychologist tomorrow, but he seems just fine. He knows that Ryan is dead, but he hasn't talked about it. Not yet, anyway."

"I just don't want him to hate me for killing his father."

"Mikey could never hate you. He loves you, Pierson," Theresa reassured him.

"No, I love that kid, and his mother's not bad, either," Pierson joked.

"I'm glad to hear that because his mother thinks you're pretty cool, too."

"Come here," Pierson said, pulling Theresa closer to the bed.

"I'm about as close to you as I can get. I don't want to hurt you, Pierson."

"I just survived two bullet wounds." He tried to move over. "Ow, ow, ow, get on up here."

"See, you're going to hurt yourself, and you want me to help you." Nevertheless, Theresa climbed on the hospital bed and lay next to him.

"So," he began, once she was settled next to him. "Theresa, I just had a life-altering experience. And I know that you're not supposed to make rash decisions around life-altering experiences, but I was wondering if you'd consider—"

"Hey, there he is," Michael said, opening the hospital door wide and making room for the rest of the family to enter. "The man of the hour, Superman's half brother."

Suddenly balloons and flowers filled the private hospital room as the crowd gathered and began extending their well wishes. Theresa left the bed, despite his protest, and Mikey quickly took her place.

"Later," he said, before she got too far away.

Theresa smiled and nodded her head. "Later."

ABOUT THE AUTHOR

Michele Sudler lives in the small East Coast town of Smyrna, Delaware. Busy raising her children, she finds time for her second passion, writing, in the evenings and on weekends. After attending Delaware State College, majoring in Business Administration, she continues to work in the corporate banking industry. Enrolling back in school, she currently is working hard on time management skills in order to balance family, work, and school.

Stolen Jewels is the second Philips family novel. *Stolen Memories* first introduced the Philips family in February 2008. The third novel in the Philips saga is in the works. Also, please be on the look-out for the author's previous novels. *Intentional Mistakes, One of these Days,* and *Waiting in the Shadows* are from the Avery family saga. *Three Doors Down,* the first novel dealing with the memorable Jarnette brothers, was released in September 2008. A second novel is in the works. *Best Foot Forward,* released in June 2009, introduced the interesting Perkins siblings.

Besides spending time with her children and writing, Michele enjoys playing and watching basketball, traveling, and reading. She would also love to hear what you think of her novels. Please send any comments to her email address: *micheleasudler@yahoo.com.*

2010 Mass Market Titles

January

Show Me The Sun
Miriam Shumba
ISBN: 978-158571-405-6
$6.99

Promises of Forever
Celya Bowers
ISBN: 978-1-58571-380-6
$6.99

February

Love Out Of Order
Nicole Green
ISBN: 978-1-58571-381-3
$6.99

Unclear and Present Danger
Michele Cameron
ISBN: 978-158571-408-7
$6.99

March

Stolen Jewels
Michele Sudler
ISBN: 978-158571-409-4
$6.99

Not Quite Right
Tammy Williams
ISBN: 978-158571-410-0
$6.99

April

Oak Bluffs
Joan Early
ISBN: 978-1-58571-379-0
$6.99

Crossing The Line
Bernice Layton
ISBN: 978-158571-412-4
$6.99

How To Kill Your Husband
Keith Walker
ISBN: 978-158571-421-6
$6.99

May

The Business of Love
Cheris F. Hodges
ISBN: 978-158571-373-8
$6.99

Wayward Dreams
Gail McFarland
ISBN: 978-158571-422-3
$6.99

June

The Doctor's Wife
Mildred Riley
ISBN: 978-158571-424-7
$6.99

Mixed Reality
Chamein Canton
ISBN: 978-158571-423-0
$6.99

2010 Mass Market Titles (continued)
July

Blue Interlude
Keisha Mennefee
ISBN: 978-158571-378-3
$6.99

Always You
Crystal Hubbard
ISBN: 978-158571-371-4
$6.99

Unbeweavable
Katrina Spencer
ISBN: 978-158571-426-1
$6.99

August

Small Sensations
Crystal V. Rhodes
ISBN: 978-158571-376-9
$6.99

Let's Get It On
Dyanne Davis
ISBN: 978-158571-416-2
$6.99

September

Unconditional
A.C. Arthur
ISBN: 978-158571-413-1
$6.99

Swan
Africa Fine
ISBN: 978-158571-377-6
$6.99$6.99

October

Friends in Need
Joan Early
ISBN:978-1-58571-428-5
$6.99

Against the Wind
Gwynne Forster
ISBN:978-158571-429-2
$6.99

That Which Has Horns
Miriam Shumba
ISBN:978-1-58571-430-8
$6.99

November

A Good Dude
Keith Walker
ISBN:978-1-58571-431-5
$6.99

Reye's Gold
Ruthie Robinson
ISBN:978-1-58571-432-2
$6.99

December

Still Waters...
Crystal V. Rhodes
ISBN:978-1-58571-433-9
$6.99

Burn
Crystal Hubbard
ISBN: 978-1-58571-406-3
$6.99

Other Genesis Press, Inc. Titles

Other Genesis Press, Inc. Titles (continued)

Other Genesis Press, Inc. Titles (continued)

Other Genesis Press, Inc. Titles (continued)

Other Genesis Press, Inc. Titles (continued)

Other Genesis Press, Inc. Titles (continued)

Secret Library Vol. 1	Nina Sheridan	$18.95
Secret Library Vol. 2	Cassandra Colt	$8.95
Secret Thunder	Annetta P. Lee	$9.95
Shades of Brown	Denise Becker	$8.95
Shades of Desire	Monica White	$8.95
Shadows in the Moonlight	Jeanne Sumerix	$8.95
Sin	Crystal Rhodes	$8.95
Singing A Song…	Crystal Rhodes	$6.99
Six O'Clock	Katrina Spencer	$6.99
Small Whispers	Annetta P. Lee	$6.99
So Amazing	Sinclair LeBeau	$8.95
Somebody's Someone	Sinclair LeBeau	$8.95
Someone to Love	Alicia Wiggins	$8.95
Song in the Park	Martin Brant	$15.95
Soul Eyes	Wayne L. Wilson	$12.95
Soul to Soul	Donna Hill	$8.95
Southern Comfort	J.M. Jeffries	$8.95
Southern Fried Standards	S.R. Maddox	$6.99
Still the Storm	Sharon Robinson	$8.95
Still Waters Run Deep	Leslie Esdaile	$8.95
Stolen Memories	Michele Sudler	$6.99
Stories to Excite You	Anna Forrest/Divine	$14.95
Storm	Pamela Leigh Starr	$6.99
Subtle Secrets	Wanda Y. Thomas	$8.95
Suddenly You	Crystal Hubbard	$9.95
Sweet Repercussions	Kimberley White	$9.95
Sweet Sensations	Gwyneth Bolton	$9.95
Sweet Tomorrows	Kimberly White	$8.95
Taken by You	Dorothy Elizabeth Love	$9.95
Tattooed Tears	T. T. Henderson	$8.95
Tempting Faith	Crystal Hubbard	$6.99
The Color Line	Lizzette Grayson Carter	$9.95
The Color of Trouble	Dyanne Davis	$8.95
The Disappearance of Allison Jones	Kayla Perrin	$5.95
The Fires Within	Beverly Clark	$9.95
The Foursome	Celya Bowers	$6.99
The Honey Dipper's Legacy	Myra Pannell-Allen	$14.95
The Joker's Love Tune	Sidney Rickman	$15.95
The Little Pretender	Barbara Cartland	$10.95
The Love We Had	Natalie Dunbar	$8.95
The Man Who Could Fly	Bob & Milana Beamon	$18.95

Other Genesis Press, Inc. Titles (continued)